THE SCORCHED FACE

The Complete

I0661210

Cases of the Continental Op

Volume 3: 1925–26

DASHIELL HAMMETT

introduction by Bob Byrne

BLACK MASK

2025

Table of Contents

Introduction / *vii*

1 The Scorched Face / *1*

2 Corkscrew / *59*

3 Dead Yellow Women / *143*

4 The Gutting of Couffignal / *221*

5 Creeping Siamese / *269*

Introduction

WELCOME TO VOLUME. Hammett had written fifteen Op stories of varying quality for Black Mask, and one rejection found its way into *True Detective Mysteries* (though they weren't actually 'true').

He had followed hard on the heels of Caroll John Daly, whose Three-Gun Terry Mack appeared in May of 1923, and just two weeks and one issue later came the first Race Williams story, "Knights of the Open Palm."

After one more Williams shoot-fest, *Black Mask* printed "Arson Plus," and Dash Hammett began reshaping the fresh clay that was the new hardboiled school. The quality of Hammett's work immediately surpassed that of Daly's, though it was up-and-down. Hammett's drinking, health issues, personal life, and problems with (his second) editor Phil Cody, made the Continental Op a bumpy ride.

Here we have the final five stories he wrote for Cody before he quit *Black Mask*. Yep. Quit. Had Joseph 'Cap' Shaw not been committed to bringing back Hammett, we would not have had *Red Harvest*, or *The Maltese Falcon*. Hammett was willing to quit the Pulps, rather than continue to labor under Cody's financially-unrewarding yoke.

"The Whosis Kid" had appeared in the March, 1925 issue of *Black Mask*. After a few lackluster efforts, it marked a return to form for the ailing author. His tuberculosis had flared up and was possibly contagious, so his wife and daughter had gone back to Montana.

Our first story, "The Scorched Face," certainly has an intriguing title, and it was in the May, 1925 issue of *Black Mask*. Alfred Banbrock's two daughters said they were going for a visit, never showed up, and seemed to have vanished. It's not your typical missing person's case.

Race Williams stories are full of action and violence. I've talked in the prior introductions about the realism which Hammett included in his Op stories, drawing on his experiences working for the Pinkertons. There are elements of a "detective procedural" in the stories. Here, having gathered information from the client and his wife, the Op goes back to the office. He arranges to have operatives in other branches reach out to the girls' out-of-town friends, using a list from Mrs. Banbrock. He has the car placed on the police's stolen vehicles list, hoping to locate it. And he also has copies of the girls' photographs made. Then he heads out to interview some local friends. He sets the 'agency machinery' in motion; this is the grind of detecting.

He draws blank after blank, wearing out shoe leather, until his last visitor is so nervous, he decides to dig into her a bit the next day. Except as he reads the morning paper over his eggs, toast, grapefruit, and coffee, he discovers she killed herself that very evening. There's something going on.

One sister is found dead in another county, and then the case peters out. The police move on to other matters, and the Op prepares to tell the client that he is giving up, when he has a sudden inspiration. He and police detective Pat Reddy compile a huge list of murdered/disappeared/committed suicide women, then dig through it. It's dull police work, but it provides the break for a nearly dead case. Hammett manages to have the Op do boring but realistic work, without making it boring to read. That should be appreciated.

THERE ARE ELEVEN short chapters in this novelette. Things are a bit dull for the first seven, and it really does read like a detective procedural. But it explodes in violence and mayhem in chapters eight and nine. An angry, under-clothed mob savaging the policeman, shootings, thrown objects, physical attacks from unseen assailants, jumping down staircases, chokings, pistol whippings: the sheer frenzy of violence is like a scene from *Daredevil* (the fantastic web series).

The explosion comes out of nowhere, and it leaves the reader breathless.

Hammett shifts gears and everything slows down. The surviving sister is found locked in a basement room behind a steel door, gun in hand, a dead body with a bullet hole, on the floor. After the prior mayhem, it's like a stillness descending. She killed him, though with understandable reasons. The readers' sympathy is with the girl, not the dead man. The girl is guilty, but the Op echoes Sherlock Holmes in "The Adventure of the Abbey Grange:"

> Once or twice in my career I feel that I have done more real harm by my discovery of the criminal than ever he had done by his crime. I have learned caution now, and I had rather play tricks with the law of England than with my own conscience.

Here, the Op sees enforcing the law, and doing the right/best thing, as different. But he needs to convince his erstwhile police friend to share that view. I'll let you see for yourself how that works out. And it wraps up with a very short O. Henry-esque ending. Henry was known for providing a twist at the end of his stories. It was nice to see Hammett use the technique in a subtle way.

I'm not gonna belabor the point, but the reader can find some elements that Hammett would use in the complex *The Dain Curse*. Though, smarmy cult leaders were not an uncommon trope in Pulp mysteries. And in my reading experience, they seemed more common on the West Coast.

"Corkscrew" appeared four months (September) after "The Scorched Face," which means Hammett missed a *Black Mask* payday, whether of his own doing, or Cody just not printing him, I don't know. Hammett's ill-feelings towards Cody may have left him less 'enthused' to crank out another Op story, quickly.

Though, only one month after the prior story, a long letter from Hammett—"Finger-Prints"—ran in the July issue. A Mr. Reeves had sent a letter to *Black Mask* that seemed critical of Hammett's story, "Slippery Fingers." The author, whose stories were infused with realism, gave his detailed thoughts on Reeves' commentary. One can envision Hammett devoting more time and energy to this pointed rebuttal, than to a new story for an editor he disliked—remuneration notwithstanding.

I said this in the intro to volume one, *Zigzags of Treachery:*

> The immensely popular (Race) Williams was the prototypical gun-slinging Western cowboy who solved every problem with hot lead, but now wearing a suit and transplanted to the urban setting of city streets.

"Corkscrew" turns that on its head and takes the big city private eye into cowboy country. It reads like Hammett meets Robert E. Howard. And if you only know Howard from his Conan stories, he wrote some pretty good Westerns as well.

This story foreshadows the classic serialized novel, *Red Harvest*. The Op is hired to clean up a town. And he stirs up the local elements against each other, getting them to do much of the work for him. Here, though, the reforming crusaders provide comic relief, whereas they are his employer in *Red Harvest*.

The Op is appointed a deputy sheriff, which makes him the only Law in the area. With three different factions (two of which have partnered together), he is under-gunned and chooses his moments to stand firm, or to walk (or ride) away.

This is the Op functioning completely out of his element. He can't tap agency resources or other operatives. There's no Dick Foley, or a cooperative police detective, to help out. He does recruit a local cowboy—with the distinctive name of "Milk River"—who doesn't have very strong ties to the faction he is working for.

Clio Landes is a NYC girl who had moved out West. Like Doc Holliday, she's a lunger: she has tuberculosis, and the local moral majority consider her a strumpet of the worst type. She does an underhanded thing to the Op, but not as a femme fatale. She is just an attractive female who used to live in the big city, but is now in the Old West. This is no Jeanne Delano.

It strikes me that Hammett wanted to do a Western, while dropping the typical trappings of an Op story. The dogged, routine detective work is missing. The Op doesn't wear out his shoe leather interviewing people and trying to rustle up clues. Though he does get in a fair share of horse riding to go see people. And he puts his deductive skills to work regarding a rope (can't have a Western without some cowboy rope, right?).

I really like "Corkscrew." I don't think I'd want the Op to be permanently assigned out West, but Hammett changes things up, and it works. And it's a little bit of a dress rehearsal for *Red Harvest:* albeit in a completely different setting.

Phil Cody encouraged Hammett to ratchet up the violence and action, and he certainly did so in this story. The Op uses (other people's) violence as a tool in his limited arsenal.

Two months after "Corkscrew," the Op was back in familiar environs, investigating the murder of some servants in China-town.

Hammett knew Chinatown well, living in San Francisco, and this story basks in its aura. It feels like an entirely different city, and the Op is a stranger in a strange land. He baits a trap that nearly delivers more than he can handle. The Op's response is the polar opposite of what Race Williams would have done.

This is a convoluted story, with the agency investigating the murder of a rich woman's servant. There are shenanigans, with the Op bringing things out into the light in the final part. But the story wasn't the strength of this one.

Hammett was good at providing supporting characters with depth. "The Girl with the Silver Eyes" was a prime example of that. Here, we get Dummy Uhl. Uhl had been a dummerer: a beggar who pretends they can't speak or hear (I had to look that up). Heroin addiction made him too jumpy to continue pulling off that scam and he became an errand boy to support his habit. The Op had used him before.

Hammett tells us that Uhl's eyes didn't show the pinpoint pupils of the heroin addict. But the Op observes that it doesn't mean that he was off the stuff. He had put belladonna in them to distend them to normal size, and the Op wondered why. This was the kind of layering that Hammett added to his characters—and sometimes subtly developed the plot though it as well. The Op definitely uses Uhl in surprising ways in this story.

I don't really know what to make of this one, and the Op manipulates a couple different sides. There are some arrests, some deaths, and sort of a detente with a crime boss. There's nothing fundamentally wrong with this story, but it's not one I go back to.

Appearing in December of 1925, "The Gutting of Couffignal" was the twentieth of twenty-one stories which Hammett wrote for Sutton or Cody. He would walk away from *Black Mask* after the next one. I don't know what 'got into him' here, but I think it's different from all the prior ones.

The Op is assigned to guard the presents from a wedding that had been attended by rich and politically notable people from around the world, on the island of Couffignal. Couffignal is a "privileged people" community on San Pablo Bay, two hours north of San Francisco.

Hammett's disdain of the rich comes through in the Op. "Most of them are well-fed gentlemen who, the profits they took from the world with both hands in their younger days now stowed away at safe percentages, have brought into the island colony so they may spend what is left of their lives nursing their livers and improving their golf game among their kind."

He can't wait to finish this mundane job and get off the island.

I liked the Wild West gunslinger theme of "Corkscrew." "Gutting…" is like a Day Keene paperback, or a story from *Manhunt*.

The action is more something out of a Robert Ludlum or Clive Cussler novel (two of my favorites) than a typical hard-boiled private eye story. A gang blows the bridge connecting the island to the mainland, kills the phone lines, sets up a car in the middle of the town square with a machine gun mounted on it, and instigates a night of terror. The lone law officer is killed when they blow up the bank.

This is a hostile takeover of an entire town, houses looted one by one. The only "poor people" who live there are the shop-keepers and servants. This is essentially a paramilitary gang that is robbing an entire resort community. A Russian princess is staying on the island, with a general who leads an under-armed resistance.

I don't want to give away any spoilers. I think this is a fast-paced, violent, action-adventure with the Op dead-center in the middle. He takes on the role of a military commander, but also functions like a Clone Trooper. It's safe to say that the bad guys would have succeeded if the Op hadn't been around.

Hammett later himself criticized his denouement, saying he didn't make the most of the situation. He said this in relation to *The Maltese Falcon*, and you can see some similarity to Sam Spade and Brigid O'Shaughnessy here. But his final scene does give some insight into the Op's emotions.

TO ME, THIS is an atypical Op story, and I suspect Hammett was of the "Okay, you want action? I'll give you plenty of action" mindset towards Cody, who he quite disliked by now. Hammett had learned in September of 1925 that his wife Josie was pregnant with their second child. The Veterans Administration had ended payments to Hammett in 1924 and Hammett threatened to quit if Cody wouldn't pay him more. I like this story, but all things considered, it feels like a "Here, jackass" piece, to Cody. Hammett would quit *Black Mask* after the next story.

Hammett describes a man who walks into the Continental offices, has him utter "Hell," then pitch over dead. THAT is an opening! There's not a whole lot more to "Creeping Siamese," though.

It's a slight story. The Op works in lockstep with Detective Sergeant O'Gar, who summons him on a hot lead. There are only two additional locations, and this feels like it could have been a play. No shooting, barely any on-page violence. The hot open open becomes lots of talking and the Op figuring things out as he listens. It's not a bad story, it's just not much of one.

There are only two parts and it wraps up rather abruptly. It almost feels like something he had written before and pulled out of a drawer and sent off to Cody for a (small) paycheck. There's no evidence of that, and since he always needed money, it's unlikely he had it sitting around, unused. But there's not a lot to say about this one.

I do wanna talk about his word-smithing a little. Hammett is justifiably lauded for his lean, direct prose style. It's the polar opposite of the over-the-top caricature style of Daly. Frederick Nebel wrote this way also. I think of it as writing well, but without too much flourish.

But sometimes, for me, Hammett flashes a similarity to Robert E. Howard. "Corkscrew" opens with the Op taking "an automobile stage" from California through the Arizona desert. Hammett is quite evocative in the first few paragraphs:

> Boiling like a coffeepot before we were five miles out of Filmer, the automobile stage carried me south into the shimmering heart and bitter white dust of the Arizona desert.

Those first words of the story paint a picture of a city man moving into the brutal heat of the Southwestern desert. Hammett was rarely so descriptive of the environment:

> The car crept through the soft sifting sand, wound between steep-walled red mesas, dipped into dry arroyos where clumps of dusty mesquite were like white lace in the glare, and skirted sharp-edged barrancas.

Finally arriving in Corkscrew without "banging out of existence in one explosive flash" due to the heat, he paints a picture of a town so unimpressive that calling it a village would have been flattery. This is a sad little town, baking under the desert sun. And the Op, a fat little man sweltering in a strange environment, is a fish out of water.

Hammett could just have had the Op get out of the cab in the deserted town square and comment on the heat and the shabbiness. Of course, getting paid by the word, that wouldn't pay the bills. But instead, he showed that he could paint word pictures with the best of his fellow Pulpsters.

Hammett wanted more money, and Cody said "No." He alleged that the magazine owed him $300, and Cody denied it. We've already seen that Cody refused to publish Hammett more than once every two months. Dash had had enough.

So, the best hardboiled Pulp writer took a full-time job as an advertising manager for a jewelry store and quit *Black Mask*. The Cody Era was over. Joe "Cap" Shaw would replace Cody, give Hammett the disputed $300, and build him up as "his guy." The author returned in February of 1927 with "The Big Knock-Over." Following that with "$106,000 Blood Money," Hammett would definitely be better than ever.

There is a false narrative that Cap Shaw made Hammett, and made *Black Mask*, hardboiled. As these first three volumes have shown, Hammett was fashioning the new genre (alongside Daly) under Phil Cody and George W. Sutton. The Continental Op came before Shaw.

What we'll see in ensuing volumes is that Hammett flourished and became the all-time greatest hardboiled writer (he's got my vote over Chandler) under Shaw. And *Black Mask* became the standard every other hardboiled/crime Pulp strove to match.

Hammett doesn't write *Red Harvest*, and *The Maltese Falcon*, without Shaw as editor. But Sutton, and then Cody, were his editors as Hammett developed. You've read all those stories. Next up, Hammett and Shaw.

—Bob Byrne

The Scorched Face

Here's another realistic detective tale by Mr.
Hammett, formerly of the Pinkertons. It has
a ring of truth in it that makes you forget
that you are only reading and not actually
following the San Francisco sleuth around.

1

"WE EXPECTED THEM home yesterday," Alfred Banbrock wound up his story. "When they had not come by this morning, my wife telephoned Mrs. Walden. Mrs. Walden said they had not been down there—had not been expected, in fact."

"On the face of it, then," I suggested, "it seems that your daughters went away of their own accord, and are staying away on their own accord?"

Banbrock nodded gravely. Tired muscles sagged in his fleshy face.

"It would seem so," he agreed. "That is why I came to your agency for help instead of going to the police."

"Have they ever disappeared before?"

"No. If you read the papers and magazines, you've no doubt seen hints that the younger generation is given to irregularity. My daughters came and went pretty much as they pleased. But, though I can't say I ever knew what they were up to, we always knew where they were in a general way."

"Can you think of any reason for their going away like this?"

He shook his weary head.

"Any recent quarrels?" I probed.

"N—" He changed it to: "Yes—although I didn't attach any importance to it, and wouldn't have recalled it if you hadn't jogged my memory. It was Thursday evening—the evening before they went away."

"And it was about—?"

"Money, of course. We never disagreed over anything else. I gave each of my daughters an adequate allowance—perhaps a very liberal one. Nor did I keep them strictly within it. There were few months in which they didn't exceed it. Thursday evening they asked for an amount of money even more than usual in excess of what two girls should need. I wouldn't give it to them, though I finally did give them a somewhat smaller amount. We didn't exactly quarrel—not in the strict sense of the word—but there was a certain lack of friendliness between us."

"And it was after this disagreement that they said they were going down to Mrs. Walden's, in Monterey, for the week-end?"

"Possibly. I'm not sure of that point. I don't think I heard of it until the next morning, but they may have told my wife before that. I shall ask her if you wish."

"And you know of no other possible reason for their running away?"

"None. I can't think that our dispute over money—by no means an unusual one—had anything to do with it."

"What does their mother think?"

"Their mother is dead," Banbrock corrected me. "My wife is their stepmother. She is only two years older than Myra, my older daughter. She is as much at sea as I."

"Did your daughters and their stepmother get along all right together?"

"Yes! Yes! Excellently! If there was a division in the family, I usually found them standing together against me."

"Your daughters left Friday afternoon?"

"At noon, or a few minutes after. They were going to drive down."

"The car, of course, is still missing?"

"Naturally."

"What was it?"

"A Locomobile, with a special cabriolet body. Black."

"You can give me the license and engine numbers?"

"I think so."

He turned in his chair to the big roll-top desk that hid a quarter of one office wall, fumbled with papers in a compartment, and read the numbers over his shoulder to me. I put them on the back of an envelope.

"I'm going to have this car put on the police department list of stolen machines," I told him. "It can be done without mentioning your daughters. The police bulletin might find the car for us. That would help us find your daughters."

"Very well," he agreed, "if it can be done without disagreeable publicity. As I told you at first, I don't want any more advertising than is absolutely necessary—unless it becomes likely that harm has come to the girls."

I nodded understanding, and got up.

"I want to go out and talk to your wife," I said. "Is she home now?"

"Yes, I think so. I'll phone her and tell her you are coming."

2

IN A BIG limestone fortress on top a hill in Sea Cliff, looking down on ocean and bay, I had my talk with Mrs. Banbrock.
She was a tall dark girl of not more than twenty-two years,
inclined to plumpness.

She couldn't tell me anything her husband hadn't at least
mentioned, but she could give me finer details.

I got descriptions of the two girls:

Myra—20 years old; 5 feet 8 inches; 150 pounds; athletic;
brisk, almost masculine manner and carriage; bobbed brown
hair; brown eyes; medium complexion; square face, with large
chin and short nose; scar over left ear, concealed by hair; fond
of horses and all outdoor sports. When she left the house she
wore a blue and green wool dress, small blue hat, short black
seal coat, and black slippers.

Ruth—18 years; 5 feet 4 inches; 105 pounds; brown eyes;
brown bobbed hair; medium complexion; small oval face; quiet,
timid, inclined to lean on her more forceful sister. When last
seen she had worn a tobacco-brown coat trimmed with brown
fur over a grey silk dress, and a wide brown hat.

I got two photographs of each girl, and an additional snap-
shot of Myra standing in front of the cabriolet. I got a list of
the things they had taken with them—such things as would
naturally be taken on a week-end visit. What I valued most
of what I got was a list of their friends, relatives, and other
acquaintances, so far as Mrs. Banbrock knew them.

"Did they mention Mrs. Walden's invitation before their

quarrel with Mr. Banbrock?" I asked, when I had my lists stowed away.

"I don't think so," Mrs. Banbrock said thoughtfully. "I didn't connect the two things at all. They didn't really quarrel with their father, you know. It wasn't harsh enough to be called a quarrel."

"Did you see them when they left?"

"Assuredly! They left at about half-past twelve Friday afternoon. They kissed me as usual when they went, and there was certainly nothing in their manner to suggest anything out of the ordinary."

"You've no idea at all where they might have gone?"

"None."

"Can't even make a guess?"

"I can't. Among the names and addresses I have given you are some of friends and relatives of the girls in other cities. They may have gone to one of those. Do you think we should—?"

"I'll take care of that," I promised. "Could you pick out one or two of them as the most likely places for the girls to have gone?"

She wouldn't try it.

"No," she said positively, "I could not."

From this interview I went back to the Agency, and put the Agency machinery in motion; arranging to have operatives from some of the Continental's other branches call on the out-of-town names on my list; having the missing Locomobile put on the police department list; turning one photograph of each girl over to a photographer to be copied.

That done, I set out to talk to the persons on the list Mrs. Banbrock had given me. My first call was on a Constance

Delee, in an apartment building on Post Street. I saw a maid. The maid said Miss Delee was out of town. She wouldn't tell me where her mistress was, or when she would be back.

From there I went up on Van Ness Avenue and found a Wayne Ferris in an automobile salesroom: a sleek-haired young man whose very nice manners and clothes completely hid anything else—brains for instance—he might have had. He was very willing to help me, and he knew nothing. It took him a long time to tell me so. A nice boy.

Another blank: "Mrs. Scott is in Honolulu."

In a real estate office on Montgomery Street I found my next one—another sleek, stylish, smooth-haired young man with nice manners and nice clothes. His name was Raymond Elwood. I would have thought him a no more distant relative of Ferris than cousin if I hadn't known that the world—especially the dancing, teaing world—was full of their sort. I learned nothing from him.

Then I drew some more blanks: "Out of town," "Shopping," "I don't know where you can find him."

I found one more of the Banbrock girls' friends before I called it a day. Her name was Mrs. Stewart Correll. She lived in Presidio Terrace, not far from the Banbrocks. She was a small woman, or girl, of about Mrs. Banbrock's age. A little fluffy blonde person with wide eyes of that particular blue which always looks honest and candid no matter what is going on behind it.

"I haven't seen either Ruth or Myra for two weeks or more," she said in answer to my question.

"At that time—the last time you saw them—did either say anything about going away?"

"No."

Her eyes were wide and frank. A little muscle twitched in her upper lip.

"And you've no idea where they might have gone?"

"No."

Her fingers were rolling her lace handkerchief into a little ball.

"Have you heard from them since you last saw them?"

"No."

She moistened her mouth before she said it.

"Will you give me the names and addresses of all the people you know who were also known by the Banbrock girls?"

"Why—? Is there—?"

"There's a chance that some of them may have seen them more recently than you," I explained. "Or may even have seen them since Friday."

Without enthusiasm, she gave me a dozen names. All were already on my list. Twice she hesitated as if about to speak a name she did not want to speak. Her eyes stayed on mine, wide and honest. Her fingers, no longer balling the handkerchief, picked at the cloth of her skirt.

I didn't pretend to believe her. But my feet weren't solidly enough on the ground for me to put her on the grill. I gave her a promise before I left, one that she could get a threat out of if she liked.

"Thanks, very much," I said. "I know it's hard to remember things exactly. If I run across anything that will help your memory, I'll be back to let you know about it."

"Wha—? Yes, do!" she said.

Walking away from the house, I turned my head to look

back just before I passed out of sight. A curtain swung into place at a second-floor window. The street lights weren't bright enough for me to be sure the curtain had swung in front of a blonde head.

My watch told me it was nine-thirty: too late to line up any more of the girls' friends. I went home, wrote my report for the day, and turned in, thinking more about Mrs. Correll than about the girls.

She seemed worth an investigation.

3

SOME TELEGRAPHIC REPORTS were in when I got to the office the next morning. None was of any value. Investigation of the names and addresses in other cities had revealed nothing. An investigation in Monterey had established reasonably—which is about as well as anything is ever established in the detecting business—that the girls had not been there recently; that the Locomobile had not been there.

The early editions of the afternoon papers were on the street when I went out to get some breakfast before taking up the grind where I had dropped it the previous night. I bought a paper to prop behind my grapefruit.

It spoiled my breakfast for me.

BANKER'S WIFE SUICIDE

Mrs. Stewart Correll, wife of the vice-president of the Golden Gate Trust Company, was found dead early this morning by her maid in her bedroom, in her home in Presidio Terrace. A bottle believed to have contained poison was on the floor beside the bed.

The dead woman's husband could give no reason for his wife's suicide. He said she had not seemed depressed or....

I gave my eggs and toast a quick play, put my coffee down in a lump, and got going.

At the Correll residence I had to do a lot of talking before I could get to Correll. He was a tall, slim man of less than thirty-five, with a sallow, nervous face and blue eyes that fidgeted.

"I'm sorry to disturb you at a time like this," I apologized when I had finally insisted my way into his presence. "I won't take up more of your time than necessary. I am an operative of the Continental Detective Agency. I have been trying to find Ruth and Myra Banbrock, who disappeared several days ago. You know them, I think."

"Yes," he said without interest. "I know them."

"You knew they had disappeared?"

"No." His eyes switched from a chair to a rug. "Why should I?"

"Have you seen either of them recently?" I asked, ignoring his question.

"Last week—Wednesday, I think. They were just leaving—standing at the door talking to my wife—when I came home from the bank."

"Didn't your wife say anything to you about their vanishing?"

"No. Really, I can't tell you anything about the Misses Banbrock. If you'll excuse me—"

"Just a moment longer," I said. "I wouldn't have bothered you if it hadn't been necessary. I was here last night, to question Mrs. Correll. She seemed nervous. My impression was that some of her answers to my questions were—uh—evasive. I want—"

He was up out of his chair. His face was red in front of mine.

"You!" he cried. "I can thank you for—"

"Now, Mr. Correll," I tried to quiet him, "there's no use—"

But he had himself all worked up.

"You drove my wife to her death," he accused me. "You killed her with your damned prying—with your bulldozing threats; with your—"

That was silly. I felt sorry for this young man whose wife had killed herself. Apart from that, I had work to do. I tightened the screws.

"We won't argue, Correll," I told him. "The point is that I came here to see if your wife could tell me anything about the Banbrocks. She told me less than the truth. Later, she committed suicide. I want to know why. Come through for me, and I'll do what I can to keep the papers and the public from linking her death with the girls' disappearance."

"Linking her death with their disappearance?" he exclaimed. "That's absurd!"

"Maybe—but the connection is there!" I hammered away at him. I felt sorry for him, but I had work to do. "It's there. If you'll give it to me, maybe it won't have to be advertised. I'm going to get it, though. You give it to me—or I'll go after it out in the open."

For a moment I thought he was going to take a poke at me. I wouldn't have blamed him. His body stiffened—then sagged, and he dropped back into his chair. His eyes fidgeted away from mine.

"There's nothing I can tell," he mumbled. "When her maid went to her room to call her this morning, she was dead. There was no message, no reason, nothing."

"Did you see her last night?"

"No. I was not home for dinner. I came in late and went straight to my own room, not wanting to disturb her. I hadn't seen her since I left the house that morning."

"Did she seem disturbed or worried then?"

"No."

"Why do you think she did it?"

"My God, man, I don't know! I've thought and thought, but I don't know!"

"Health?"

"She seemed well. She was never ill, never complained."

"Any recent quarrels?"

"We never quarreled—never in the year and a half we have been married!"

"Financial trouble?"

He shook his head without speaking or looking up from the floor.

"Any other worry?"

He shook his head again.

"Did the maid notice anything peculiar in her behavior last night?"

"Nothing."

"Have you looked through her things—for papers, letters?"

"Yes—and found nothing." He raised his head to look at me. "The only thing"—he spoke very slowly—"there was a little pile of ashes in the grate in her room, as if she had burned papers, or letters."

Correll held nothing more for me—nothing I could get out of him, anyway.

The girl at the front gate in Alfred Banbrock's Shoreman's Building suite told me he was in conference. I sent my name in. He came out of conference to take me into his private office. His tired face was full of questions.

I didn't keep him waiting for the answers. He was a grown man. I didn't edge around the bad news.

"Things have taken a bad break," I said as soon as we were locked in together. "I think we'll have to go to the police and newspapers for help. A Mrs. Correll, a friend of your daughters, lied to me when I questioned her yesterday. Last night she committed suicide."

"Irma Correll? Suicide?"

"You knew her?"

"Yes! Intimately! She was—that is, she was a close friend of my wife and daughters. She killed herself?"

"Yes. Poison. Last night. Where does she fit in with your daughters' disappearance?"

"Where?" he repeated. "I don't know. Must she fit in?"

"I think she must. She told me she hadn't seen your daughters for a couple of weeks. Her husband told me just now that they were talking to her when he came home from the bank last Wednesday afternoon. She seemed nervous when I questioned her. She killed herself shortly afterward. There's hardly a doubt that she fits in somewhere."

"And that means—?"

"That means," I finished for him, "that your daughters may be perfectly safe, but that we can't afford to gamble on that possibility."

"You think harm has come to them?"

"I don't think anything," I evaded, "except that with a death tied up closely with their going, we can't afford to play around."

Banbrock got his attorney on the phone—a pink-faced, white-haired old boy named Norwall, who had the reputation of knowing more about corporations than all the Morgans, but who hadn't the least idea as to what police procedure was all about—and told him to meet us at the Hall of Justice.

We spent an hour and a half there, getting the police turned loose on the affair, and giving the newspapers what we wanted them to have. That was plenty of dope on the girls, plenty of photographs and so forth; but nothing about the connection between them and Mrs. Correll. Of course we let the police in on that angle.

4

AFTER BANBROCK AND his attorney had gone away together, I went back to the detectives' assembly room to chew over the job with Pat Reddy, the police sleuth assigned to it.

Pat was the youngest member of the detective bureau—a big blond Irishman who went in for the spectacular in his lazy way.

A couple of years ago he was a new copper, pounding his feet in harness on a hillside beat. One night he tagged an automobile that was parked in front of a fireplug. The owner came out just then and gave him an argument. She was Althea Wallach, only and spoiled daughter of the owner of the Wallach Coffee Company—a slim, reckless youngster with hot eyes. She must have told Pat plenty. He took her over to the station and dumped her in a cell.

Old Wallach, so the story goes, showed up the next morning with a full head of steam and half the lawyers in San Francisco. But Pat made his charge stick, and the girl was fined. Old Wallach did everything but take a punch at Pat in the corridor afterward. Pat grinned his sleepy grin at the coffee importer, and drawled:

"You better lay off me—or I'll stop drinking your coffee."

That crack got into most of the newspapers in the country, and even into a Broadway show.

But Pat didn't stop with the snappy come-back. Three days later he and Althea Wallach went over to Alameda and got themselves married. I was in on that part. I happened to be on the ferry they took, and they dragged me along to see the deed done.

Old Wallach immediately disowned his daughter, but that didn't seem to worry anybody else. Pat went on pounding his beat, but, now that he was conspicuous, it wasn't long before his qualities were noticed. He was boosted into the detective bureau. Old Wallach relented before he died, and left Althea both of his millions.

Pat took the afternoon off to go to the funeral, and went back to work that night, catching a wagonload of gunmen. He kept on working. I don't know what his wife did with her money, but Pat didn't even improve the quality of his cigars—though he should have. He lived now in the Wallach mansion, true enough, and now and then on rainy mornings he would be driven down to the Hall in a Hispano-Suiza brougham; but there was no difference in him beyond that.

That was the big blond Irishman who sat across a desk from me in the assembly room and fumigated me with something shaped like a cigar.

He took the cigar-like thing out of his mouth presently, and spoke through the fumes.

"This Correll woman you think's tied up with the Banbrocks—she was stuck-up a couple of months back and nicked for eight hundred dollars. Know that?"

I hadn't known it.

"Lose anything besides cash?" I asked.

"No."

"You believe it?"

He grinned.

"That's the point," he said. "We didn't catch the bird who did it. With women who lose things that way—especially money—it's always a question whether it's a hold-up or a hold-out."

He teased some more poison-gas out of the cigar-thing, and added:

"The hold-up might have been on the level, though. What are you figuring on doing now?"

"Let's go up to the Agency and see if anything new has turned up. Then I'd like to talk to Mrs. Banbrock again. Maybe she can tell us something about the Correll woman."

At the office I found that reports had come in on the rest of the out-of-town names and addresses. Apparently none of these people knew anything about the girls' whereabouts. Reddy and I went on up to Sea Cliff to the Banbrock home.

Banbrock had telephoned the news of Mrs. Correll's death to his wife, and she had read the papers. She told us she could think of no reason for the suicide. She could imagine no possible connection between the suicide and her stepdaughters' vanishing.

"Mrs. Correll seemed as nearly contented and happy as usual the last time I saw her, two or three weeks ago," Mrs. Banbrock said. "Of course she was by nature inclined to be dissatisfied with things, but not to the extent of doing a thing like this."

"Do you know of any trouble between her and her husband?"

"No. So far as I know, they were happy, though—"

She broke off. Hesitancy, embarrassment showed in her dark eyes.

"Though?" I repeated.

"If I don't tell you now, you'll think I am hiding something," she said, flushing, and laughing a little laugh that held more nervousness than amusement. "It hasn't any bearing, but I was always just a little jealous of Irma. She and my husband were—well, everyone thought they would marry. That was a little before he and I married. I never let it show, and I dare say it was a foolish idea, but I always had a suspicion that Irma married Stewart more in pique than for any other reason, and that she was still fond of Alfred—Mr. Banbrock."

"Was there anything definite to make you think that?"

"No, nothing—really! I never thoroughly believed it. It was just a sort of vague feeling. Cattiness, no doubt, more than anything else."

It was getting along toward evening when Pat and I left the Banbrock house. Before we knocked off for the day, I called up the Old Man—the Continental's San Francisco branch manager, and therefore my boss—and asked him to sic an operative on Irma Correll's past.

I took a look at the morning papers—thanks to their custom of appearing almost as soon as the sun is out of sight—before I went to bed. They had given our job a good spread. All the facts except those having to do with the Correll angle were there, plus photographs, and the usual assortment of guesses and similar garbage.

The following morning I went after the friends of the missing girls to whom I had not yet talked. I found some of them, and got nothing of value from them. Late in the morning I telephoned the office to see if anything new had turned up.

It had.

"We've just had a call from the sheriff's office at Martinez," the Old Man told me. "An Italian grapegrower near Knob Valley picked up a charred photograph a couple of days ago, and recognized it as Ruth Banbrock when he saw her picture in this morning's paper. Will you get up there? A deputy sheriff and the Italian are waiting for you in the Knob Valley marshal's office."

"I'm on my way," I said.

At the ferry building I used the four minutes before my boat left trying to get Pat Reddy on the phone, with no success.

Knob Valley is a town of less than a thousand people, a dreary, dirty town in Contra Costa county. A San Francisco-Sacramento local set me down there while the afternoon was still young.

I knew the marshal slightly—Tom Orth. I found two men in the office with him. Orth introduced us. Abner Paget, a gawky man of forty-something, with a slack chin, scrawny face, and pale intelligent eyes, was the deputy sheriff. Gio Cereghino, the Italian grapegrower, was a small, nut-brown man with strong yellow teeth that showed in an everlasting smile under his black mustache, and soft brown eyes.

Paget showed me the photograph. A scorched piece of paper the size of a half-dollar, apparently all that had not been burned of the original picture. It was Ruth Banbrock's face. There was little room for doubting that. She had a peculiarly excited—almost drunken—look, and her eyes were larger than in the other pictures of her I had seen. But it was her face.

"He says he found it day 'fore yesterday," Paget explained dryly, nodding at the Italian. "The wind blew it against his foot when he was walkin' up a piece of road near his place. He picked it up an' stuck it in his pocket, he says, for no special reason, I guess, except maybe that guineas like pictures."

He paused to regard the Italian meditatively. The Italian nodded his head in vigorous affirmation.

"Anyways," the deputy sheriff went on, "he was in town this mornin', an' seen the pictures in the papers from 'Frisco. So he come in here an' told Tom about it. Tom an' me decided the best thing was to phone your agency—since the papers said you was workin' on it."

I looked at the Italian.

Paget, reading my mind, explained:

"Cereghino lives over in the hills. Got a grape-ranch there. Been around here five or six years, an' ain't killed nobody that I know of."

"Remember the place where you found the picture?" I asked the Italian.

His grin broadened under his mustache, and his head went up and down.

"For sure, I remember that place."

"Let's go there," I suggested to Paget.

"Right. Comin' along, Tom?"

The marshal said he couldn't. He had something to do in town. Cereghino, Paget and I went out and got into a dusty Ford that the deputy sheriff drove.

We rode for nearly an hour, along a county road that bent up the slope of Mount Diablo. After a while, at a word from the Italian, we left the county road for a dustier and ruttier one.

A mile of this one.

"This place," Cereghino said.

Paget stopped the Ford. We got out in a clearing. The trees and bushes that had crowded the road retreated here for twenty feet or so on either side, leaving a little dusty circle in the woods.

"About this place," the Italian was saying. "I think by this stump. But between that bend ahead and that one behind, I know for sure."

5

PAGET WAS A countryman. I am not. I waited for him to move.

He looked around the clearing, slowly, standing still between the Italian and me. His pale eyes lighted presently. He went around the Ford to the far side of the clearing. Cereghino and I followed.

Near the fringe of brush at the edge of the clearing, the scrawny deputy stopped to grunt at the ground. The wheel-marks of an automobile were there. A car had turned around here.

Paget went on into the woods. The Italian kept close to his heels. I brought up the rear. Paget was following some sort of track. I couldn't see it, either because he and the Italian blotted it out ahead of me, or because I'm a shine Indian.

We went back quite a way.

Paget stopped. The Italian stopped.

Paget said, "Uh-huh," as if he had found an expected thing.

The Italian said something with the name of God in it.

I trampled a bush, coming beside them to see what they saw. I saw it.

At the base of a tree, on her side, her knees drawn up close to her body, a girl was dead.

She wasn't nice to see. Birds had been at her.

A tobacco-brown coat was half on, half off her shoulders. I knew she was Ruth Banbrock before I turned her over to look at the side of her face the ground had saved from the birds.

Cereghino stood watching me while I examined the girl. His face was mournful in a calm way. The deputy sheriff paid little attention to the body. He was off in the brush, moving around, looking at the ground.

He came back as I finished my examination.

"Shot," I told him, "once in the right temple. Before that, I think, there was a fight. There are marks on the arm that was under her body. There's nothing on her—no jewelry, money—nothing."

"That goes," Paget said. "Two women got out of the car back in the clearin', an' came here. Could've been three women—if the others carried this one. Can't make out how many went back. One of 'em was larger than this one. There was a scuffle here. Find the gun?"

"No," I said.

"Neither did I. It went away in the car, then. There's what's left of a fire over there." He ducked his head to the left. "Paper an' rags burnt. Not enough left to do us any good. I reckon the photo Cereghino found blew away from the fire. Late Friday, I'd put it, or maybe Saturday mornin'… No nearer than that."

I took the deputy sheriff's word for it. He seemed to know his stuff.

"Come here. I'll show you somethin'," he said, and led me over to a little black pile of ashes.

He hadn't anything to show me. He wanted to talk to me away from the Italian's ears.

"I think the guinea's all right," he said, "but I reckon I'd best hold him a while to make sure. This is some way from his place, an' he stuttered a little bit too much tellin' me how he happened to be passin' here. Course, that don't mean nothin' much. All these guineas peddle vino, an' I guess that's what brought him out this way. I'll hold him a day or two, anyways."

"Good," I agreed. "This is your country, and you know the people. Can you visit around and see what you can pick up? Whether anybody saw anything? Saw a Locomobile cabriolet? Or anything else? You can get more than I could."

"I'll do that," he promised.

"All right. Then I'll go back to San Francisco now. I suppose you'll want to camp here with the body?"

"Yeah. You drive the Ford back to Knob Valley, an' tell Tom what's what. He'll come or send out. I'll keep the guinea here with me."

Waiting for the next west-bound train out of Knob Valley, I got the office on the telephone. The Old Man was out. I told my story to one of the office men and asked him to get the news to the Old Man as soon as he could.

Everybody was in the office when I got back to San Francisco. Alfred Banbrock, his face a pink-grey that was deader than solid grey could have been. His pink and white old lawyer. Pat Reddy, sprawled on his spine with his feet on another chair. The Old Man, with his gentle eyes behind gold spectacles and his mild smile, hiding the fact that fifty years of sleuthing had left him without any feelings at all on any subject. (Whitey Clayton used to say the Old Man could spit icicles in August.)

Nobody said anything when I came in. I said my say as briefly as possible.

"Then the other woman—the woman who killed Ruth was—?"

Banbrock didn't finish his question. Nobody answered it.

"We don't know what happened," I said after a while. "Your

daughter and someone we don't know may have gone there. Your daughter may have been dead before she was taken there. She may have—"

"But Myra!" Banbrock was pulling at his collar with a finger inside. "Where is Myra?"

I couldn't answer that, nor could any of the others.

"You are going up to Knob Valley now?" I asked him.

"Yes, at once. You will come with me?"

I wasn't sorry I could not.

"No. There are things to be done here. I'll give you a note to the marshal. I want you to look carefully at the piece of your daughter's photograph the Italian found—to see if you remember it."

Banbrock and the lawyer left.

6

REDDY LIT ONE of his awful cigars. "We found the car," the Old Man said.

"Where?"

"In Sacramento. It was left in a garage there either late Friday night or early Saturday. Foley has gone up to investigate it. And Reddy has uncovered a new angle."

Pat nodded through his smoke.

"A hock-shop dealer came in this morning," Pat said, "and told us that Myra Banbrock and another girl came to his joint last week and hocked a lot of stuff. They gave him phoney names, but he swears one of them was Myra. He recognized her picture as soon as he saw it in the paper. Her companion wasn't Ruth. It was a little blonde."

"Mrs. Correll?"

"Uh-huh. The shark can't swear to that, but I think that's the answer. Some of the jewelry was Myra's, some Ruth's, and some we don't know. I mean we can't prove it belonged to Mrs. Correll—though we will."

"When did all this happen?"

"They soaked the stuff Monday before they went away."

"Have you seen Correll?"

"Uh-huh," Pat said. "I did a lot of talking to him, but the answers weren't worth much. He says he don't know whether any of her jewelry is gone or not, and doesn't care. It was hers, he says, and she could do anything she wanted with it. He was kind of disagreeable. I got along a little better with one of the maids. She says some of Mrs. Correll's pretties disappeared last week. Mrs. Correll said she had lent them to a friend. I'm going to show the stuff the hock-shop has to the maid tomorrow, to see if she can identify it. She didn't know anything else—except that Mrs. Correll was out of the picture for a while on Friday—the day the Banbrock girls went away."

"What do you mean, out of the picture?" I asked.

"She went out late in the morning and didn't show up until somewhere around three the next morning. She and Correll had a row over it, but she wouldn't tell him where she had been."

I liked that. It could mean something.

"And," Pat went on, "Correll has just remembered that his wife had an uncle who went crazy in Pittsburgh in 1902, and that she had a morbid fear of going crazy herself, and that she had often said she would kill herself if she thought she was going crazy. Wasn't it nice of him to remember those things at last? To account for her death?"

"It was," I agreed, "but it doesn't get us anywhere. It doesn't even prove that he knows anything. Now my guess is—"

"To hell with your guess," Pat said, getting up and pushing his hat in place. "Your guesses all sound like a lot of static to me. I'm going home, eat my dinner, read my Bible, and go to bed."

I suppose he did. Anyway, he left us.

We all might as well have spent the next three days in bed for all the profit that came out of our running around. No place we visited, nobody we questioned, added to our knowledge. We were in a blind alley.

We learned that the Locomobile was left in Sacramento by Myra Banbrock, and not by anyone else, but we didn't learn where she went afterward. We learned that some of the jewelry in the pawnshop was Mrs. Correll's. The Locomobile was brought back from Sacramento. Mrs. Correll was buried. Ruth Banbrock was buried. The newspapers found other mysteries. Reddy and I dug and dug, and all we brought up was dirt.

The following Monday brought me close to the end of my rope. There seemed nothing more to do but sit back and hope that the circulars with which we had plastered North America would bring results. Reddy had already been called off and put to running out fresher trails. I hung on because Banbrock wanted me to keep at it so long as there was the shadow of anything to keep at. But by Monday I had worked myself out.

Before going to Banbrock's office to tell him I was licked, I dropped in at the Hall of Justice to hold a wake over the job with Pat Reddy. He was crouched over his desk, writing a report on some other job.

"Hello!" he greeted me, pushing his report away and smearing it with ashes from his cigar. "How do the Banbrock doings?"

"They don't," I admitted. "It doesn't seem possible, with the stack-up what it is, that we should have come to a dead stop! It's there for us, if we can find it. The need of money before both the Banbrock and the Correll calamities: Mrs. Correll's suicide after I had questioned her about the girls; her burning things before she died and the burning of things immediately before or after Ruth Banbrock's death."

"Maybe the trouble is," Pat suggested, "that you're not such a good sleuth."

"Maybe."

We smoked in silence for a minute or two after that insult.

"You understand," Pat said presently, "there doesn't have to be any connection between the Banbrock death and disappearance and the Correll death."

"Maybe not. But there has to be a connection between the Banbrock death and the Banbrock disappearance. There was a connection—in a pawnshop—between the Banbrock and Correll actions before these things. If there is that connection, then—"

I broke off, all full of ideas.

"What's the matter?" Pat asked. "Swallow your gum?"

"Listen!" I let myself get almost enthusiastic. "We've got what happened to three women hooked up together. If we could tie up some more in the same string—I want the names and addresses of all the women and girls in San Francisco who have committed suicide, been murdered, or have disappeared within the past year."

"You think this is a wholesale deal?"

"I think the more we can tie up together, the more lines we'll have to run out. And they can't all lead nowhere. Let's get our list, Pat!"

We spent all the afternoon and most of the night getting it. Its size would have embarrassed the Chamber of Commerce. It looked like a hunk of the telephone book. Things happen in a city in a year. The section devoted to strayed wives and daughters was the largest; suicides next; and even the smallest division—murders—wasn't any too short.

We could check off most of the names against what the police department had already learned of them and their motives, weeding out those positively accounted for in a manner nowise connected with our present interest. The remainder we split into two classes; those of unlikely connection, and those of more possible connection. Even then, the second list was longer than I had expected, or hoped.

There were six suicides in it, three murders, and twenty-one disappearances.

Reddy had other work to do. I put the list in my pocket and went calling.

7

FOR FOUR DAYS I ground at the list. I hunted, found, questioned, and investigated friends and relatives of the women and girls on my list. My questions all hit in the same direction. Had she been acquainted with Myra Banbrock? Ruth? Mrs. Correll? Had she been in need of money before her death or disappearance? Had she destroyed anything before her death or disappearance? Had she known any of the other women on my list?

Three times I drew yeses.

Sylvia Varney, a girl of twenty, who had killed herself on November 5th, had drawn six hundred dollars from the bank the week before her death. No one in her family could say what she had done with the money. A friend of Sylvia Varney's—Ada Youngman, a married woman of twenty-five or -six—had disappeared on December 2nd, and was still gone. The Varney girl had been at Mrs. Youngman's home an hour before she—the Varney girl—killed herself.

Mrs. Dorothy Sawdon, a young widow, had shot herself on the night of January 13th. No trace was found of either the money her husband had left her or the funds of a club whose treasurer she was. A bulky letter her maid remembered having given her that afternoon was never found.

These three women's connection with the Banbrock-Correll affair was sketchy enough. None of them had done anything that isn't done by nine out of ten women who kill themselves or run away. But the troubles of all three had come to a head within the past few months—and all three were women of about the same financial and social position as Mrs. Correll and the Banbrocks.

Finishing my list with no fresh leads, I came back to these three.

I had the names and addresses of sixty-two friends of the Banbrock girls. I set about getting the same sort of catalogue on the three women I was trying to bring into the game. I didn't have to do all the digging myself. Fortunately, there were two or three operatives in the office with nothing else to do just then.

We got something.

Mrs. Sawdon had known Raymond Elwood. Sylvia Varney had known Raymond Elwood. There was nothing to show Mrs. Youngman had known him, but it was likely she had. She and the Varney girl had been thick.

I had already interviewed this Raymond Elwood in connection with the Banbrock girls, but had paid no especial attention to him. I had considered him just one of the sleek-headed, high-polished young men of whom there was quite a few listed.

I went back at him, all interest now. The results were promising.

He had, as I have said, a real estate office on Montgomery Street. We were unable to find a single client he had ever served, or any signs of one's existence. He had an apartment out in the Sunset District, where he lived alone. His local record seemed to go back no farther than ten months, though we couldn't find its definite starting point. Apparently he had no relatives in San Francisco. He belonged to a couple of fashionable clubs. He was vaguely supposed to be "well connected in the East." He spent money.

I couldn't shadow Elwood, having too recently interviewed him. Dick Foley did. Elwood was seldom in his office during the first three days Dick tailed him. He was seldom in the financial district. He visited his clubs, he danced and tead and so forth, and each of those three days he visited a house on Telegraph Hill.

The first afternoon Dick had him, Elwood went to the Telegraph Hill house with a tall fair girl from Burlingame. The second day—in the evening—with a plump young woman who came out of a house out on Broadway. The third evening with a very young girl who seemed to live in the same building as he.

Usually Elwood and his companion spent from three to four hours in the house on Telegraph Hill. Other people—all apparently well-to-do—went in and out of the house while it was under Dick's eye.

I climbed Telegraph Hill to give the house the up-and-down. It was a large house—a big frame house painted egg-yellow. It hung dizzily on a shoulder of the hill, a shoulder that was sharp where rock had been quarried away. The house seemed about to go ski-ing down on the roofs far below.

It had no immediate neighbors. The approach was screened by bushes and trees.

I gave that section of the hill a good strong play, calling at all the houses within shooting distance of the yellow one. Nobody knew anything about it, or about its occupants. The folks on the Hill aren't a curious lot—perhaps because most of them have something to hide on their own account.

My climbing uphill and downhill got me nothing until I succeeded in learning who owned the yellow house. The owner was an estate whose affairs were in the hands of the West Coast Trust Company.

I took my investigations to the trust company, with some satisfaction. The house had been leased eight months ago by Raymond Elwood, acting for a client named T.F. Maxwell.

We couldn't find Maxwell. We couldn't find anybody who knew Maxwell. We couldn't find any evidence that Maxwell was anything but a name.

One of the operatives went up to the yellow house on the hill, and rang the bell for half an hour with no result. We didn't try that again, not wanting to stir things up at this stage.

I made another trip up the hill, house-hunting. I couldn't find a place as near the yellow house as I would have liked, but I succeeded in renting a three-room flat from which the approach to it could be watched.

Dick and I camped in the flat—with Pat Reddy, when he wasn't off on other duties—and watched machines turn into the screened path that led to the egg-tinted house. Afternoon and night there were machines. Most of them carried women. We saw no one we could place as a resident of the house. Elwood came daily, once alone, the other time with women whose faces we couldn't see from our window.

We shadowed some of the visitors away. They were without exception reasonably well off financially, and some were socially prominent. We didn't go up against any of them with talk. Even a carefully planned pretext is as likely as not to tip your mitt when you're up against a blind game.

Three days of this—and our break came.

It was early evening, just dark. Pat Reddy had phoned that he had been up on a job for two days and a night, and was going to sleep the clock around. Dick and I were sitting at the window of our flat, watching automobiles turn toward the yellow house, writing down their license numbers as they passed through the blue-white patch of light an arc-lamp put in the road just beyond our window.

A woman came climbing the hill, afoot. She was a tall woman, strongly built. A dark veil, not thick enough to advertise the fact that she wore it to hide her features, nevertheless did hide them. Her way was up the hill, past our flat, on the other side of the roadway.

A night-wind from the Pacific was creaking a grocer's sign down below, swaying the arc-light above. The wind caught the woman as she passed out of our building's sheltered area. Coat and skirts tangled. She put her back to the wind, a hand to her hat. Her veil whipped out straight from her face.

Her face was a face from a photograph—Myra Banbrock's face.

Dick made her with me.

"Our Baby!" he cried, bouncing to his feet.

"Wait," I said. "She's going into the joint on the edge of the hill. Let her go. We'll go after her when she's inside. That's our excuse for frisking the joint."

I went into the next room, where our telephone was, and called Pat Reddy's number.

"She didn't go in," Dick called from the window. "She went past the path."

"After her!" I ordered. "There's no sense to that! What's the matter with her?" I felt sort of indignant about it. "She's got to go in! Tail her. I'll find you after I get Pat."

Dick went.

Pat's wife answered the telephone. I told her who I was.

"Will you shake Pat out of the covers and send him up here? He knows where I am. Tell him I want him in a hurry."

"I will," she promised. "I'll have him there in ten minutes—wherever it is."

Outdoors, I went up the road, hunting for Dick and Myra Banbrock. Neither was in sight. Passing the bushes that masked the yellow house, I went on, circling down a stony path to the left. No sign of either.

I turned back in time to see Dick going into our flat. I followed.

"She's in," he said when I joined him. "She went up the road, cut across through some bushes, came back to the edge of the cliff, and slid feet-first through a cellar window."

That was nice. The crazier the people you are sleuthing act, as a rule, the nearer you are to an ending of your troubles.

Reddy arrived within a minute or two of the time his wife had promised. He came in buttoning his clothes.

"What the hell did you tell Althea?" he growled at me. "She gave me an overcoat to put over my pajamas, dumped the rest of my clothes in the car, and I had to get in them on the way over."

"I'll cry with you after awhile," I dismissed his troubles. "Myra Banbrock just went into the joint through a cellar window. Elwood has been there an hour. Let's knock it off."

Pat is deliberate.

"We ought to have papers, even at that," he stalled.

"Sure," I agreed, "but you can get them fixed up afterward. That's what you're here for. Contra Costa county wants her—maybe to try her for murder. That's all the excuse we need to get into the joint. We go there for her. If we happen to run into anything else—well and good."

Pat finished buttoning his vest.

"Oh, all right!" he said sourly. "Have it your way. But if you get me smashed for searching a house without authority, you'll have to give me a job with your law-breaking agency."

"I will." I turned to Foley. "You'll have to stay outside, Dick. Keep your eye on the getaway. Don't bother anybody else, but if the Banbrock girl gets out, stay behind her."

"I expected it," Dick howled. "Any time there's any fun I can count on being stuck off somewhere on a street corner!"

8

PAT REDDY AND I went straight up the bush-hidden path to the yellow house's front door, and rang the bell.

A big black man in a red fez, red silk jacket over red-striped silk shirt, red zouave pants and red slippers, opened the door. He filled the opening, framed in the black of the hall behind him.

"Is Mr. Maxwell home?" I asked.

The black man shook his head and said words in a language I don't know.

"Mr. Elwood, then?"

Another shaking of the head. More strange language.

"Let's see whoever is home then," I insisted.

Out of the jumble of words that meant nothing to me, I picked three in garbled English, which I thought were "master," "not," and "home."

The door began to close. I put a foot against it.

Pat flashed his buzzer.

Though the black man had poor English, he had knowledge of police badges.

One of his feet stamped on the floor behind him. A gong boomed deafeningly in the rear of the house.

The black man bent his weight to the door.

My weight on the foot that blocked the door, I leaned sidewise, swaying to the negro.

Slamming from the hip, I put my fist in the middle of him.

Reddy hit the door and we went into the hall.

" 'Fore God, Fat Shorty," the black man gasped in good black Virginian, "you done hurt me!"

Reddy and I went by him, down the hall whose bounds were lost in darkness.

The bottom of a flight of steps stopped my feet.

A gun went off upstairs. It seemed to point at us. We didn't get the bullets.

A babel of voices—women screaming, men shouting—came and went upstairs; came and went as if a door was being opened and shut.

"Up, my boy!" Reddy yelped in my ear.

We went up the stairs. We didn't find the man who had shot at us.

At the head of the stairs, a door was locked. Reddy's bulk forced it.

We came into a bluish light. A large room, all purple and gold. Confusion of overturned furniture and rumpled rugs. A gray slipper lay near a far door. A green silk gown was in the center of the floor. No person was there.

I raced Pat to the curtained door beyond the slipper. The door was not locked. Reddy yanked it wide.

A room with three girls and a man crouching in a corner, fear in their faces. Neither of them was Myra Banbrock, or Raymond Elwood, or anyone we knew.

Our glances went away from them after the first quick look. The open door across the room grabbed our attention.

The door gave to a small room.

The room was chaos.

A small room, packed and tangled with bodies. Live bodies, seething, writhing. The room was a funnel into which men and women had been poured. They boiled noisily toward the one small window that was the funnel's outlet. Men and women, youths and girls, screaming, struggling, squirming, fighting. Some had no clothes.

"We'll get through and block the window!" Pat yelled in my ear.

"Like hell—" I began, but he was gone ahead into the confusion.

I went after him.

I didn't mean to block the window. I meant to save Pat from his foolishness. No five men could have fought through that boiling turmoil of maniacs. No ten men could have turned them from the window.

Pat—big as he is—was down when I got to him. A half dressed girl—a child—was driving at his face with sharp high-heels. Hands, feet, were tearing him apart.

I cleared him with a play of gun-barrel on shins and wrists—dragged him back.

"Myra's not there!" I yelled into his ear as I helped him up. "Elwood's not there!"

I wasn't sure, but I hadn't seen them, and I doubted that they would be in this mess. These savages, boiling again to the window, with no attention for us, whoever they were, weren't insiders. They were the mob, and the principals shouldn't be among them.

"We'll try the other rooms," I yelled again. "We don't want these."

Pat rubbed the back of his hand across his torn face and laughed.

"It's a cinch I don't want 'em any more," he said.

We went back to the head of the stairs the way we had come. We saw no one. The man and girls who had been in the next room were gone.

At the head of the stairs we paused. There was no noise behind us except the now fainter babel of the lunatics fighting for their exit.

A door shut sharply downstairs.

A body came out of nowhere, hit my back, flattened me to the landing.

The feel of silk was on my cheek. A brawny hand was fumbling at my throat.

I bent my wrist until my gun, upside down, lay against my cheek. Praying for my ear, I squeezed.

My cheek took fire. My head was a roaring thing, about to burst.

The silk slid away.

Pat hauled me upright.

We started down the stairs.

Swish!

A thing came past my face, stirring my bared hair.

A thousand pieces of glass, china, plaster, exploded upward at my feet.

I tilted head and gun together.

A negro's red-silk arms were still spread over the balustrade above.

I sent him two bullets. Pat sent him two.

The negro teetered over the rail.

He came down on us, arms out-flung—a dead man's swan-dive.

We scurried down the stairs from under him.

He shook the house when he landed, but we weren't watching him then.

The smooth sleek head of Raymond Elwood took our attention.

In the light from above, it showed for a furtive split-second around the newel-post at the foot of the stairs. Showed and vanished.

Pat Reddy, closer to the rail than I, went over it in a one-hand vault down into the blackness below.

I made the foot of the stairs in two jumps, jerked myself around with a hand on the newel, and plunged into the suddenly noisy dark of the hall.

A wall I couldn't see hit me. Caroming off the opposite wall, I spun into a room whose curtained grayness was the light of day after the hall.

9

PAT REDDY STOOD with one hand on a chair-back, holding his belly with the other. His face was mouse-colored under its blood. His eyes were glass agonies. He had the look of a man who had been kicked.

The grin he tried failed. He nodded toward the rear of the house. I went back.

In a little passageway I found Raymond Elwood.

He was sobbing and pulling frantically at a locked door. His face was the hard white of utter terror.

I measured the distance between us.

He turned as I jumped.

I put everything I had in the downswing of my gun-barrel—

A ton of meat and bone crashed into my back.

I went over against the wall, breathless, giddy, sick.

Red-silk arms that ended in brown hands locked around me.

I wondered if there was a whole regiment of these gaudy negroes—or if I was colliding with the same one over and over.

This one didn't let me do much thinking.

He was big. He was strong. He didn't mean any good.

My gun-arm was flat at my side, straight down. I tried a shot at one of the negro's feet. Missed. Tried again. He moved his feet. I wriggled around, half facing him.

Elwood piled on my other side.

The negro bent me backward, folding my spine on itself like an accordion.

I fought to hold my knees stiff. Too much weight was hanging on me. My knees sagged. My body curved back.

Pat Reddy, swaying in the doorway, shone over the negro's shoulder like the Angel Gabriel.

Gray pain was in Pat's face, but his eyes were clear. His right hand held a gun. His left was getting a blackjack out of his hip pocket.

He swung the sap down on the negro's shaven skull.

The black man wheeled away from me, shaking his head.

Pat hit him once more before the negro closed with him— hit him full in the face, but couldn't beat him off.

Twisting my freed gun-hand up, I drilled Elwood neatly through the chest, and let him slide down me to the floor.

The negro had Pat against the wall, bothering him a lot. His broad red back was a target.

But I had used five of the six bullets in my gun. I had more in my pocket, but reloading takes time.

I stepped out of Elwood's feeble hands, and went to work with the flat of my gun on the negro. There was a roll of fat where his skull and neck fit together. The third time I hit it, he flopped, taking Pat with him.

I rolled him off. The blond police detective—not very blond now—got up.

At the other end of the passageway, an open door showed an empty kitchen.

Pat and I went to the door that Elwood had been playing with. It was a solid piece of carpentering, and neatly fastened.

Yoking ourselves together, we began to beat the door with our combined three hundred and seventy or eighty pounds.

It shook, but held. We hit it again. Wood we couldn't see tore. Again.

The door popped away from us. We went through—down a flight of steps—rolling, snowballing down—until a cement floor stopped us.

Pat came back to life first.

"You're a hell of an acrobat," he said. "Get off my neck!"

I stood up. He stood up. We seemed to be dividing the evening between falling on the floor and getting up from the floor.

A light-switch was at my shoulder. I turned it on.

If I looked anything like Pat, we were a fine pair of nightmares. He was all raw meat and dirt, with not enough clothes left to hide much of either.

I didn't like his looks, so I looked around the basement in which we stood. To the rear was a furnace, coal-bins and a woodpile. To the front was a hallway and rooms, after the manner of the upstairs.

The first door we tried was locked, but not strongly. We smashed through it into a photographer's dark-room.

The second door was unlocked, and put us in a chemical laboratory: retorts, tubes, burners and a small still. There was a little round iron stove in the middle of the room. No one was there.

We went out into the hallway and to the third door, not so cheerfully. This cellar looked like a bloomer. We were wasting our time here, when we should have stayed upstairs. I tried the door.

It was firm beyond trembling.

We smacked it with our weight, together, experimentally. It didn't shake.

"Wait."

Pat went to the woodpile in the rear and came back with an axe.

He swung the axe against the door, flaking out a hunk of wood. Silvery points of light sparkled in the hole. The other side of the door was an iron or steel plate.

Pat put the axe down and leaned on the helve.

"You write the next prescription," he said.

I didn't have anything to suggest, except:

"I'll camp here. You beat it upstairs, and see if any of your coppers have shown up. This is a God-forsaken hole, but somebody may have sent in an alarm. See if you can find another way into this room—a window, maybe—or man-power enough to get us in through this door."

Pat turned toward the steps.

A sound stopped him—the clicking of bolts on the other side of the iron-lined door.

A jump put Pat on one side of the frame. A step put me on the other.

Slowly the door moved in. Too slowly.

I kicked it open.

Pat and I went into the room on top of my kick.

His shoulder hit the woman. I managed to catch her before she fell.

Pat took her gun. I steadied her back on her feet.

Her face was a pale blank square.

She was Myra Banbrock, but she now had none of the masculinity that had been in her photographs and description.

Steadying her with one arm—which also served to block her arms—I looked around the room.

A small cube of a room whose walls were brown-painted

metal. On the floor lay a queer little dead man.

A little man in tight-fitting black velvet and silk. Black velvet blouse and breeches, black silk stockings and skull cap, black patent leather pumps. His face was small and old and bony, but smooth as stone, without line or wrinkle.

A hole was in his blouse, where it fit high under his chin. The hole bled very slowly. The floor around him showed it had been bleeding faster a little while ago.

Beyond him, a safe was open. Papers were on the floor in front of it, as if the safe had been tilted to spill them out.

The girl moved against my arm.

"You killed him?" I asked.

"Yes," too faint to have been heard a yard away.

"Why?"

She shook her short brown hair out of her eyes with a tired jerk of her head.

"Does it make any difference?" she asked. "I did kill him."

"It might make a difference," I told her, taking my arm away, and going over to shut the door. People talk more freely in a room with a closed door. "I happen to be in your father's employ. Mr. Reddy is a police detective. Of course, neither of us can smash any laws, but if you'll tell us what's what, maybe we can help you."

"My father's employ?" she questioned.

"Yes. When you and your sister disappeared, he engaged me to find you. We found your sister, and—"

Life came into her face and eyes and voice.

"I didn't kill Ruth!" she cried. "The papers lied! I didn't kill her! I didn't know she had the revolver. I didn't know it! We were going away to hide from—from everything. We stopped in the woods to burn the—those things. That's the first time I knew she had the revolver. We had talked about suicide at first, but I had persuaded her—thought I had persuaded her—not to. I tried to take the revolver away from her, but I couldn't. She shot herself while I was trying to get it away. I tried to stop her. I didn't kill her!"

This was getting somewhere.

"And then?" I encouraged her.

"And then I went to Sacramento and left the car there, and came back to San Francisco. Ruth told me she had written Raymond Elwood a letter. She told me that before I persuaded her not to kill herself—the first time. I tried to get the letter from Raymond. She had written him she was going to kill herself. I tried to get the letter, but Raymond said he had given it to Hador.

"So I came here this evening to get it. I had just found it when there was a lot of noise upstairs. Then Hador came in and found me. He bolted the door. And—and I shot him with the revolver that was in the safe. I—I shot him when he turned around, before he could say anything. It had to be that way, or I couldn't."

"You mean you shot him without being threatened or attacked by him?" Pat asked.

"Yes. I was afraid of him, afraid to let him speak. I hated him! I couldn't help it. It had to be that way. If he had talked I couldn't have shot him. He—he wouldn't have let me!"

"Who was this Hador?" I asked.

She looked away from Pat and me, at the walls, at the ceiling, at the queer little dead man on the floor.

10

"HE WAS A—" She cleared her throat, and started again, staring down at her feet. "Raymond Elwood brought us here the first time. We thought it was funny. But Hador was a devil. He told you things and you believed them. You couldn't help it. He told you everything and you believed it. Perhaps we were drugged. There was always a warm bluish wine. It must have been drugged. We couldn't have done those things if it hadn't. Nobody would— He called himself a priest—a priest of Alzoa. He taught a freeing of the spirit from the flesh by—"

Her voice broke huskily. She shuddered.

"It was horrible!" she went on presently in the silence Pat and I had left for her. "But you believed him. That is the whole thing. You can't understand it unless you understand that. The things he taught could not be so. But he said they were, and you believed they were. Or maybe—I don't know—maybe you pretended you believed them, because you were crazy and drugs were in your blood. We came back again and again, for weeks, months, before the disgust that had to come drove us away.

"We stopped coming, Ruth and I—and Irma. And then we found out what he was. He demanded money, more money than we had been paying while we believed—or pretended belief— in his cult. We couldn't give him the money he demanded. I told him we wouldn't. He sent us photographs—of us—taken during the—the times here. They were—pictures—you— couldn't—explain. And they were true! We knew them true!

What could we do? He said he would send copies to our father, every friend, everyone we knew—unless we paid.

"What could we do—except pay? We got the money somehow. We gave him money—more—more—more. And then we had no more—could get no more. We didn't know what to do! There was nothing to do, except— Ruth and Irma wanted to kill themselves. I thought of that, too. But I persuaded Ruth not to. I said we'd go away. I'd take her away—keep her safe. And then—then—this!"

She stopped talking, went on staring at her feet.

I looked again at the little dead man on the floor, weird in his black cap and clothes. No more blood came from his throat.

It wasn't hard to put the pieces together. This dead Hador, self-ordained priest of something or other, staging orgies under the alias of religious ceremonies. Elwood, his confederate, bringing women of family and wealth to him. A room lighted for photography, with a concealed camera. Contributions from his converts so long as they were faithful to the cult. Blackmail—with the help of the photographs—afterward.

I looked from Hador to Pat Reddy. He was scowling at the dead man. No sound came from outside the room.

"You have the letter your sister wrote Elwood?" I asked the girl.

Her hand flashed to her bosom, and crinkled paper there. "Yes."

"It says plainly she meant to kill herself?"

"Yes."

"That ought to square her with Contra Costa county," I said to Pat.

He nodded his battered head.

"It ought to," he agreed. "It's not likely that they could prove murder on her even without that letter. With it, they'll not take her into court. That's a safe bet. Another is that she won't have any trouble over this shooting. She'll come out of court free, and thanked in the bargain."

Myra Banbrock flinched away from Pat as if he had hit her in the face.

I was her father's hired man just now. I saw her side of the affair.

I lit a cigarette and studied what I could see of Pat's face through blood and grime. Pat is a right guy.

"Listen, Pat," I wheedled him, though with a voice that was as if I were not trying to wheedle him at all. "Miss Banbrock can go into court and come out free and thanked, as you say. But to do it, she's got to use everything she knows. She's got to have all the evidence there is. She's got to use all those photographs Hador took—or all we can find of them.

"Some of those pictures have sent women to suicide, Pat—at least two that we know. If Miss Banbrock goes into court, we've got to make the photographs of God knows how many other women public property. We've got to advertise things that will put Miss Banbrock—and you can't say how many other women and girls—in a position that at least two women have killed themselves to escape."

Pat scowled at me and rubbed his dirty chin with a dirtier thumb.

I took a deep breath and made my play.

"Pat, you and I came here to question Raymond Elwood, having traced him here. Maybe we suspected him of being tied up with the mob that knocked over the St. Louis bank last month. Maybe we suspected him of handling the stuff that was taken from the mail cars in that stick-up near Denver week before last. Anyway, we were after him, knowing that he had a lot of money that came from nowhere, and a real estate office that did no real estate business.

"We came here to question him in connection with one of these jobs I've mentioned. We were jumped by a couple of the shines upstairs when they found we were sleuths. The rest of it grew out of that. This religious cult business was just something we ran into, and didn't interest us especially. So far as we knew, all these folks jumped us just through friendship for the man we were trying to question. Hador was one of them, and, tussling with you, you shot him with his own gun, which, of course, is the one Miss Banbrock found in the safe."

Reddy didn't seem to like my suggestion at all. The eyes with which he regarded me were decidedly sour.

"You're goofy," he accused me. "What'll that get anybody? That won't keep Miss Banbrock out of it. She's here, isn't she, and the rest of it will come out like thread off a spool."

"But Miss Banbrock wasn't here," I explained. "Maybe the upstairs is full of coppers by now. Maybe not. Anyway, you're going to take Miss Banbrock out of here and turn her over to Dick Foley, who will take her home. She's got nothing to do with this party. Tomorrow she, and her father's lawyer, and I, will all go up to Martinez and make a deal with the prosecuting attorney of Contra Costa county. We'll show him how Ruth killed herself. If somebody happens to connect the Elwood who I hope is dead upstairs with the Elwood who knew the girls and Mrs. Correll, what of it? If we keep out of court— as we'll do by convincing the Contra Costa people they can't possibly convict her of her sister's murder—we'll keep out of the newspapers—and out of trouble."

Pat hung fire, thumb still to chin.

"Remember," I urged him, "it's not only Miss Banbrock we're doing this for. It's a couple of dead ones, and a flock of live ones, who certainly got mixed up with Hador of their own accords, but who don't stop being human beings on that account."

Pat shook his head stubbornly.

"I'm sorry," I told the girl with faked hopelessness. "I've done all I can, but it's a lot to ask of Reddy. I don't know that I blame him for being afraid to take a chance on—"

Pat is Irish.

"Don't be so damned quick to fly off," he snapped at me, cutting short my hypocrisy. "But why do I have to be the one that shot this Hador? Why not you?"

I had him!

"Because," I explained, "you're a bull and I'm not. There'll be less chance of a slip-up if he was shot by a bona fide, star-wearing, flat-footed officer of the peace. I killed most of those birds upstairs. You ought to do something to show you were here."

That was only part of the truth. My idea was that if Pat took the credit, he couldn't very well ease himself out afterward, no matter what happened. Pat's a right guy, and I'd trust him anywhere—but you can trust a man just as easily if you have him sewed up.

Pat grumbled and shook his head, but:

"I'm ruining myself, I don't doubt," he growled, "but I'll do it, this once."

"Attaboy!" I went over to pick up the girl's hat from the

corner in which it lay. "I'll wait here until you come back from turning her over to Dick." I gave the girl her hat and orders together. "You go to your home with the man Reddy turns you over to. Stay there until I come, which will be as soon as I can make it. Don't tell anybody anything, except that I told you to keep quiet. That includes your father. Tell him I told you not to tell him even where you saw me. Got it?"

"Yes, and I—"

Gratitude is nice to think about afterward, but it takes time when there's work to be done.

"Get going, Pat!"

They went.

11

AS SOON AS I was alone with the dead man I stepped over him and knelt in front of the safe, pushing letters and papers away, hunting for photographs. None was in sight. One compartment of the safe was locked.

I frisked the corpse. No key. The locked compartment wasn't very strong, but neither am I the best safe-burglar in the West. It took me a while to get into it.

What I wanted was there. A thick sheaf of negatives. A stack of prints—half a hundred of them.

I started to run through them, hunting for the Banbrock girls' pictures. I wanted to have them pocketed before Pat came back. I didn't know how much farther he would let me go.

Luck was against me—and the time I had wasted getting into the compartment. He was back before I had got past the sixth print in the stack. Those six had been—pretty bad.

"Well, that's done," Pat growled at me as he came into the room. "Dick's got her. Elwood is dead, and so is the only one of the negroes I saw upstairs. Everybody else seems to have beat it. No bulls have shown—so I put in a call for a wagonful."

I stood up, holding the sheaf of negatives in one hand, the prints in the other.

"What's all that?" he asked.

I went after him again.

"Photographs. You've just done me a big favor, Pat, and I'm not hoggish enough to ask another. But I'm going to put something in front of you, Pat. I'll give you the lay, and you can name it.

"These"—I waved the pictures at him—"are Hador's meal-tickets—the photos he was either collecting on or planning to collect on. They're photographs of people, Pat, mostly women and girls, and some of them are pretty rotten.

"If tomorrow's papers say that a flock of photos were found in this house after the fireworks, there's going to be a fat suicide-list in the next day's papers, and a fatter list of disappearances. If the papers say nothing about the photos, the lists may be a little smaller, but not much. Some of the people whose pictures are here know they are here. They will expect the police to come hunting for them. We know this much about the photographs—two women have killed themselves to get away from them. This is an armful of stuff that can dynamite a lot of people, Pat, and a lot of families—no matter which of those two ways the papers read.

"But, suppose, Pat, the papers say that just before you shot Hador he succeeded in burning a lot of pictures and papers, burning them beyond recognition. Isn't it likely, then, that there won't be any suicides? That some of the disappearances of recent months may clear themselves up? There she is, Pat—you name it."

Looking back, it seems to me I had come a lot nearer being eloquent than ever before in my life.

But Pat didn't applaud.

He cursed me. He cursed me thoroughly, bitterly, and with an amount of feeling that told me I had won another point in my little game. He called me more things than I ever listened to before from a man who was built of meat and bone, and who therefore could be smacked.

When he was through, we carried the papers and photographs and a small book of addresses we found in the safe into the next room, and fed them to the little round iron stove there. The last of them was ash before we heard the police overhead.

"That's absolutely all!" Pat declared when we got up from our work. "Don't ever ask me to do anything else for you if you live to be a thousand."

"That's absolutely all," I echoed.

I like Pat. He is a right guy. The sixth photograph in the stack had been of his wife—the coffee importer's reckless, hot-eyed daughter.

Corkscrew

1

BOILING LIKE A coffee pot before we were five miles out of Filmer, the automobile stage carried me south into the shimmering heat, blinding sunlight, and bitter white dust of the Arizona desert.

I was the only passenger. The driver felt as little like talking as I. All morning we rode through cactus-spiked, sage-studded oven-country, without conversation, except when the driver cursed the necessity of stopping to feed his clattering machine more water. The car crept through soft sifting sand; wound between steep-walled red mesas; dipped into dry arroyas where clumps of dusty mesquite were like white lace in the glare; and skirted sharp-edged barrancos.

All these things were hot. All of them tried to get rid of their heat by throwing it on the car. My fat melted in the heat. The heat dried my perspiration before I could feel its moisture. The dazzling light scorched my eyeballs; puckered my lids; cooked my mouth. Alkali stung my nose; was gritty between my teeth.

It was a nice ride! I understood why the natives were a hard lot. A morning like this would put any man in a mood to kill his brother, and would fry his brother into not caring whether he was killed.

The sun climbed up in the brazen sky. The higher it got, the larger and hotter it got. I wondered how much hotter it would have to get to explode the cartridges in the gun under my arm. Not that it mattered—if it got any hotter, we would all blow up anyway. Car, desert, chauffeur and I would all bang out of existence in one explosive flash. I didn't care if we did!

That was my frame of mind as we pushed up a long slope, topped a sharp ridge, and slid down into Corkscrew.

Corkscrew wouldn't have been impressive at any time. It especially wasn't this white-hot Sunday afternoon. One sandy street following the crooked edge of the Tirabuzon Cañon, from which, by translation, the town took its name. A town, it was called, but village would have been flattery: fifteen or eighteen shabby buildings slumped along the irregular street, with tumble-down shacks leaning against them, squatting close to them, and trying to sneak away from them.

That was Corkscrew. One look at it, and I believed all I had heard about it!

In the street, four dusty automobiles cooked. Between two buildings I could see a corral where half a dozen horses bunched their dejection under a shed. No person was in sight. Even the stage driver, carrying a limp and apparently empty mail sack, had vanished into a building labelled "Adderly's Emporium."

Gathering up my two grey-powdered bags, I climbed out and crossed the road to where a weather-washed sign, on which Cañon House was barely visible, hung over the door of a two-story, iron-roofed, adobe house.

I crossed the wide, unpainted and unpeopled porch, and pushed a door open with my foot, going into a dining-room, where a dozen men and a woman sat eating at oilcloth-covered tables. In one corner of the room, was a cashier's desk; and, on the wall behind it, a key-rack. Between rack and desk, a pudgy man whose few remaining hairs were the exact shade of his sallow skin, sat on a stool, and pretended he didn't see me.

"A room and a lot of water," I said, dropping my bags, and reaching for the glass that sat on top of a cooler in the corner.

"You can have your room," the sallow man growled, "but water won't do you no good. You won't no sooner drink and wash, than you'll be thirsty and dirty all over again. Where in hell is that register?"

He couldn't find it, so he pushed an old envelope across the desk at me.

"Register on the back of that. Be with us a spell?"

"Most likely."

A chair upset behind me.

I turned around as a lanky man with enormous red ears reared himself upright with the help of his hands on the table—one of them flat in the plate of ham and eggs he had been eating.

"Ladiesh an' gentsh," he solemnly declaimed, "th' time hash came for yuh t' give up y'r evil waysh an' git out y'r knittin'. Th' law hash came to Orilla County!"

The drunk bowed to me, upset his ham and eggs, and sat down again. The other diners applauded with thump of knives and forks on tables and dishes.

I looked them over while they looked me over. A miscellaneous assortment: weather-beaten horsemen, clumsily muscled laborers, men with the pasty complexions of night workers. The one woman in the room didn't belong to Arizona. She was a thin girl of maybe twenty-five, with too-bright dark eyes, dark, short hair, and a sharp prettiness that was the mark of a larger settlement than this. You've seen her, or her sisters, in the larger cities, in the places that get going after the theatres let out.

The man with her was range country—a slim lad in the early

twenties, not very tall, with pale blue eyes that were startling in so dark-tanned a face. His features were a bit too perfect in their clean-cut regularity.

"So you're the new deputy sheriff?" the sallow man questioned the back of my head.

Somebody had kept my secret right out in the open! There was no use trying to cover up.

"Yes." I hid my annoyance under a grin that took in him and the diners. "But I'll trade my star right now for that room and water we were talking about."

He took me through the dining-room and upstairs to a board-walled room in the rear second floor, said, "This is it," and left me.

I did what I could with the water in a pitcher on the washstand to free myself from the white grime I had accumulated. Then I dug a grey shirt and a suit of whipcords out of my bags, and holstered my gun under my left shoulder, where it wouldn't be a secret.

In each side pocket of my coat I stowed a new .32 automatic—small, snub-nosed affairs that weren't much better than toys. Their smallness let me carry them where they'd be close to my hands without advertising the fact that the gun under my shoulder wasn't all my arsenal.

The dining-room was empty when I went downstairs again. The sallow pessimist who ran the place stuck his head out of a door.

"Any chance of getting something to eat?" I asked.

"Hardly any," jerking his head toward a sign that said: "Meals 6 to 8 A.M., 12 to 2 and 5 to 7 P.M."

"You can grub up at the Jew's—if you ain't particular," he

added sourly.

I went out, across the porch that was too hot for idlers, and into the street that was empty for the same reason. Huddled against the wall of a large one-story adobe building, which had Border Palace painted all across its front, I found the Jew's.

It was a small shack—three wooden walls stuck against the adobe wall of the Border Palace—jammed with a lunch counter, eight stools, a stove, a handful of cooking implements, half the flies in the world, an iron cot behind a half-drawn burlap curtain, and the proprietor. The interior had once been painted white. It was a smoky grease-color now, except where home-made signs said:

"Meals At All Hours. No Credit" and gave the prices of various foods. These signs were a fly-specked yellow-grey.

The proprietor wasn't a Jew—an Armenian or something of the sort, I thought. He was a small man, old, scrawny, dark-skinned, wrinkled and cheerful.

"You the new sheriff?" he asked, and when he grinned I saw he had no teeth.

"Deputy," I admitted, "and hungry. I'll eat anything you've got that won't bite back, and that won't take long to get ready."

"Sure!" He turned to his stove and began banging pans around. "We need sheriffs," he said over his shoulder. "Sure, we need them!"

"Somebody been picking on you?"

He showed his empty gums in another grin.

"Nobody pick on me—I tell you that!" He flourished a stringy hand at a sugar barrel under the shelves behind his counter. "I fix them decidedly!"

A shotgun butt stuck out of the barrel. I pulled it out: a

double-barrel shotgun with the barrels sawed off short: a mean weapon close up.

I slid it back into its resting place as the old man began thumping dishes down in front of me.

2

THE FOOD INSIDE me and a cigarette burning, I went out into the crooked street again. From the Border Palace came the clicking of pool balls. I followed the sound through the door.

In a large room, four men were leaning over a couple of pool tables, while five or six more watched them from chairs along the wall. On one side of the room was an oak bar, with nobody behind it. Through an open door in the rear came the sound of shuffling cards.

A big man whose paunch was dressed in a white vest, over a shirt in the bosom of which a diamond sparkled, came toward me; his triple-chinned red face expanding into the professionally jovial smile of a confidence man.

"I'm Bardell," he greeted me, stretching out a fat and shiny-nailed hand on which more diamonds glittered. "This is my joint. I'm glad to know you, sheriff! By God, we need you, and I hope you can spend a lot of your time here. These waddies"— and he chuckled, nodding at the pool players—"cut up rough on me sometimes, and I'm glad there's going to be somebody around who can handle them."

I let him pump my hand up and down.

"Let me make you known to the boys," he went on, turning with one arm across my shoulders. "These are Circle H.A.R. riders"—waving some of his rings at the pool players—"except this Milk River hombre, who, being a peeler, kind of looks down on ordinary hands."

The Milk River hombre was the slender youth who had sat beside the girl in the Cañon House dining-room. His companions were young—though not quite so young as he—sun-marked, wind-marked, pigeontoed in high-heeled boots. Buck Small was sandy and pop-eyed; Smith was sandy and short; Dunne was a rangy Irishman.

The men watching the game were mostly laborers from the Orilla Colony, or hands from some of the smaller ranches in the neighborhood. There were two exceptions: Chick Orr, short, thick-bodied, heavy-armed, with the shapeless nose, battered ears, gold front teeth and gnarled hands of a pugilist; and Gyp Rainey, a slack-chinned, ratty individual whose whole front spelled cocaine.

Conducted by Bardell, I went into the back room to meet the poker players. There were only four of them. The other six card tables, the keno outfit, and the dice table were idle.

One of the players was the big-eared drunk who had made the welcoming speech at the hotel. Slim Vogel was the name. He was a Circle H.A.R. hand, as was Red Wheelan, who sat beside him. Both of them were full of hooch. The third player was a quiet, middle-aged man named Keefe. Number four was Mark Nisbet, a pale, slim man. Gambler was written all over him, from his heavy-lidded brown eyes to the slender sureness of his white fingers.

Nisbet and Vogel didn't seem to be getting along so good.

It was Nisbet's deal, and the pot had already been opened. Vogel, who had twice as many chips as anybody else, threw away two cards.

"I want both of 'em off'n th' top—this time!" and he didn't say it nicely.

Nisbet dealt the cards, with nothing in his appearance to show he had heard the crack. Red Wheelan took three cards. Keefe was out. Nisbet drew one. Wheelan bet. Nisbet stayed. Vogel raised. Wheelan stayed. Nisbet raised. Vogel bumped it again. Wheelan dropped out. Nisbet raised once more.

"I'm bettin' you took your draw off'n th' top, too," Vogel snarled across the table at Nisbet, and tilted the pot again.

Nisbet called. He had aces over kings. The cowpuncher had three nines.

Vogel laughed noisily as he raked in the chips.

" 'F I could keep a sheriff behind you t' watch you all th' time, I'd do somethin' for myself!"

Nisbet pretended to be busy straightening his chips. I sympathized with him. He had played his hand rotten—but how else can you play against a drunk?

"How d'you like our little town?" Red Wheelan asked me.

"I haven't seen much of it yet," I stalled. "The hotel, the lunch-counter—they're all I've seen outside of here."

Wheelan laughed.

"So you met the Jew? That's Slim's friend!"

Everybody except Nisbet laughed, including Slim Vogel.

"Slim tried to beat the Jew out of two bits' worth of Java and sinkers once. He says he forgot to pay for 'em, but it's more likely he sneaked out. Anyways, the next day, here comes the Jew, stirring dust into the ranch, a shotgun under his arm. He'd lugged that instrument of destruction fifteen miles across the desert, on foot, to collect his two bits. He collected, too! He took his little two bits away from Slim right there between the corral and the bunkhouse—at the cannon's mouth, as you might say!"

Slim Vogel grinned ruefully and scratched one of his big ears.

"The old son-of-a-gun done came after me just like I was a damned thief! 'F he'd of been a man I'd of seen him in hell 'fore I'd of gave it to him. But what can y' do with an old buzzard that ain't even got no teeth to bite you with?"

His bleary eyes went back to the table, and the laughter went out of them. The laugh on his loose lips changed to a sneer.

"Let's play," he growled, glaring at Nisbet. "It's a honest man's deal this time!"

Bardell and I went back to the front of the building, where the cowboys were still knocking the balls around. I sat in one of the chairs against the wall, and let them talk around me. The conversation wasn't exactly fluent. Anybody could tell there was a stranger present.

My first job was to get over that.

"Got any idea," I asked nobody in particular, "where I could pick up a horse? One that can run pretty good, but that isn't too tricky for a bum rider to sit."

The Milk River hombre was playing the seven ball in a side pocket. He made the shot, and his pale eyes looked at the pocket into which the ball had gone for a couple of seconds before he straightened up. Lanky Dunne was looking fixedly at nothing, his mouth puckered a bit. Buck Small's pop-eyes were intent on the tip of his cue.

"You might get one at Echlin's stable," Milk River said slowly, meeting my gaze with guileless blue eyes; "though it ain't likely he's got anything that'll live long if you hurry it. I tell you what—Peery, out to the ranch, has got a buckskin that'd just fit you. He won't want to let him go, but if you took some real money along and flapped it in his face, maybe you could deal. He does need money."

"You're not steering me into a horse I can't handle, are you?" I asked.

The pale eyes went blank.

"I ain't steering you into nothing whatsomever, Mister," he said. "You asked for information. I give it to you. But I don't mind telling you that anybody that can stay in a rocking chair can sit that buckskin."

"That's fine. I'll go out tomorrow."

Milk River put his cue down, frowning.

"Come to think of it, Peery's going down to the lower camp tomorrow. I tell you—if you got nothing else to do, we'll mosey out there right now. It's Sunday, and we'll be sure of catching him."

"Good," I said, and stood up.

"You boys going home?" Milk River asked his companions.

"Yeah," Smith spoke casually. "We gotta roll out early in the mornin', so I s'pose we'd ought to be shakin' along out there. I'll see if Slim an' Red are ready."

They weren't. Vogel's disagreeable voice came through the open door.

"I'm camped right here! I got this reptile on th' run, an' it's only a matter o' time 'fore he'll have t' take a chance on pullin' 'em off'n th' bottom t' save his hide. An' that's exac'ly what I'm awaitin' for! Th' first time he gets fancy, I'm goin' t' open him up from his Adam's apple plumb down to his ankles!"

Smith returned to us.

"Slim an' Red are gonna play 'em a while. They'll git a lift out when they git enough."

Milk River, Smith, Dunne, Small and I went out of the Border Palace.

3

THREE STEPS FROM the door, a stooped, white-mustached man in a collarless stiff-bosomed shirt swooped down on me, as if he had been lying in wait.

"My name's Adderly," he introduced himself, holding out one hand toward me while flicking the other at Adderly's Emporium. "Got a minute or two to spare? I'd like to make you acquainted with some of the folks."

The Circle H.A.R. men were walking slowly toward one of the machines in the street.

"Can you wait a couple of minutes?" I called after them.

Milk River looked back over his shoulder.

"Yes. We got to gas and water the flivver. Take yor time."

Adderly led me toward his store, talking as he walked.

"Some of the better element is at my house—danged near all the better element. The folks who'll back you up if you'll put the fear of God in Corkscrew. We're tired and sick of this perpetual hell-raising."

We went through his store, across a yard, and into his house. There were a dozen or more people in his living-room.

The Reverend Dierks—a gangling, emaciated man with a tight mouth in a long, thin face—made a speech at me. He called me brother, he told me what a wicked place Corkscrew was, and he told me he and his friends were prepared to swear out warrants for the arrest of various men who had committed sixty-some crimes during the past two years.

He had a list of them, with names, dates, and hours, which

he read to me. Everybody I had met that day—except those here—was on that list at least once, along with a lot of names I didn't know. The crimes ranged from murder to intoxication and the use of profane language.

"If you'll let me have that list, I'll study it," I promised.

He gave it to me, but he wasn't to be put off with promises.

"To refrain even for an hour from punishing wickedness is to be a partner to that wickedness, brother. You have been inside that house of sin operated by Bardell. You have heard the Sabbath desecrated with the sound of pool-balls. You have smelled the foul odor of illegal rum on men's breaths!

"Strike now, brother! Let it not be said that you condoned evil from your first day in Corkscrew! You have seen men whose garments did not conceal the deadly weapons under them! In that list is the black record of many months' unatoned sinfulness. Strike now, brother, for the Lord and righteousness! Go into those hells and do your duty as an officer of the law and a Christian!"

This was a minister; I didn't like to laugh.

I looked at the others. They were sitting—men and women—on the edges of their chairs. On their faces were the same expressions you see around a prize ring just before the gong rings.

Mrs. Echlin, the livery man's wife, an angular-faced, angular-bodied woman, caught my gaze with her pebble-hard eyes.

"And that brazen scarlet woman who calls herself Señora Gaia—and the three hussies who pretend they're her daughters! You ain't much of a deputy sheriff if you leave 'em in that house of theirs one night longer—to poison the manhood of Orilla County!"

The others nodded vigorously. Echlin's eyes had lit up at his wife's words, and he licked his lips as he nodded.

Miss Janey, school teacher, false-toothed, sour-faced, put in her part:

"And even worse than those—those creatures, is that Clio Landes! Worse, because at least those—those hussies"—she looked down, managed a blush, looked out of the corners of her eyes at the minister—"those hussies are at least openly what they are. While she—who knows how bad she really is?"

"I don't know about her," Adderly began, but his wife shut him up.

"I do!" she snapped. She was a large, mustached woman whose corsets made knobs and points in her shiny black dress. "Miss Janey is perfectly right. That woman is worse than the rest!"

"Is this Clio Landes person on your list?" I asked, not remembering it.

"No, brother, she is not," the Reverend Dierks said regretfully. "But only because she is more subtle than the others. Corkscrew would indeed be better without her—a woman of obviously low moral standards, with no visible means of support, associating with our worst element."

"I'm glad to have met you folks," I said as I folded the list and put it in my pocket. "And I'm glad to know you'll back me up."

I edged toward the door, hoping to get away without much more talk. Not a chance. The Reverend Dierks followed me up.

"You will strike now, brother? You will carry God's war immediately into blind tiger and brothel and gambling hell?"

The others were on their feet now, closing in.

"I'll have to look things over first," I stalled.

"Brother, are you evading your duty? Are you procrastinating in the face of Satan? If you are the man I hope you are, you will march now, with the decent citizens of Corkscrew at your heels, to wipe from the face of our town the sin that blackens it!"

So that was it. I was to lead one of these vice-crusading mobs. I wondered how many of these crusaders would be standing behind me if one of the devil's representatives took a shot at me. The minister maybe—his thin face was grimly pugnacious. But I couldn't imagine what good he'd be in a row. The others would scatter at the first sign of trouble.

I stopped playing politics and said my say.

"I'm glad to have your support," I said, "but there isn't going to be any wholesale raiding—not for a while, anyway. Later, I'll try to get around to the bootleggers and gamblers and similar small fry, though I'm not foolish enough to think I can put them all out of business. Just now, so long as they don't cut up too rough, I don't expect to bother them. I haven't the time.

"This list you've given me—I'll do what I think ought to be done after I've examined it, but I'm not going to worry a lot over a batch of petty misdemeanors that happened a year ago. I'm starting from scratch. What happens from now on is what interests me. See you later."

And I left.

The cowboys' car was standing in front of the store when I came out.

"I've been meeting the better element," I explained as I found a place in it between Milk River and Buck Small.

Milk River's brown face wrinkled around his eyes.

"Then you know what kind of riff-raff we are," he said.

4

DUNNE DRIVING, THE car carried us out of Corkscrew at the street's southern end, and then west along the sandy and rocky bottom of a shallow draw. The sand was deep and the rocks were numerous; we didn't make very good time. An hour and a half of jolting, sweltering and smothering in this draw, and we climbed up out of it and crossed to a larger and greener draw, where the mesquite grew in small trees and bees zizzed among wild flowers.

Around a bend in this draw the Circle H.A.R. buildings sat. We got out of the automobile under a low shed, where another car already stood. A heavily muscled, heavily boned man came around a white-washed building toward us. His face was square and dark. His close-clipped mustache and deep-set small eyes were dark.

This, I learned, was Peery, who bossed the ranch for the owner, who lived in the East.

"He wants a nice, mild horse," Milk River told Peery, "and we thought maybe you might sell him that Rollo horse of yours. That's the nicest, mildest horse I ever heard tell of."

Peery tilted his high-crowned sombrero back on his head and rocked on his heels.

"What was you figuring on paying for this here horse?"

"If it suits me," I said, "I'm willing to pay what it takes to buy him."

"That ain't so bad," he said. "S'pose one of you boys dab a rope on that buckskin and bring him around for the gent to look at."

Smith and Dunne set out together, pretending they weren't going eagerly.

"Where's Red and Slim?" Peery asked.

"Stayin' in a while," Small told him. "Slim's a million ahead in a poker game."

Presently the two cowhands came back, riding, with the buckskin between them, already saddled and bridled. I noticed each of them had a rope on him. He was a loose-jointed pony of an unripe lemon color, with a sad, drooping, Roman-nosed head.

"There he is," Peery said. "Try him out and we'll talk dinero. I warn you, I ain't so damned anxious to get rid of him that I'll let him go for nothing. But you try him first—trot him down the draw a little ways and back. He's downright sweet."

I chucked away my cigarette and went over to the buckskin. He cocked one mournful eye at me, twitched one ear, and went on looking sadly at the ground. Dunne and Smith took their lines off him, and I got into the saddle.

Rollo stood still under me until the other horses had left his side.

Then he showed me what he had.

He went straight up in the air—and hung there long enough to turn around before he came down. He stood on his front feet and then on his hind ones, and then he got off all of them again.

I didn't like this, but it wasn't a surprise. I had known I was a lamb being led to the slaughter. This was the third time it had happened to me. I might as well get it over with. A city man in range country is bound to find himself sitting on a disagreeable bone sooner or later. I'm a city man. I can sit any street car or taxicab in the world, and I can even ride a horse if he'll coöperate. But when the horse doesn't want to stay under me—the horse wins.

Rollo was going to win. I wasn't foolish enough to waste strength fighting him.

So the next time he traded ends, I went away from him, holding myself limp, so the tumble wouldn't ruin me.

Smith had caught the yellow pony, and was holding its head, when I took my knees off my forehead and stood up.

Peery, squatting on his heels, was frowning at me. Milk River was looking at Rollo with what was supposed to be a look of utter amazement.

"Now whatever did you do to Rollo to make him act that-away?" Peery asked me.

"Maybe he was only fooling," I suggested. "I'll try him again."

Once more Rollo stood still and sad until I was securely up on him. Then he went into convulsions under me—convulsions that lasted until I piled on my neck and one shoulder in a clump of brush.

I stood up, rubbing my left shoulder, which had hit a rock. Smith was holding the buckskin. The faces of all five men were serious and solemn—too serious and solemn.

"Maybe he don't like you," Buck Small gave his opinion.

"Might be," I admitted as I climbed into the saddle for the third time.

The lemon-tinted devil was getting warmed up by now, was beginning to take pride in his work. He let me stay aboard longer than before, so he could slam me off harder.

I was sick when I hit the ground in front of Peery and Milk

River. It took me a little while to get up, and I had to stand still for a moment, until I could feel the ground under my feet.

"Hold him a couple of seconds—" I began.

Peery's big frame stood in front of me.

"That's enough," he said. "I ain't going to have you killed on my hands."

I shook my head violently, trying to clear it, so I could see him better.

"Get out of my way," I growled. "I like this. I want more of it."

"You don't top my pony no more," he growled back at me. "He ain't used to playing so rough. You're liable to hurt him, falling off carelessly like that."

I tried to get past him. He barred my way with a thick arm. I drove my right fist at his dark face.

He went back, busy trying to keep his feet under him.

I went over and hoisted myself up on Rollo.

I had the buckskin's confidence by this time. We were old friends. He didn't mind showing me his secret stuff. He did things no horse could possibly do. Looking down, I was surprised not to see his kidneys and liver—because I knew damned well he was turning himself inside out.

I landed in the same clump of brush that had got me once before.

I couldn't see much when I got up—only the yellow of Rollo.

I heard Peery's bass voice, protesting to somebody:

"No, let the damned fool kill himself if he wants to."

I heaved myself wearily into the saddle again.

For a while I thought Rollo had had enough. He was a well-behaved animal under me. That was fine. I had ridden him at last.

Nonsense! He was fooling.

He put his nose in the sand. He put it in the sky. And, using his head for a base, he wagged his body as a puppy would wag its tail.

I went away from him—and stayed where I landed.

I didn't know whether I could have got up again if I had wanted to. But I didn't want to. I closed my eyes and rested. If I hadn't done what I had set out to do, I was willing to fail.

Small, Dunne and Milk River carried me indoors and spread me on a bunk.

"I don't think that horse would be much good to me," I told them. "Maybe I'd better look at another."

"You don't want to get discouraged like that," Small advised me.

"You better lay still and rest, fella," Milk River said. "You're liable to fall apart if you start moving around."

I took his advice.

5

WHEN I WOKE up it was morning, and Milk River was
prodding me with a finger.

"You figuring on getting up for breakfast, or would you like
it brung to you?"

I moved cautiously until I found I was all in one piece.

"I can crawl that far."

He sat down on a bunk across the room and rolled a cigarette while I put on my shoes—the only things, except my hat,
I hadn't slept in. He had something to say, so I gave him time,
lacing my shoes slowly.

Presently he said it:

"I always had the idea that nobody that couldn't sit a horse
some couldn't amount to nothing much. I ain't so sure now. You
can't ride any, and never will. You don't seem to have the least
notion what to do after you get in the middle of the animal!
But, still and all, a hombre that'll let a bronc dirty him up three
times handrunning and then ties into a gent who tries to keep
him from making it permanent, ain't exactly hay wire."

He lit his cigarette, and broke the match in half.

"I got a sorrel horse you can have for a hundred dollars. He
don't take no interest in handling cows, but he's all horse, and
he ain't mean."

I went into my money-belt—slid five twenties over into his lap.

"Better look at him first," he objected.

"You've seen him," I yawned, standing up. "Where's that
breakfast you were bragging about?"

Six men were eating in the chuck-shack when we came in. Three of them were hands I hadn't seen before. Neither Peery, Wheelan, nor Vogel was there. Milk River introduced me to the strangers as the high-diving deputy sheriff, and, between bites of the food the one-eyed Chinese cook put on the table, the meal was devoted almost exclusively to wise cracks about my riding ability.

That suited me. I was sore and stiff, but my bruises weren't wasted. I had bought myself a place of some sort in this desert community, and maybe even a friend or two. In less than a day I had accomplished what, by milder means, would have taken weeks, or months. These cowhands were kidding me just about as they would have kidded each other.

We were following the smoke of our cigarettes outdoors when running hoofs brought a swirl of dust up the draw.

Red Wheelan slid off his horse and staggered out of the sand-cloud.

"Slim's dead!" he said thickly.

Half a dozen voices shot questions at him. He stood swaying, trying to answer them. He was drunk as a lord!

"Nisbet shot him. I heard about it when I woke up this mornin'. He was shot early this mornin'—in front of Bardell's. I left 'em aroun' midnight last night, an' went down to Gaia's. I heard about it this mornin'. I went after Nisbet, but"—he looked down sheepishly at his empty belt—"Bardell took m' gun away."

He swayed again. I caught him, steadying him.

"Horses!" Peery bawled over my shoulder. "We're going to town!"

I let go of Wheelan and turned around.

"We're going to town," I repeated, "but no foolishness when we get there. This is my job, and if I want any help I'll tell you."

Peery's eyes met mine.

"Slim belonged to us," he said.

"And whoever killed Slim belongs to me," I said.

That was all on the subject, but I didn't think I had made the point stick.

6

AN HOUR LATER we were dismounting in front of the Border Palace, going indoors.

A long, thin, blanket-wrapped body lay on two tables that had been pushed together. Half the citizens of Corkscrew were there. Behind the bar, Chick Orr's battered face showed, hard and watchful. Gyp Rainey was sitting in a corner, rolling a cigarette with shaky fingers that sprinkled the floor with tobacco crumbs. Beside him, paying no attention to anything, not even looking up at our arrival, Mark Nisbet sat.

"By God, I'm glad to see you!" Bardell was telling me, his fat face not quite so red as it had been the day before. "This thing of having men killed at my front door has got to stop, and you're the man to stop it!"

I noticed that the Circle H.A.R. men had not followed me into the center of the room, but had stopped in a loose semi-circle just inside the street door.

I lifted a flap of the blanket and looked at the dead man. A small hole was in his forehead, over his right eye.

"Has a doctor seen him?" I asked.

"Yes," Bardell said. "Doc Haley saw him, but couldn't do anything. He must have been dead before he fell."

"Can you send for Haley?"

"I reckon I can." Bardell called to Gyp Rainey, "Run across the street and tell Doc Haley that the deputy sheriff wants to talk to him."

Gyp went gingerly through the cowboys grouped at the door

and vanished.

I didn't like this public stuff. I'd rather do my questioning on the side. But to try that here would probably call for a show-down with Peery and his men, and I wasn't quite ready for that.

"What do you know about the killing, Bardell?" I began.

"Nothing," he said emphatically, and then went on to tell me what he knew. "Nisbet and I were in the back room, count-ing the day's receipts. Chick was straightening the bar up. Nobody else was in here. It was about half-past one this morn-ing, maybe.

"We heard the shot—right out front, and all run out there, of course. Chick was closest, so he got there first. Slim was laying in the street—dead."

"And what happened after that?"

"Nothing. We brought him in here. Adderly and Doc Haley—who lives right across the street—and the Jew next door had heard the shot, too, and they came out and—and that's all there was to it."

I turned to Gyp.

He spit in a cuspidor and hunched his shoulders.

"Bardell's give it all to you."

"Didn't see anything before or after except what Bardell has said?"

"Nothin'."

"Don't know who shot him?"

"Nope."

I saw Adderly's white mustache near the front of the room, and I put him on the stand next. He couldn't contribute anything. He had heard the shot, had jumped out of bed, put on pants and shoes, and had arrived in time to see Chick kneeling beside the dead man. He hadn't seen anything Bardell hadn't mentioned.

Dr. Haley had not arrived by the time I was through with Adderly, and I wasn't ready to open on Nisbet yet. Nobody else there seemed to know anything.

"Be back in a minute," I said, and went through the cowboys at the door to the street.

The Jew was giving his joint a much-needed cleaning.

"Good work," I praised him; "it needed it."

He climbed down from the counter on which he had been standing to reach the ceiling. The walls and floor were already comparatively clean.

"I not think it was so dirty," he grinned, showing his empty gums, "but when the sheriff come in to eat and make faces at my place, what am I going to do but clean him up?"

"Know anything about the killing last night?"

"Sure, I know. I am in my bed, and I hear that shot. I jump out of my bed, grab that shotgun, and run to the door. There is that Slim Vogel in the street, and that Chick Orr on his knees alongside him. I stick my head out. There is Mr. Bardell and that Nisbet standing in their door.

"Mr. Bardell say, 'How is he, Chick?'

"That Chick Orr, he say, 'He's dead enough.'

"That Nisbet, he does not say anything, but he turn around and go back into the place. And then comes the doctor and Mr. Adderly, and I go out, and after the doctor looks at him and says he is dead, we carry him into Mr. Bardell's place and put him on those tables."

That was all the Jew knew. I returned to the Border Palace. Dr. Haley—a fussy little man whose nervous fingers played with his lips—was there.

The sound of the shot had awakened him, he said, but he had seen nothing beyond what the others had already told me. The bullet was a .38. Death had been instantaneous.

So much for that.

I sat on a corner of a pool table, facing Mark Nisbet. Feet shuffled on the floor behind me and I could feel tension making.

"What can you tell me, Nisbet?" I asked.

He didn't look up from the floor. No muscle moved in his face except those that shaped his mouth to his words.

"Nothing that is likely to help," he said, picking his words slowly and carefully. "You were in in the afternoon and saw Slim, Wheelan, Keefe and I playing. Well, the game went on like that. He won a lot of money—or he seemed to think it was a lot—as long as we played poker. But Keefe left before midnight, and Wheelan shortly after. Nobody else came in the game, so we were kind of short-handed for poker. We quit it and played some high-card. I cleaned Vogel—got his last nickel. It was about one o'clock when he left, say half an hour before he was shot."

"You and Vogel get along pretty well?"

The gambler's eyes switched up to mine, turned to the floor again.

"You know better than that. You heard him riding me ragged. Well, he kept that up—maybe was a little rawer toward the last."

"And you let him ride?"

"I did just that. I make my living out of cards, not out of picking fights."

"There was no trouble over the table, then?"

"I didn't say that. There was trouble. He made a break for his gun after I cleaned him."

"And you?"

"I shaded him on the draw—took his gun—unloaded it—gave it back to him—told him to beat it. He went."

"No shooting in here?"

"Not a shot."

"And you didn't see him again until after he had been killed?"

"That's right."

I got down from my perch on the table and walked over to Nisbet, holding out one hand.

"Let me look at your gun."

He slid it swiftly out of his clothes—butt-first—into my hand. A .38 S. & W., loaded in all six chambers.

"Don't lose it," I said as I handed it back to him, "I may want it later."

A roar from Peery turned me around. As I turned I let my hands go into my coat pockets to rest on the .32 toys.

Peery's right hand was near his neck, within striking distance of the gun I knew he had under his vest. Spread out behind him, his men were as ready for action as he. Their hands hovered close to the bulges that showed where their weapons were packed.

"Maybe that's a deputy sheriff's idea of what had ought to be done," Peery was bellowing, "but it ain't mine! That skunk killed Slim. Slim went out of here toting too much money. That skunk shot him down without even giving him a chance to go for his iron, and took his dirty money back. If you think we're going to stand for—"

"Maybe somebody's got some evidence I haven't heard," I cut in. "The way it stands, I haven't got enough to convict Nisbet, and I don't see any sense in arresting a man just because it looks as if he might have done a thing."

"Evidence be damned! Facts are facts, and you know this—"

"The first fact for you to study," I interrupted him again, "is that I'm running this show—running it my own way. Got anything against that?"

"Plenty!"

A worn .45 appeared in his fist. Guns blossomed in the hands of the men behind him.

I got between Peery's gun and Nisbet, feeling ashamed of the little popping noise my .32s were going to make compared with the roar of the guns facing me.

"What I'd like"—Milk River had stepped away from his fellows, and was leaning his elbows on the bar, facing them, a gun in each hand, a purring quality in his drawling voice—"would be for whosoever wants to swap lead with our high-diving deputy to wait his turn. One at a time is my idea. I don't like this idea of crowding him."

Peery's face went purple.

"What I don't like," he bellowed at the boy, "is a yellow puppy that'll throw down the men he rides with!"

Milk River's dark face flushed, but his voice was still a purring drawl.

"Mister jigger, what you don't like and what you do like are so damned similar to me that I can't tell 'em apart. And you don't want to forget that I ain't one of your rannies. I got a contract to gentle some horses for you at ten dollars per gentle. Outside of that, you and yours are strangers to me."

The excitement was over. The action that had been brewing had been talked to death by now.

"Your contract expired just about a minute and a half ago," Peery was telling Milk River. "You can show up at the Circle H.A.R. just once more—that's when you come for whatever stuff you left behind you. You're through!"

He pushed his square-jawed face at me.

"And you needn't think all the bets are in!"

He spun on his heel, and his hands trailed him out to their horses.

7

MILK RIVER AND I were sitting in my room in the Cañon House an hour later, talking. I had sent word to the county seat that the coroner had a job down here, and had found a place to stow Vogel's body until he came.

"Can you tell me who spread the grand news that I was a deputy sheriff?" I asked Milk River, who was making a cigarette while I lit one of the Fatimas he had refused. "It was supposed to be a secret."

"Was it? Nobody would of thought it. Our Mr. Turney didn't do nothing else for two days but run around telling folks what was going to happen when the new deputy come. He sure laid out a reputation for you! According to his way of telling it, you was the toughest, hardest, strongest, fastest, sharpest, biggest, wisest and meanest man west of the Mississippi River."

"Who is this Turney?"

"You mean you don't know him? From the way he talked, I took it you and him ate off the same plate."

"Never even heard any rumors about him. Who is he?"

"He's the gent that bosses the Orilla County Company outfit up the way."

So my client's local manager was the boy who had tipped my mitt!

"Got anything special to do the next few days?" I asked.

"Nothing downright special."

"I've got a place on the payroll for a man who knows this country and can chaperon me around it."

He poured a mouthful of grey smoke at the ceiling.

"I'd have to know what the play was before I'd set in," he said slowly. "You ain't a regular deputy, and you don't belong in this country. It ain't none of my business, but I wouldn't want to tie in with a blind game."

That was sensible enough.

"I'll spread it out for you," I offered. "I'm a private detective—the San Francisco branch of the Continental Detective Agency. The stockholders of the Orilla Colony Company sent me down here. They've spent a lot of money irrigating and developing their land, and now they're about ready to start selling it.

"According to them, the combination of heat and water makes it ideal farm land—as good as the Imperial Valley. Nevertheless, there doesn't seem to be any great rush of customers. What's the matter, so the stockholders figure, is that you original inhabitants of this end of the state are such a hard lot that peaceful farmers don't want to come among you.

"It's no secret from anybody that both borders of this United States are sprinkled with sections that are as lawless now as they ever were in the old days. There's too much money in running immigrants over the line, and it's too easy, not to have attracted a lot of gentlemen who don't care how they get their money. With only 450 immigration inspectors divided between the two borders, the government hasn't been able to do much. The official guess is that some 135,000 foreigners were run into the country last year through back and side doors. Compared to this graft, rum-running—even dope-running—is kid stuff!

"Because this end of Orilla County isn't railroaded or telephoned up, it has got to be one of the chief smuggling sections, and therefore, according to these men who hired me, full of assorted thugs. On another job a couple of months ago, I happened to run into a smuggling game, and knocked it over. The Orilla Colony people thought I could do the same thing for them down here. So hither I come to make this part of Arizona nice and lady-like.

"I stopped over at the county seat and got myself sworn in as deputy sheriff, in case the official standing came in handy. The sheriff said he didn't have a deputy down here and hadn't the money to hire one, so he was glad to sign me on. But we thought it was a secret—until I got here."

"I think you're going to have one hell of a lot of fun," Milk River grinned at me, "so I reckon I'll take that job you was offering. But I ain't going to be no deputy myself. I'll play around with you, but I don't want to tie myself up, so I'll have to enforce no laws I don't like. If you want to have me hanging around you sort of loose and individual-like, I'm with you."

"It's a bargain. Now what can you tell me that I ought to know?"

He blew more smoke at the ceiling.

"Well, you needn't bother none about the Circle H.A.R. They're plenty tough, but they ain't running nothing over the line."

"That's all right as far as it goes," I agreed, "but my job is to clean out trouble-makers, and from what I've seen of them they come under that heading."

"You're going to have one hell of a lot of fun," Milk River repeated. "Of course they're troublesome! But how could Peery raise cows down here if he didn't get hisself a crew that's a match for the gunmen your Orilla Colony people don't like? And you know how cowhands are. Set 'em down in a hard neighborhood and they're hell-bent on proving to everybody that they're just as tough as the next one—and tougher."

"I've nothing against them—if they behave. Now about these border-running folks?"

"I reckon Bardell's your big meat. Whether you'll ever get anything on him is another thing—something for you to work up a lather over. Next to him—Big 'Nacio. You ain't seen him yet? A big, black-whiskered Mex that's got a rancho down the cañon—four-five mile this side of the line. Anything that comes over the line comes through that rancho. But proving that's another item for you to beat your head about."

"He and Bardell work together?"

"Uh-huh—I reckon he works for Bardell. Another thing you got to include in your tally is that these foreign gents who buy their way across the line don't always—nor even mostly—wind up where they want to. It ain't nothing unusual these days to find some bones out in the desert beside what was a grave until the coyotes opened it. And the buzzards are getting fat! If the immigrant's got anything worth taking on him, or if a couple of government men happen to be nosing around, or if anything happens to make the smuggling gents nervous, they usually drop their customer and dig him in where he falls."

The racket of the dinner-bell downstairs cut off our conference at this point.

8

THERE WERE ONLY eight or ten diners in the dining-room. None of Peery's men was there. Milk River and I sat at a table back in one corner of the room. Our meal was about half eaten when the dark-eyed girl I had seen the previous day came in.

She came straight to our table. I stood up to learn her name was Clio Landes. She was the girl the better element wanted floated. She gave me a flashing smile, a strong, thin hand, and sat down.

"I hear you've lost your job again, you big bum," she laughed at Milk River.

I had known she didn't belong to Arizona. Her voice was New York.

"If that's all you heard, I'm still 'way ahead of you," Milk River grinned back at her. "I gone and got me another job—riding herd on law and order."

Something that could have been worry flashed into her dark eyes, and out again.

"You might just as well start looking for another hired man right away," she advised me. "He never kept a job longer than a few days in his life."

From the distance came the sound of a shot.

I went on eating.

Clio Landes said:

"Don't you coppers get excited over things like that?"

"The first rule," I told her, "is never to let anything interfere with your meals, if you can help it."

An overalled man came in from the street.

"Nisbet's been killed down in Bardell's!" he yelled.

To Bardell's Border Palace Milk River and I went, half the diners running ahead of us, with half the town.

We found Nisbet in the back room, stretched out on the floor, dead. A hole that a .45 could have made was in his chest, which the men around him had bared.

Bardell's fingers gripped my arm.

"Never give him a chance, the dogs!" he cried thickly. "Cold murder!"

"He say anything before he died?"

"No. He was dead when we got to him."

"Who shot him?"

"One of the Circle H.A.R., you can bet your neck on that!"

"Didn't anybody see it?"

"Nobody here admits they saw it."

"How did it happen?"

"Mark was out front. Me and Chick and five or six of these men were there. Mark came back here. Just as he stepped through the door—bang!"

Bardell shook his fist at the open window.

I crossed to the window and looked out. A five-foot strip of rocky ground lay between the building and the sharp edge of the Tirabuzon Cañon. A close-twisted rope was tight around a small knob of rock at the cañon's edge.

I pointed at the rope. Bardell swore savagely.

"If I'd of seen that we'd of got him! We didn't think anybody could get down there, and didn't look very close. We ran up and down the ledge, looking between buildings."

We went outside, where I lay on my belly and looked down

into the cañon. The rope—one end fastened to the knob—ran straight down the rock wall for twenty feet, and disappeared among the trees and bushes of a narrow shelf that ran along the wall there. Once on that shelf, a man could find ample cover to shield his retreat.

"What do you think?" I asked Milk River, who lay beside me.

"A clean getaway."

I stood up, pulling up the rope. A rope such as any one of a hundred cowhands might have owned, in no way distinguishable from any other to my eyes. I handed it to Milk River.

"It don't mean nothing to me. Might be anybody's," he said.

"The ground tell you anything?"

He shook his head again.

"You go down into the cañon and see what you can pick up," I told him. "I'll ride out to the Circle H.A.R. If you don't find anything, ride out that way."

I went back indoors, for further questioning. Of the seven men who had been in Bardell's place at the time of the shooting, three seemed to be fairly trustworthy. The testimony of those three agreed with Bardell's in every detail.

"Didn't you say you were going out to see Peery?" Bardell asked.

"Yes."

"Chick, get horses! Me and you'll ride out there with the deputy, and as many of you other men as want to go. He'll need guns behind him!"

"Nothing doing!" I stopped Chick. "I'm going by myself. This posse stuff is out of my line."

Bardell scowled, but he nodded his head in agreement.

"You're running it," he said. "I'd like to go out there with you, but if you want to play it different, I'm gambling you're right."

9

IN THE LIVERY stable, where we had put our horses, I found Milk River saddling them, and we rode out of town together.

Half a mile out, we split. He turned to the left, down a trail that led into the cañon, calling over his shoulder to me:

"If you get through out there sooner than you think, you can maybe pick me up by following the draw the ranch-house is in down to the cañon. Don't be too hard on the boys!"

I turned into the draw that led toward the Circle H.A.R., the long-legged, long-bodied horse Milk River had sold me carrying me along easily and swiftly. It was too soon after midday for riding to be pleasant. Heat waves boiled out of the draw-bottom, the sun hurt my eyes, dust caked my throat. That same dust rose behind me in a cloud that advertised me to half the state, notwithstanding that I was riding below the landscape.

Crossing from this draw into the larger one the Circle H.A.R. occupied, I found Peery waiting for me.

He didn't say anything, didn't move a hand. He just sat his horse and watched me approach. Two .45s were holstered on his legs.

I came alongside and held out the lariat I had taken from the rear of the Border Palace. As I held it out I noticed that no rope decorated his saddle.

"Know anything about this?" I asked.

He looked at the rope, but made no move to take it.

"Looks like one of those things hombres use to drag steers

around with."

"Can't fool you, can I?" I grunted. "Ever see this particular one before?"

He took a minute or more to think up an answer to that.

"Yeah," finally. "Fact is, I lost that same rope somewheres between here and town this morning."

"Know where I found it?"

"Don't hardly make no difference." He reached for it. "The main thing is you found it."

"It might make a difference," I said, moving the rope out of his reach. "I found it strung down the cañon wall, behind Bardell's, where you could slide down it after you potted Nisbet."

His hands went to his guns. I turned so he could see the shape of one of the pocketed automatics I was holding.

"Don't do anything you'll be sorry for," I advised him.

"Shall I gun this la-ad now?" Dunne's brogue rolled from behind me, "or will we wa-ait a bit?"

I looked around to see him standing behind a boulder, a .30-30 rifle held on me. Above other rocks, other heads and other weapons showed.

I took my hand out of my pocket and put it on my saddle horn.

Peery spoke past me to the others.

"He tells me Nisbet's been shot."

"Now ain't that provokin'?" Buck Small grieved. "I hope it didn't hurt him none."

"Dead," I supplied.

"Whoever could 'a' done th' like o' that?" Dunne wanted to know.

"It wasn't Santa Claus," I gave my opinion.

"Got anything else to tell me?" Peery demanded.

"Isn't that enough?"

"Yeah. Now if I was you, I'd ride right back to Corkscrew and go to bed."

"You mean you don't want to go back with me?"

"Not any. If you want to try and take me, now—"

I didn't want to try, and I said so.

"Then there's nothing keeping you here," he pointed out.

I grinned at him and his friends, pulled the sorrel around, and started back the way I had come.

A few miles down, I swung off to the south again, found the lower end of the Circle H.A.R. draw, and followed it down into the Tirabuzon Cañon. Then I started to work up toward the point where the rope had been let down.

The cañon deserved its name—a rough and stony, tree and bush-choked, winding gutter across the face of Arizona. But it was nicely green and cool compared to most of the rest of the State.

I hadn't gone far when I ran into Milk River, leading his horse toward me. He shook his head.

"Not a damned thing! I can cut sign with the rest of 'em, but there's too many rocky ridges here."

I dismounted. We sat under a tree and smoked some tobacco.

"How'd you come out?" he wanted to know.

"So-so. The rope is Peery's, but he didn't want to come along with me. I figure we can find him when we want him, so I didn't insist. It would have been kind of uncomfortable."

He looked at me out of the end of his pale eyes.

"A hombre might guess," he said slowly, "that you was playing the Circle H.A.R. against Bardell's crew, encouraging each side to eat up the other, and save you the trouble."

"You could be either right or wrong. Do you think that'd be a dumb play?"

"I don't know. I reckon not—if you're making it, and if you're sure you're strong enough to take hold when you have to."

10

NIGHT WAS COMING on when Milk River and I turned into Corkscrew's crooked street. It was too late for the Cañon House's dining-room, so we got down in front of the Jew's shack.

Chick Orr was standing in the Border Palace doorway. He turned his hammered mug to call something over his shoulder. Bardell appeared beside him, looked at me with a question in his eyes, and the pair of them stepped out into the street.

"What result?" Bardell asked.

"No visible ones."

"You didn't make the pinch?" Chick Orr demanded, incredulously.

"That's right. I invited a man to ride back with me, but he said no."

The ex-pug looked me up and down and spit on the ground at my feet.

"Ain't you a swell mornin'-glory?" he snarled. "I got a great mind to smack you down, you shine elbow, you!"

"Go ahead," I invited him. "I don't mind skinning a knuckle on you."

His little eyes brightened. Stepping in, he let an open hand go at my face. I took my face out of the way, and turned my back, taking off coat and shoulder-holster.

"Hold these, Milk River. And make the spectators behave while I take this pork-and-beaner for a romp."

Corkscrew came running as Chick and I faced each other.

We were pretty much alike in size and age, but his fat was softer than mine, I thought. He had been a professional. I had battled around a little, but there was no doubt that he had me shaded on smartness. To offset that, his hands were lumpy and battered, while mine weren't. And he was—or had been—used to gloves, while bare knuckles was more in my line.

Popular belief has it that you can do more damage with bare hands than with gloves, but, as usual, popular belief is wrong. The chief value of gloves is the protection they give your hands. Jaw-bones are tougher than finger-bones, and after you've pasted a tough face for a while with bare knuckles you find your hands aren't holding up very well, that you can't get the proper snap into your punches. If you don't believe me, look up the records. You'll find that knock-outs began to come quicker as soon as the boys in the profession began to pad their fists.

So I figured I hadn't anything to fear from this Chick Orr— or not a whole lot. I was in better shape, had stronger hands, and wasn't handicapped with boxing-glove training. I wasn't altogether right in my calculations.

He crouched, waiting for me to come to him. I went, trying to play the boob, faking a right swing for a lead.

Not so good! He stepped outside instead of in. The left I chucked at him went wide. He rapped me on the cheek-bone.

I stopped trying to out-smart him. His left hand played a three-note tune on my face before I could get in to him.

I smacked both hands into his body, and felt happy when the flesh folded softly around them. He got away quicker than I could follow, and shook me up with a sock on the jaw.

He left-handed me some more—in the eye, in the nose. His right scraped my forehead, and I was in again.

Left, right, left, I dug into his middle. He slashed me across the face with forearm and fist, and got clear.

He fed me some more lefts, splitting my lip, spreading my nose, stinging my face from forehead to chin. And when I finally got past that left hand I walked into a right uppercut that came up from his ankle to click on my jaw with a shock that threw me back half a dozen steps.

Keeping after me, he swarmed all over me. The evening air was full of fists. I pushed my feet into the ground and stopped the hurricane with a couple of pokes just above where his shirt ran into his pants.

He copped me with his right again—but not so hard. I laughed at him, remembering that something had clicked in his hand when he landed that uppercut, and plowed into him, hammering at him with both hands.

He got away again—cut me up with his left. I smothered his left arm with my right, hung on to it, and whaled him with my own left, keeping them low. His right banged into me. I let it bang. It was dead.

He nailed me once more before the fight ended—with a high straight left that smoked as it came. I managed to keep my feet under me, and the rest of it wasn't so bad. He chopped me a lot more, but his steam was gone.

He went down after a while, from an accumulation of punches rather than from any especial one, and couldn't get up.

His face didn't have a mark on it that I was responsible for. Mine must have looked as if it had been run through a grinder.

"Maybe I ought to wash up before we eat," I said to Milk River as I took my coat and gun.

"Hell, yes!" he agreed, staring at my face.

A plump man in a Palm Beach suit got in front of me, taking my attention.

"I am Mr. Turney of the Orilla Colony Company," he introduced himself. "Am I to understand that you have not made an arrest since you have been here?"

This was the bird who had advertised me! I didn't like that, and I didn't like his round, aggressive face.

"Yes," I confessed.

"There have been two murders in two days," he ran on, "concerning which you have done nothing, though in each case the evidence seems clear enough. Do you think that is satisfactory? Do you think you are performing the duties for which you were employed?"

I didn't say anything.

"Let me tell you that it is not at all satisfactory," he supplied the answers to his own questions. "Neither is it satisfactory that you should have employed this man"—stabbing a plump finger in Milk River's direction—"who is notoriously one of the most lawless men in the county. I want you to understand clearly that unless there is a distinct improvement in your work—unless you show some disposition to do the things you were engaged to do—that engagement will be terminated!"

"Who'd you say you arc?" I asked, when he had talked himself out.

"Mr. Turney, general superintendent of the Orilla Colony."

"So? Well, Mr. General Superintendent Turney, your owners forgot to tell me anything about you when they employed me. So I don't know you at all. Any time you've got anything to say to me, you turn it over to your owners, and if it's important enough, maybe they'll pass it on to me."

He puffed himself up.

"I shall certainly inform them that you have been extremely remiss in your duty, however proficient you may be in street brawls!"

"Will you put a postscript on for me," I called after him as he walked away. "Tell 'em I'm kind of busy just now and can't use any advice—no matter who it comes from."

Milk River and I went ten steps toward the Cañon House, and came face to face with the Reverend Dierks, Miss Janey, and old Adderly. None of them looked at me with anything you could call pleasure.

"You should be ashamed of yourself!" Miss Janey ground out between her false teeth. "Fighting in the street—you who are supposed to keep the peace!"

"As a deputy sheriff you're terrible," Adderly put in. "There's been more trouble here since you came than there ever was before!"

"I must say, brother, that I am deeply disappointed in your actions as a representative of the law!" was the minister's contribution.

I didn't like to say, "Go to hell!" to a group that included a minister and a woman, and I couldn't think of anything else, so, with Milk River making a poor job of holding in his laughter, I stepped around the better element, and we went on to the Cañon House.

Vickers, the sallow, pudgy proprietor, was at the door.

"If you think I got towels to mop up the blood from every hombre that gets himself beat up, you're mistaken," he growled at me. "And I don't want no sheets torn up for bandages, neither!"

"I never seen such a disagreeable cuss as you are," Milk River insisted as we climbed the stairs. "Seems like you can't get along with nobody. Don't you never make no friends?"

"Only with saps!"

I did what I could with water and adhesive tape to reclaim my face, but the result was a long way from beauty. Milk River sat on the bed and grinned and watched me.

"How does a fellow go about winning a fight he gets the worst of?" he inquired.

"It's a gift," was the only answer I could think up.

"You're a lot gifted. That Chick give you more gifts than a Christmas tree could hold."

11

MY PATCHING FINISHED, we went down to the Jew's for food. Three eaters were sitting at the counter. I had to exchange comments on the battle with them while I ate.

We were interrupted by the running of horses in the street. A dozen or more men went past the door, and we could hear them pulling up sharply, dismounting, in front of Bardell's.

Milk River leaned sidewise until his mouth was close to my ear.

"Big 'Nacio's crew from down the cañon. You better hold on tight, chief, or they'll shake the town from under you."

We finished our meal and went out to the street.

In the glow from the big lamp over Bardell's door a Mexican lounged against the wall. A big black-bearded man, his clothes gay with silver buttons, two white-handled guns holstered low on his thighs, the holsters tied down.

"Will you take the horses over to the stable?" I asked Milk River. "I'm going up and lie across the bed and grow strength again."

He looked at me curiously, and went over to where we had left the ponies.

I stopped in front of the bearded Mexican, and pointed with my cigarette at his guns.

"You're supposed to take those things off when you come to town," I said pleasantly. "Matter of fact, you're not supposed to bring 'em in at all, but I'm not inquisitive enough to look under a man's coat for them. You can't wear them out in the open, though."

Beard and mustache parted to show a smiling curve of yellow teeth.

"Mebbe if el senor jerife no lak t'ese t'ings, he lak try take t'em 'way?"

"No. You put 'em away."

His smile spread.

"I lak t'em here. I wear t'em here."

"You do what I tell you," I said, still pleasantly, and left him, going back to the Jew's shack.

Leaning over the counter, I picked the sawed-off shotgun out of its nest.

"Can I borrow this? I want to make a believer out of a guy."

"Yes, sir, sure! You help yourself!"

I cocked both barrels before I stepped outdoors.

The big Mexican wasn't in sight. I found him inside, telling his friends about it. Some of his friends were Mexican, some American, some God knows what. All wore guns. All had the look of thugs.

The big Mexican turned when his friends gaped past him at me. His hands dropped to his guns as he turned, but he didn't draw.

"I don't know what's in this cannon," I told the truth, centering the riot gun on the company, "maybe pieces of barbed wire and dynamite shavings. We'll find out if you birds don't start piling your guns on the bar right away—because I'll sure—God splash you with it!"

They piled their weapons on the bar. I didn't blame them. This thing in my hands would have mangled them plenty!

"After this, when you come to Corkscrew, put your guns out of sight."

Fat Bardell pushed through them, putting joviality back on his face.

"Will you tuck these guns away until your customers are ready to leave town?" I asked him.

"Yes! Yes! Be glad to!" he exclaimed when he had got over his surprise.

I returned the shotgun to its owner and went up to the Cañon House.

A door just a room or two from mine opened as I walked down the hall. Chick Orr came out, saying:

"Don't do nothin' I wouldn't do," over his shoulder.

I saw Clio Landes standing inside the door.

Chick turned from the door, saw me, and stopped, scowling at me.

"You can't fight worth a damn!" he said. "All you know is how to hit!"

"That's right."

He rubbed a swollen hand over his belly.

"I never could learn to take 'em down there. That's what beat me in the profesh."

I tried to look sympathetic, while he studied my face carefully.

"I messed you up, for a fact." His scowl curved up in a gold-toothed grin. The grin went away. The scowl came back. "Don't pick no more fights with me—I might hurt you!"

He poked me in the ribs with a thumb, and went on past me, down the stairs.

The girl's door was closed when I passed it. In my room, I dug out my fountain pen and paper, and had three words of my report written when a knock sounded on my door.

"Come in," I called, having left the door unlocked for Milk River.

Clio Landes pushed the door open.

"Busy?"

"No. Come in and make yourself comfortable. Milk River will be along in a few minutes."

I switched over to the bed, giving her my only chair.

"You're not foxing Milk River, are you?" she asked point-blank.

"No. I got nothing to hang on him. He's right so far as I'm concerned. Why?"

"Nothing, only I thought there might be a caper or two you were trying to cop him for. You're not fooling me, you know! These hicks think you're a bust, but I know different."

"Thanks for those few kind words. But don't be press-agenting my wisdom around. I've had enough advertising. What are you doing out here in the sticks?"

"Lunger!" She tapped her chest. "A croaker told me I'd last longer out here. Like a boob, I fell for it. Living out here isn't any different from dying in the big city."

"How long have you been away from the noise?"

"Three years—a couple up in Colorado, and then this hole. Seem like three centuries."

"I was back there on a job in April," I led her on, "for two or three weeks."

"You were?"

It was just as if I'd said I had been to heaven. She began to shoot questions at me: was this still so-and-so? Was that still thus?

We had quite a little gabfest, and I found I knew some of

her friends. A couple of them were high-class swindlers, one was a bootleg magnate, and the rest were a mixture of bookies, conmen, and the like. When I was living in New York, back before the war, I had spent quite a few of my evenings in Dick Malloy's Briar Patch, a cabaret on Seventh Avenue, near where the Ringside opened later. This girl had been one of the Briar Patch's regular customers a few years after my time there.

I couldn't find out what her grift was. She talked a blend of thieves' slang and high-school English, and didn't say much about herself.

We were getting along fine when Milk River came in.

"My friends still in town?" I asked.

"Yes. I hear 'em bubbling around down in Bardell's. I hear you've been makin' yourself more unpopular."

"What now?"

"Your friends among the better element don't seem to think a whole lot of that trick of yours of giving Big 'Nacio's guns, and his hombres', to Bardell to keep. The general opinion seems to be you took the guns out of their right hands and put 'em back in the left."

"I only took 'em to show that I could," I explained. "I didn't want 'em. They would have got more anyway. I think I'll go down and show myself to 'em. I won't be long."

The Border Palace was noisy and busy. None of Big 'Nacio's friends paid any attention to me. Bardell came across the room to tell me:

"I'm glad you backed the boys down. Saved me a lot of trouble, maybe."

I nodded and went out, around to the livery stable, where I found the night man hugging a little iron stove in the office.

"Got anybody who can ride to Filmer with a message tonight?"

"Maybe I can find somebody," he said without enthusiasm.

"Give him a good horse and send him up to the hotel as soon as you can," I requested.

I sat on the edge of the Cañon House porch until a long-legged lad of eighteen or so arrived on a pinto pony and asked for the deputy sheriff. I left the shadow I had been sitting in, and went down into the street, where I could talk to the boy without having an audience.

"Th' old man said yuh wanted to send somethin' to Filmer."

"Can you head out of here toward Filmer, and then cross over to the Circle H.A.R.?"

"Yes, suh, I c'n do that."

"Well, that's what I want. When you get there, tell Peery that Big 'Nacio and his men are in town, and might be riding that way before morning. And don't let the information get out to anybody else."

"I'll do jus' that, suh."

"This is yours, I'll pay the stable bill later." I slid a bill into his hand. "Get going."

Up in my room again, I found Milk River and the girl sitting around a bottle of liquor. I gave my oath of office the laugh to the extent of three drinks. We talked and smoked a while, and then the party broke up. Milk River told me he had the room next to mine.

I added another word to the report I had started, decided I needed sleep more than the client needed the report, and went to bed.

12

MILK RIVER'S KNUCKLES on the door brought me out of bed to shiver in the cold of five-something in the morning.

"This isn't a farm!" I grumbled at him as I let him in. "You're in the city now. You're supposed to sleep until the sun comes up."

"The eye of the law ain't never supposed to sleep," he grinned at me, his teeth clicking together, because he hadn't any more clothes on than I. "Fisher, who's got a ranch out that-away, sent a man in to tell you that there's a battle going on out at the Circle H.A.R. He hit my door instead of yours. Do we ride out that-away, chief?"

"We do. Hunt up some rifles, water, and the horses. I'll be down at the Jew's, ordering breakfast and getting some lunch wrapped up."

Forty minutes later Milk River and I were out of Corkscrew.

The morning warmed as we rode, the sun making long violet pictures on the desert, raising the dew in a softening mist. The mesquite was fragrant, and even the sand—which would be as nice as a dusty stove-top later—had a fresh, pleasant odor. There was nothing to hear but the creaking of leather, the occasional clink of metal, and the plop-plop of the horses' feet on hard ground, which changed to a shff-shff when we struck loose sand.

The battle seemed to be over, unless the battlers had run out of bullets and were going at it hand to hand.

Up over the ranch buildings, as we approached, three blue spots that were buzzards circled, and a moving animal showed against the sky for an instant on a distant ridge.

"A bronc that ought to have a rider and ain't," Milk River pronounced it.

Farther along, we passed a bullet-riddled Mexican sombrero, and then the sun sparkled on a handful of empty brass cartridges.

One of the ranch buildings was a charred black pile. Nearby another one of the men I had disarmed in Bardell's lay dead on his back.

A bandaged head poked around a building-corner, and its owner stepped out, his right arm in a sling, a revolver in his left. Behind him trotted the one-eyed Chinese cook, swinging a cleaver.

Milk River recognized the bandaged man.

"Howdy, Red! Been quarreling?"

"Some. We took all th' advantage we could of th' warnin' you sent out, an' when Big 'Nacio an' his herd showed up just 'fore daylight, we Injuned them all over the county. I stopped a couple o' slugs, so I stayed to home whilst th' rest o' th' boys followed 'em south. 'F you listen sharp, you can hear a pop now an' then."

"Do we follow 'em, or head 'em?" Milk River asked me.

"Can we head 'em?"

"Might. If Big 'Nacio's running, he'll circle back to his rancho along about dark. If we cut into the cañon and slide along down, maybe we can be there first. He won't make much speed having to fight off Peery and the boys as he goes."

"We'll try it."

Milk River leading, we went past the ranch buildings, and on down the draw, going into the cañon at the point where I had entered it the previous day. After a while the footing got better, and we made better time.

The sun climbed high enough to let its rays down on us, and the comparative coolness in which we had been riding went away. At noon we stopped to rest the horses, eat a couple of sandwiches, and smoke a bit. Then we went on.

Presently the sun passed, began to crawl down on our right, and shadows grew in the cañon. The welcome shade had reached the east wall when Milk River, in front, stopped.

"Around this next bend it is."

We dismounted, took a drink apiece, blew the sand off our rifles, and went forward afoot, toward a clump of bushes that covered the crooked cañon's next twist.

Beyond the bend, the floor of the cañon ran downhill into a round saucer. The saucer's sides sloped gently up to the desert floor. In the middle of the saucer, four low adobe buildings sat. In spite of their exposure to the desert sun, they looked somehow damp and dark. From one of them a thin plume of bluish smoke rose. Water ran out of a rock-bordered hole in one sloping cañon-wall, disappearing in a thin stream that curved behind one of the buildings.

No man, no animal was in sight.

"I'm going to prospect down there," Milk River said, handing me his hat and rifle.

"Right," I agreed. "I'll cover you, but if anything breaks, you'd better get out of the way. I'm not the most dependable rifle-shot in the world!"

For the first part of his trip Milk River had plenty of cover.

He went ahead rapidly. The screening plants grew fewer. His pace fell off. Flat on the ground, he squirmed from clump to boulder, from hummock to bush.

Thirty feet from the nearest building, he ran out of places to hide. I thought he would scout the buildings from that point, and then come back. Instead, he jumped up and sprinted to the shelter of the nearest building.

Nothing happened. He crouched against the wall for several long minutes, and then began to work his way toward the rear.

A hatless Mexican came around the corner.

I couldn't make out his features, but I saw his body stiffen.

His hand went to his waist.

Milk River's gun flashed.

The Mexican dropped. The bright steel of his knife glittered high over Milk River's head, and rang when it landed on a stone.

Milk River went out of my sight around the building. When I saw him again he was charging at the black doorway of the second building.

Fire-streaks came out of the door to meet him.

I did what I could with the two rifles—laying a barrage ahead of him—pumping lead at the open door, as fast as I could get it out. I emptied the second rifle just as he got too close to the door for me to risk another shot.

Dropping the rifle, I ran back to my horse, and rode to my crazy assistant's assistance.

He didn't need any. It was all over when I arrived.

He was driving another Mexican and Gyp Rainey out of the building with the nozzles of his guns.

"This is the crop," he greeted me. "Leastways, I couldn't find no more."

"What are you doing here?" I asked Rainey.

But the hop-head didn't want to talk. He looked sullenly at the ground and made no reply.

"We'll tie 'em up," I decided, "and then look around."

Milk River did most of the tying, having had more experience with ropes.

He trussed them back to back on the ground, and we went exploring.

13

EXCEPT FOR PLENTY of guns of all sizes and more than plenty of ammunition to fit, we didn't find anything very exciting until we came to a heavy door—barred and padlocked—set half in the foundation of the principal building, half in the mound on which the building sat.

I found a broken piece of rusty pick, and knocked the padlock off with it. Then we took the bar off and swung the door open.

Men came eagerly toward us out of an unventilated, unlighted cellar. Seven men who talked a medley of languages as they came.

We used our guns to stop them.

Their jabbering went high, excited.

"Quiet!" I yelled at them.

They knew what I meant, even if they didn't understand the word. The babel stopped and we looked them over. All seven seemed to be foreigners—and a hard-looking gang of cutthroats. A short Jap with a scar from ear to ear; three Slavs, one bearded, barrel-bodied, red-eyed, the other two bullet-headed, cunning-faced; a swarthy husky who was unmistakably a Greek; a bowlegged man whose probable nationality I couldn't guess; and a pale fat man whose china-blue eyes and puckered red mouth were probably Teutonic.

Milk River and I tried them out with English first, and then with what Spanish we could scrape up between us. Both attempts brought a lot of jabbering from them, but nothing in either of those languages.

"Got anything else?" I asked Milk River.

"Chinook is all that's left."

That wouldn't help much. I tried to remember some of the words we used to think were French in the A.E.F.

"Que désirez-vous?" brought a bright smile to the fat face of the blue-eyed man.

I caught "Nous allons à les États-Unis" before the speed with which he threw the words at me confused me beyond recognizing anything else.

That was funny. Big 'Nacio hadn't let these birds know that they were already in the United States. I suppose he could manage them better if they thought they were still in Mexico.

"Montrez-moi votre passe-port."

That brought a sputtering protest from Blue Eyes. They had been told no passports were necessary. It was because they had been refused passports that they were paying to be smuggled in.

"Quand êtes-vous venu ici?"

He meant yesterday, regardless of what the other things he put in his answer were. Big 'Nacio had come straight to Corkscrew after bringing these men across the border and sticking them in his cellar, then.

We locked the immigrants in their cellar again, putting Rainey and the Mexican in with them. Rainey howled like a wolf when I took his hypodermic needle and his coke away from him.

"Sneak up and take a look at the country," I told Milk River, "while I plant the man you killed."

By the time he came back I had the dead Mexican arranged to suit me: slumped down in a chair a little off from the front door of the principal building, his back against the wall, a sombrero tilted down over his face.

"There's dust kicking up some ways off," Milk River reported. "Wouldn't surprise me none if we got our company along towards dark."

Darkness had been solid for an hour when they came.

By then, fed and rested, we were ready for them. A light was burning in the house. Milk River was in there, tinkling a mandolin. Light came out of the open front door to show the dead Mexican dimly—a statue of a sleeper. Beyond him, around the corner except for my eyes and forehead, I lay close to the wall.

We could hear our company long before we could see them. Two horses—but they made enough noise for ten—coming lickety-split down to the lighted door.

Big 'Nacio, in front, was out of the saddle and had one foot in the doorway before his horse's front feet—thrown high by the violence with which the big man had pulled him up—hit the ground again. The second rider was close behind him.

The bearded man saw the corpse. He jumped at it, swinging his quirt, roaring:

"Arriba, piojo!"

The mandolin's tinkling stopped.

I scrambled up.

Big 'Nacio's whiskers went down in surprise.

His quirt caught a button of the dead man's clothes, tangled there, the loop on its other end holding one of Big 'Nacio's wrists.

His other hand went to his thigh.

My gun had been in my hand for an hour. I was close. I had leisure to pick my target. When his hand touched his gun-butt, I put a bullet through hand and thigh.

As he fell, I saw Milk River knock the second man down with a clout of gun-barrel on back of his head.

"Seems like we team-up pretty good," the sunburned boy said as he stooped to take the enemy's weapons from them.

The bearded man's bellowing oaths made conversation difficult.

"I'll put this one you beaned in the cooler," I said. "Watch 'Nacio, and we'll patch him up when I come back."

I dragged the unconscious man halfway to the cellar door before he came to. I goaded him the rest of the way with my gun, shooed him indoors, shooed the other prisoners away from the door, and closed and barred it again.

The bearded man had stopped howling when I returned.

"Anybody riding after you?" I asked, as I knelt beside him and began cutting his pants away with my pocket knife.

For answer to that I got a lot of information about myself, my habits, my ancestors. None of it happened to be the truth, but it was colorful.

"Maybe we'd better put a hobble on his tongue," Milk River suggested.

"No. Let him cry!" I spoke to the bearded man again. "If I were you, I'd answer that question. If it happens that the Circle H.A.R. riders trail you here and take us unawares, it's a gut that you're in for a lynching. Ahorcar, understand?"

He hadn't thought of that.

"Sí, sí. T'at Peery an' hees hombres. T'ey seguir—mucho rapidez!"

"Any of your men left, besides you and this other?"

"No! Ningún!"

"Suppose you build as much fire as you can out here in front while I'm stopping this egg's bleeding, Milk River."

The lad looked disappointed.

"Ain't we going to bushwack them waddies none?"

"Not unless we have to."

By the time I had put a couple of tourniquets on the Mexican, Milk River had a roaring fire lighting the buildings and most of the saucer in which they sat. I had intended stowing 'Nacio and Milk River indoors, in case I couldn't make Peery talk sense. But there wasn't time. I had just started to explain my plan to Milk River when Peery's bass voice came from outside the ring of light.

"Put 'em up, everybody!"

14

"EASY!" I CAUTIONED Milk River, and stood up. But I didn't raise my hands.

"The excitement's over," I called. "Come on down."

Ten minutes passed. Peery rode into the light. His square-jawed face was grime-streaked and grim. His horse was muddy lather all over. His guns were in his hands.

Behind him rode Dunne—as dirty, as grim, as ready with his firearms.

Nobody followed Dunne. The others were spread around us in the darkness, then.

Peery leaned over his pony's head to look at Big 'Nacio, who was lying breathlessly still on the ground.

"Dead?"

"No—a slug through hand and leg. I've got some of his friends under lock and key indoors."

Mad red rims showed around Peery's eyes in the firelight.

"You can keep the others," he said harshly. "This hombre will do us."

I didn't misunderstand him.

"I'm keeping all of them."

"I ain't got a damned bit of confidence in you," Peery growled down at me. "You ain't done nothing since you been here, and it ain't likely you ever will. I'm making sure that this Big 'Nacio's riding stops right here. I'm taking care of him myself."

"Nothing stirring!"

"How you figuring on keeping me from taking him?" he

laughed viciously at me. "You don't think me and Irish are alone, do you? If you don't believe you're corralled, make a play!"

I believed him, but—

"That doesn't make any difference. If I were a grub-line rider, or a desert rat, or any lone guy with no connections, you'd rub me out quick enough. But I'm not, and you know I'm not. I'm counting on that. You've got to kill me to take 'Nacio. That's flat! I don't think you want him bad enough to go that far. Right or wrong, I'm playing it that way."

He stared at me for a while. Then his knees urged his horse toward the Mexican, 'Nacio sat up and began pleading with me to save him.

Slowly I raised my right hand to my shoulder-holstered gun.

"Drop it!" Peery ordered, both his guns close to my head.

I grinned at him, took my gun out slowly, slowly turned it until it was level between his two.

We held that pose long enough to work up a good sweat apiece. It wasn't restful!

A queer light flickered in his red-rimmed eyes.

I didn't guess what was coming until too late.

His left-hand gun swung away from me—exploded.

A hole opened in the top of Big 'Nacio's head. He pitched over on his side.

The grinning Milk River shot Peery out of the saddle.

I was under Peery's right-hand gun when it went off. I was scrambling under his rearing horse's feet.

Dunne's revolvers coughed.

"Inside!" I yelled to Milk River, and put two bullets into Dunne's pony.

Rifle bullets sang every which way across, around, under, over us.

Inside the lighted doorway Milk River hugged the floor, spouting fire and lead from both hands.

Dunne's horse was down. Dunne got up—caught both hands to his face—went down beside his horse.

Milk River turned off the fireworks long enough for me to dash over him into the house.

While I smashed the lamp chimney, blew out the flame, he slammed the door.

Bullets made music on door and wall.

"Did I do right, shooting that jigger?" Milk River asked.

"Good work!" I lied.

There was no use bellyaching over what was done, but I hadn't wanted Peery dead. Dunne's death was unnecessary, too. The proper place for guns is after talk has failed, and I hadn't run out of words by any means when this brown-skinned lad had gone into action.

The bullets stopped punching holes in our door.

"The boys have got their heads together," Milk River guessed. "They can't have a hell of a lot of caps left if they've been snapping them at 'Nacio since early morning."

I found a white handkerchief in my pocket and began stuffing one corner in a rifle muzzle.

"What's for that?" Milk River asked.

"Talk." I moved to the door. "And you're to hold your hand until I'm through."

"I never seen such a hombre for making talk," he complained.

I opened the door a cautious crack. Nothing happened. I eased the rifle through the crack and waved it in the light of the still burning fire. Nothing happened. I opened the door and stepped out.

"Send somebody down to talk!" I yelled at the outer darkness.

A voice I didn't recognize cursed bitterly, and began a threat: "We'll give yuh—"

It broke off in silence.

Metal glinted off to one side.

Buck Small, his bulging eyes dark-circled, a smear of blood on one cheek, came into the light.

"What are you people figuring on doing?" I asked.

He looked sullenly at me.

"We're figurin' on gettin' that Milk River party. We ain't got nothin' against you. You're doin' what you're paid to do. But Milk River hadn't ought of killed Peery!"

Milk River bounced stiff-legged out of the door.

"Any time you want any part of me, you pop-eyed this-and-that, all you got to do is name it!"

Small's hands curved toward his holstered guns.

"Cut it!" I growled at Milk River, getting in front of him, pushing him back to the door. "I've got work to do. I can't waste time watching you boys cut up. This is no time to be bragging about what a desperate guy you are!"

I finally got rid of him, and faced Small again.

"You boys want to take a tumble to yourselves, Buck. The wild and woolly days are over. You're in the clear so far. 'Nacio jumped you, and you did what was right when you massacred his riders all over the desert. But you've got no right to fool with my prisoners. Peery wouldn't understand that. And if we hadn't shot him, he'd have swung later!"

"For Milk River's end of it: he doesn't owe you anything. He dropped Peery under your guns—dropped him with less than an even break! You people had the cards stacked against us. Milk River took a chance you or I wouldn't have taken. You've got nothing to howl about.

"I've got ten prisoners in there, and I've got a lot of guns, and stuff to put in 'em. If you make me do it, I'm going to deal out the guns to my prisoners and let 'em fight. I'd rather lose every damned one of them that way than let you take one of 'em away from me!

"All that you boys can get out of fighting us is a lot of grief—whether you win or lose. This end of Orilla County has been left to itself longer than most of the Southwest. But those days are over. Outside money has come into it; outside people are coming. You can't buck it! Men tried that in the old days, and failed. Will you talk it over with the others?"

"Yeah," and he went away in the darkness.

I went indoors.

"I think they'll be sensible," I told Milk River, "but you can't tell. So maybe you better hunt around and see if you can find a way through the floor to our basement hoosgow, because I meant what I said about giving guns to our captives."

Twenty minutes later Buck Small was back.

"You win," he said. "We want to take Peery and Dunne with us."

15

NOTHING EVER LOOKED better to me than my bed in the Cañon House the next—Wednesday—night. My grandstand play with the yellow horse, my fight with Chick Orr, the unaccustomed riding I had been doing—these things had filled me fuller of aches than Orilla County was of sand.

Our ten prisoners were resting in an old outdoor store-room of Adderly's, guarded by volunteers from among the better element, under the supervision of Milk River. They would be safe there, I thought, until the immigration inspectors—to whom I had sent word—could come for them. Most of Big 'Nacio's men had been killed in the fight with the Circle H.A.R. hands, and I didn't think Bardell could collect men enough to try to open my prison.

The Circle H.A.R. riders would behave reasonably well from now on, I thought. There were two angles still open, but the end of my job in Corkscrew wasn't far away. So I wasn't dissatisfied with myself as I got stiffly out of my clothes and climbed into bed for the sleep I had earned.

Did I get it? No.

I was just comfortably bedded down when somebody began thumping on my door.

It was fussy little Dr. Haley.

"I was called into your temporary prison a few minutes ago to look at Rainey," the doctor said. "He tried to escape, and broke his arm in a fight with one of the guards. That isn't serious, but the man's condition is. He should be given some cocaine. I don't think it is safe to leave him without the drug any longer. I would have given him an injection, but Milk River stopped me, saying you had given orders that nothing was to be done without instructions from you."

"Is he really in bad shape?"

"Yes."

"I'll go down and talk to him," I said, reluctantly starting to dress again. "I gave him a shot now and then on the way up from the rancho—enough to keep him from falling down on us. But I want to get some information out of him now, and he gets no more until he'll talk. Maybe he's ripe now."

We could hear Rainey's howling before we reached the jail.

Milk River was squatting on his heels outside the door, talking to one of the guards.

"He's going to throw a joe on you, chief, if you don't give him a pill," Milk River told me. "I got him tied up now, so's he can't pull the splints off his arm. He's plumb crazy!"

The doctor and I went inside, the guard holding a lantern high at the door so we could see.

In one corner of the room, Gyp Rainey sat in the chair to which Milk River had tied him. Froth was in the corners of his mouth. He was writhing with cramps. The other prisoners were trying to get some sleep, their blankets spread on the floor as far from Rainey as they could get.

"For Christ's sake give me a shot!" Rainey whined at me.

"Give me a hand, Doctor, and we'll carry him out."

We lifted him, chair and all, and carried him outside.

"Now stop your bawling and listen to me," I ordered. "You shot Nisbet. I want the straight story of it. The straight story will bring you a shot, and nothing else will."

"I didn't kill him!" he screamed. "I didn't! Before God, I didn't!"

"That's a lie. You stole Peery's rope while the rest of us were in Bardell's place Monday morning, talking over Slim's death. You tied the rope where it would look like the murderer had made a getaway down the cañon. Then you stood at the window until Nisbet came into the back room—and you shot him. Nobody went down that rope—or Milk River would have found some sign. Will you come through?"

He wouldn't. He screamed and cursed and pleaded and denied knowledge of the murder.

"Back you go!" I said.

Dr. Haley put a hand on my arm.

"I don't want you to think I am interfering, but I really must warn you that what you're doing is dangerous. It is my belief, and my duty to advise you, that you are endangering this man's life by refusing him some of the drug."

"I know it, Doctor, but I'll have to risk it. He's not so far gone, or he wouldn't be lying. When the sharp edge of the drug-hunger hits him, he'll talk!"

Gyp Rainey stowed away again, I went back to my room. But not to bed.

Clio Landes was waiting for me, sitting there—I had left the door unlocked—with a bottle of whisky. She was about three-quarters lit up—one of those melancholy lushes.

She was a poor, sick, lonely, homesick girl, far away from her world. She dosed herself with alcohol, remembered her dead parents, sad bits of her childhood and unfortunate slices of her past, and cried over them. She poured out all her hopes and fears to me—including her liking for Milk River, who was a good kid even if he had never been within two thousand miles of Forty-second Street and Broadway.

The talk always came back to that: New York, New York, New York.

It was close to four o'clock Thursday morning when the whisky finally answered my prayers, and she went to sleep on my shoulder.

I picked her up and carried her down the hall to her own room. Just as I reached her door, fat Bardell came up the stairs.

"More work for the sheriff," he commented jovially, and went on.

I took her slippers off, tucked her in bed, opened the window, and went out, locking the door behind me and chucking the key over the transom.

After that I slept.

16

THE SUN WAS high and the room was hot when I woke to the familiar sound of someone knocking on the door. This time it was one of the volunteer guards—the long-legged boy who had carried the warning to Peery Monday night.

"Gyp wants t' see yuh." The boy's face was haggard. "He wants yuh more'n I ever seen a man want anything."

Rainey was a wreck when I got to him.

"I killed him! I killed him!" he shrieked at me. "Bardell knowed the Circle H.A.R. would hit back f'r Slim's killin'. He made me kill Nisbet an' stack th' deal agin Peery so's it'd be up t' you t' go up agin 'em. He'd tried it before an' got th' worst of it!"

"Gimme a shot! That's th' God's truth! I stoled th' rope, planted it, an' shot Nisbet wit' Bardell's gun when Bardell sent him back there! Th' gun's under th' tin-can dump in back o' Adderly's. Gimme th' shot! Gimme it!"

"Where's Milk River?" I asked the long-legged boy.

"Sleepin', I reckon. He left along about daylight."

"All right, Gyp! Hold it until the doc gets here. I'll send him right over!"

I found Dr. Haley in his house. A minute later he was carrying a charge over to the hypo.

The Border Palace didn't open until noon. Its doors were locked. I went up the street to the Cañon House. Milk River came out just as I stepped up on the porch.

"Hello, young fellow," I greeted him. "Got any idea which room your friend Bardell reposes in?"

He looked at me as if he had never seen me before.

"S'pose you find out for yourself. I'm through doing your chores. You can find yourself a new wet nurse, Mister, or you can go to hell!"

The odor of whisky came out with the words, but he wasn't drunk enough for that to be the whole explanation.

"What's the matter with you?" I asked.

"What's the matter is I think you're a lousy—"

I didn't let it get any farther than that.

His right hand whipped to his side as I stepped in.

I jammed him between the wall and my hip before he could draw, and got one of my hands on each of his arms.

"You may be a curly wolf with your rod," I growled, shaking him, a lot more peeved than if he had been a stranger, "but if you try any of your monkey business on me, I'll turn you over my knee!"

Clio Landes' thin fingers dug into my arm.

"Stop it!" she cried. "Stop it! Why don't you behave?" to Milk River; and to me: "He's sore over something this morning. He doesn't mean what he says!"

I was sore myself.

"I mean what I said," I insisted.

But I took my hands off him, and went indoors. Inside the door I ran into sallow Vickers, who was hurrying to see what the rumpus was about.

"What room is Bardell's?"

"214. Why?"

I went on past him and upstairs.

My gun in one hand, I used the other to knock on Bardell's door.

"Who is it?" came through.

I told him.

"What do you want?"

I said I wanted to talk to him.

He kept me waiting for a couple of minutes before he opened. He was half-dressed. All his clothes below the waist were on. Above, he had a coat on over his undershirt, and one of his hands was in his coat pocket.

His eyes jumped big when they lit on my gun.

"You're arrested for Nisbet's murder!" I informed him. "Take your hand out of your pocket."

He tried to look as if he thought I was kidding him.

"For Nisbet's murder?"

"Uh-huh. Rainey came through. Take your hand out of your pocket."

"You're arresting me on the say-so of a hop-head?"

"Uh-huh. Take your hand out of your pocket."

"You're—"

"Take your hand out of your pocket."

His eyes moved from mine to look past my head, a flash of triumph burning in them.

I beat him to the first shot by a hairline, since he had wasted time waiting for me to fall for that ancient trick.

His bullet cut my neck.

Mine took him where his undershirt was tight over his fat chest.

He fell, tugging at his pocket, trying to get the gun out for another shot.

I could have jumped him, but he was going to die anyhow. That first bullet had got his lungs. I put another into him.

The hall filled with people.

"Get the doctor!" I called to them.

But Bardell didn't need him. He was dead before I had the words out of my mouth.

Chick Orr came through the crowd, into the room.

I stood up, sticking my gun back in its holster.

"I've got nothing on you, Chick, yet," I said slowly. "You know better than I do whether there is anything to get or not. If I were you, I'd drift out of Corkscrew without wasting too much time packing up."

The ex-pug squinted his eyes at me, rubbed his chin, and made a clucking sound in his mouth.

His gold teeth showed in a grin.

"'F anybody asks for me, you tell 'em I'm off on a tour," and he pushed out through the crowd again.

When the doctor came, I took him up the hall to my room, where he patched my neck. The wound wasn't much, but my neck is fleshy, and it bled a lot—all over me, in fact.

After he had finished, I got fresh clothes from my bag and undressed. But when I went to wash, I found the doctor had used all my water. Getting into coat, pants and shoes, I went down to the kitchen for more.

The hall was empty when I came upstairs again, except for Clio Landes.

She went past me without looking at me—deliberately not looking at me.

I washed, dressed, and strapped on my gun. One more angle to be cleaned up, and I would be through. I didn't think I'd need the .32 toys any more, so I put them away. One more angle, and I was done. I was pleased with the idea of getting away from

Corkscrew. I didn't like the place, had never liked it, liked it less than ever since Milk River's break.

I was thinking about him when I stepped out of the hotel—to see him standing across the street.

I didn't give him a tumble, but turned toward the lower end of the street.

One step. A bullet kicked up dirt at my feet.

I stopped.

"Go for it, fat boy!" Milk River yelled. "It's me or you!"

I turned slowly to face him, looking for an out. But there wasn't any.

His eyes were insane-lighted slits. His face was a ghastly savage mask. He was beyond reasoning with.

"Put it away!" I ordered, though I knew the words were wasted.

"It's me or you!" he repeated, and put another bullet into the ground in front of me. "Warm your iron!"

I stopped looking for an out. Blood thickened in my head, and things began to look queer. I could feel my neck thickening. I hoped I wasn't going to get too mad to shoot straight.

I went for my gun.

He gave me an even break.

His gun swung down to me as mine straightened to him.

We pulled triggers together.

Flame jumped at me.

I smacked the ground—my right side all numb.

He was staring at me—bewildered. I stopped staring at him, and looked at my gun—the gun that had only clicked when I pulled the trigger!

When I looked up again, he was coming toward me, slowly, his gun hanging at his side.

"Played it safe, huh?" I raised my gun so he could see the broken firing-pin. "Serves me right for leaving it on the bed when I went downstairs for water."

Milk River dropped his gun—grabbed mine.

Clio Landes came running from the hotel to him.

"You're not—?"

Milk River stuck my gun in her face.

"You done that?"

"I was afraid he—" she began.

"You — —!"

With the back of an open hand, Milk River struck the girl's mouth.

He dropped down beside me, his face a boy's face. A tear fell hot on my hand.

"Chief, I didn't—"

"That's all right," I assured him, and I meant it.

I missed whatever else he said. The numbness was leaving my side, and the feeling that came in its place wasn't pleasant. Everything stirred inside me....

17

I WAS IN bed when I came to. Dr. Haley was doing disagreeable things to my side. Behind him, Milk River held a basin
in unsteady hands.

"Milk River," I whispered, because that was the best I could
do in the way of talk.

He bent his ear to me.

"Get the Jew. He killed Vogel. Careful—gun on him. Talk
self-defense—maybe confess. Lock him up with others."

Sweet sleep again.

Night, dim lamplight was in the room when I opened my
eyes again. Clio Landes sat beside my bed, staring at the floor,
woebegone.

"Good evening," I managed.

I was sorry I had said anything.

She cried all over me and kept me busy assuring her she had
been forgiven for the trickery with my gun. I don't know how
many times I forgave her. It got to be a damned nuisance. No
sooner would I say that everything was all right than she'd
begin all over again to ask me to forgive her.

"I was so afraid you'd kill him, because he's only a kid, and
somebody had told him a lot of things about you and me, and I
knew how crazy he was, and he's only a kid, and I was so afraid
you'd kill him," and so on and so on.

Half an hour of this had me woozy with fever.

"And now he won't talk to me, won't even look at me, won't let
me come in here when he's here. And nothing will ever make

things right again, and I was so afraid you'd kill him, because he's only a boy, and …"

I had to shut my eyes and pretend I had passed out to shut her up.

I must have slept some, because when I looked around again it was day, and Milk River was in the chair.

He stood up, not looking at me, his head hanging.

"I'll be moving on, Chief, now that you're coming around all right. I want you to know, though, that if I'd knowed what that—done to your gun I wouldn't never have throwed down on you."

"What was the matter with you, anyhow?" I growled at him.

His face got beet-color and he shuffled his feet.

"Crazy, I reckon," he mumbled. "I had a couple of drinks, and then Bardell filled me full of stuff about you and her, and that you was playing me for a Chinaman. And—and I just went plumb loco, I reckon."

"Any of it left in your system?"

"Hell, no, chief! I'd give a leg if none of it had never happened!"

"Then suppose you stop this foolishness and sit down and talk sense. Are you and the girl still on the outs?"

They were, most emphatically, most profanely.

"You're a big boob!" I told him. "She's a stranger out here, and homesick for her New York. I could talk her language and knew the people she knew. That's all there was—"

"But that ain't the big point, chief! Any woman that would pull a—"

"Bunk! It was a shabby trick, right enough. But a woman who'll pull a trick like that for you when you are in a jam is worth a million an ounce, and you'd know it if you had anything to know anything with. Now you run out and find this Clio person, and bring her back with you, and no nonsense!"

He pretended he was going reluctantly. But I heard her voice when he knocked on her door. And they let me lay there in my bed of pain for one solid hour before they remembered me. They came in walking so close together that they were stumbling over each other's feet.

"Now let's talk business," I grumbled. "What day is this?"

"Monday."

"Did you get the Jew?"

"I done that thing," Milk River said, dividing the one chair with the girl. "He's over to the county seat now—went over with the others. He swallowed that self-defense bait, and told me all about it. How'd you ever figure it out, chief?"

"Figure what out?"

"That the Jew killed poor old Slim. He says Slim come in there that night, woke him up, ate a dollar and ten cents' worth of grub on him, and then dared him to try and collect. In the argument that follows, Slim goes for his gun, and the Jew gets scared and shoots him—after which Slim obligingly staggers out o' doors to die. I can see all that clear enough, but how'd you hit on it?"

"I oughtn't give away my professional secrets, but I will this once. The Jew was cleaning house when I went in to ask him for what he knew about the killing, and he had scrubbed his floor before he started on the ceiling. If that meant anything at all, it meant that he had had to scrub his floor, and was making the cleaning general to cover it up. So maybe Slim had bled some on that floor.

"Starting from that point, the rest came easily enough. Slim leaving the Border Palace in a wicked frame of mind, broke after his earlier winning, humiliated by Nisbet's triumph in the gun-pulling, soured further by the stuff he had been drinking all day. Red Wheelan had reminded him that afternoon of the time the Jew had followed him to the ranch to collect two bits. What more likely than he'd carry his meanness into the Jew's shack? That Slim hadn't been shot with the shotgun didn't mean anything. I never had any faith in that shotgun from the first. If the Jew had been depending on that for his protection, he wouldn't have put it in plain sight, and under a shelf, where it wasn't easy to get out. I figured the shotgun was there for moral effect, and he'd have another one stowed out of sight for use.

"Another point you folks missed was that Nisbet seemed to be telling a straight story—not at all the sort of tale he'd have told if he were guilty. Bardell's and Chick's weren't so good, but the chances are they really thought Nisbet had killed Slim, and were trying to cover him up."

Milk River grinned at me, pulling the girl closer with the one arm that was around her.

"You ain't so downright dumb," he said. "Clio done warned me the first time she seen you that I'd best not try to run no sandies on you."

A far-away look came into his pale eyes.

"Think of all them folks that were killed and maimed and jailed—all over a dollar and ten cents. It's a good thing Slim didn't eat five dollars' worth of grub. He'd of depopulated the State of Arizona complete!"

Dead Yellow Women

1

SHE WAS SITTING straight and stiff in one of the Old Man's chairs when he called me into his office—a tall girl of perhaps twenty-four, broad-shouldered, deep-bosomed, in mannish grey clothes. That she was Oriental showed only in the black shine of her bobbed hair, in the pale yellow of her unpowdered skin, and in the fold of her upper lids at the outer eye-corners, half hidden by the dark rims of her spectacles. But there was no slant to her eyes, her nose was almost aquiline, and she had more chin than Mongolians usually have. She was modern Chinese-American from the flat heels of her tan shoes to the crown of her untrimmed felt hat.

I knew her before the Old Man introduced me. The San Francisco papers had been full of her affairs for a couple of days. They had printed photographs and diagrams, interviews, editorials, and more or less expert opinions from various sources. They had gone back to 1912 to remember the stubborn fight of the local Chinese—mostly from Fokien and Kwangtung, where democratic ideas and hatred of Manchus go together—to have her father kept out of the United States, to which he had scooted when the Manchu rule flopped. The papers had recalled the excitement in Chinatown when Shan Fang was allowed to land—insulting placards had been hung in the streets, an unpleasant reception had been planned.

But Shan Fang had fooled the Cantonese. Chinatown had never seen him. He had taken his daughter and his gold—presumably the accumulated profits of a life-time of provincial misrule—down to San Mateo County, where he had built what the papers described as a palace on the edge of the Pacific. There he had lived and died in a manner suitable to a Ta Jen and a millionaire.

So much for the father. For the daughter—this young woman who was coolly studying me as I sat down across the table from her: she had been ten-year-old Ai Ho, a very Chinese little girl, when her father had brought her to California. All that was Oriental of her now were the features I have mentioned and the money her father had left her. Her name, translated into English, had become Water Lily, and then, by another step, Lillian. It was as Lillian Shan that she had attended an eastern university, acquired several degrees, won a tennis championship of some sort in 1919, and published a book on the nature and significance of fetishes, whatever all that is or are.

Since her father's death, in 1921, she had lived with her four Chinese servants in the house on the shore, where she had written her first book and was now at work on another. A couple of weeks ago, she had found herself stumped, so she said—had run into a blind alley. There was, she said, a certain old cabalistic manuscript in the Arsenal Library in Paris that she believed would solve her troubles for her. So she had packed some clothes and, accompanied by her maid, a Chinese woman named Wang Ma, had taken a train for New York, leaving the three other servants to take care of the house during her absence. The decision to go to France for a look at the manuscript had been formed one morning—she was on the train before dark.

On the train between Chicago and New York, the key to the problem that had puzzled her suddenly popped into her head.

Dead Yellow Women

Without pausing even for a night's rest in New York, she had turned around and headed back for San Francisco. At the ferry here she had tried to telephone her chauffeur to bring a car for her. No answer. A taxicab had carried her and her maid to her house. She rang the door-bell to no effect.

When her key was in the lock the door had been suddenly opened by a young Chinese man—a stranger to her. He had refused her admittance until she told him who she was. He mumbled an unintelligible explanation as she and the maid went into the hall.

Both of them were neatly bundled up in some curtains.

Two hours later Lillian Shan got herself loose—in a linen closet on the second floor. Switching on the light, she started to untie the maid. She stopped. Wang Ma was dead. The rope around her neck had been drawn too tight.

Lillian Shan went out into the empty house and telephoned the sheriff's office in Redwood City.

Two deputy sheriffs had come to the house, had listened to her story, had poked around, and had found another Chinese body—another strangled woman—buried in the cellar. Apparently she had been dead a week or a week and a half; the dampness of the ground made more positive dating impossible. Lillian Shan identified her as another of her servants—Wan Lan, the cook.

The other servants—Hoo Lun and Yin Hung—had vanished. Of the several hundred thousand dollars' worth of furnishings old Shan Fang had put into the house during his life, not a nickel's worth had been removed. There were no signs of a struggle. Everything was in order. The closest neighboring house was nearly half a mile away. The neighbors had seen nothing, knew nothing.

That's the story the newspapers had hung headlines over, and that's the story this girl, sitting very erect in her chair, speaking with businesslike briskness, shaping each word as exactly as if it were printed in black type, told the Old Man and me.

"I am not at all satisfied with the effort the San Mateo County authorities have made to apprehend the murderer or murderers," she wound up. "I wish to engage your agency."

The Old Man tapped the table with the point of his inevitable long yellow pencil and nodded at me.

"Have you any idea of your own on the murders, Miss Shan?" I asked.

"I have not."

"What do you know about the servants—the missing ones as well as the dead?"

"I really know little or nothing about them." She didn't seem very interested. "Wang Ma was the most recent of them to come to the house, and she has been with me for nearly seven years. My father employed them, and I suppose he knew something about them."

"Don't you know where they came from? Whether they have relatives? Whether they have friends? What they did when they weren't working?"

"No," she said. "I did not pry into their lives."

"The two who disappeared—what do they look like?"

"Hoo Lun is an old man, quite white-haired and thin and stooped. He did the housework. Yin Hung, who was my chauffeur and gardener, is younger, about thirty years old, I think. He is quite short, even for a Cantonese, but sturdy. His nose has been broken at some time and not set properly. It is very flat, with a pronounced bend in the bridge."

"Do you think this pair, or either of them, could have killed the women?"

"I do not think they did."

"The young Chinese—the stranger who let you in the house—what did he look like?"

"He was quite slender, and not more than twenty or twenty-one years old, with large gold fillings in his front teeth. I think he was quite dark."

"Will you tell me exactly why you are dissatisfied with what the sheriff is doing, Miss Shan?"

"In the first place, I am not sure they are competent. The ones I saw certainly did not impress me with their brilliance."

"And in the second place?"

"Really," she asked coldly, "is it necessary to go into all my mental processes?"

"It is."

She looked at the Old Man, who smiled at her with his polite, meaningless smile—a mask through which you can read nothing.

For a moment she hung fire. Then: "I don't think they are looking in very likely places. They seem to spend the greater part of their time in the vicinity of the house. It is absurd to think the murderers are going to return."

I turned that over in my mind.

"Miss Shan," I asked, "don't you think they suspect you?"

Her dark eyes burned through her glasses at me and, if possible, she made herself more rigidly straight in her chair.

"Preposterous!"

"That isn't the point," I insisted. "Do they?"

"I am not able to penetrate the police mind," she came back. "Do you?"

"I don't know anything about this job but what I've read and what you've just told me. I need more foundation than that to suspect anybody. But I can understand why the sheriff's office would be a little doubtful. You left in a hurry. They've got your word for why you went and why you came back, and your word is all. The woman found in the cellar could have been killed just before you left as well as just after. Wang Ma, who could have told things, is dead. The other servants are missing. Nothing was stolen. That's plenty to make the sheriff think about you!"

"Do you suspect me?" she asked again.

"No," I said truthfully. "But that proves nothing."

She spoke to the Old Man, with a chin-tilting motion, as if she were talking over my head.

"Do you wish to undertake this work for me?"

"We shall be very glad to do what we can," he said, and then to me, after they had talked terms and while she was writing a check, "you handle it. Use what men you need."

"I want to go out to the house first and look the place over," I said.

Lillian Shan was putting away her check-book.

"Very well. I am returning home now. I will drive you down."

It was a restful ride. Neither the girl nor I wasted energy on conversation. My client and I didn't seem to like each other very much. She drove well.

2

THE SHAN HOUSE was a big brownstone affair, set among sodded lawns. The place was hedged shoulder-high on three sides. The fourth boundary was the ocean, where it came in to make a notch in the shore-line between two small rocky points.

The house was full of hangings, rugs, pictures, and so on—a mixture of things American, European and Asiatic. I didn't spend much time inside. After a look at the linen-closet, at the still open cellar grave, and at the pale, thick-featured Danish woman who was taking care of the house until Lillian Shan could get a new corps of servants, I went outdoors again. I poked around the lawns for a few minutes, stuck my head in the garage, where two cars, besides the one in which we had come from town, stood, and then went off to waste the rest of the afternoon talking to the girl's neighbors. None of them knew anything. Since we were on opposite sides of the game, I didn't hunt up the sheriff's men.

By twilight I was back in the city, going into the apartment building in which I lived during my first year in San Francisco. I found the lad I wanted in his cubby-hole room, getting his small body into a cerise silk shirt that was something to look at. Cipriano was the bright-faced Filipino boy who looked after the building's front door in the daytime. At night, like all the Filipinos in San Francisco, he could be found down on Kearny Street, just below Chinatown, except when he was in a Chinese gambling-house passing his money over to the yellow brothers.

I had once, half-joking, promised to give the lad a fling at gum-shoeing if the opportunity ever came. I thought I could use him now.

"Come in, sir!"

He was dragging a chair out of a corner for me, bowing and smiling. Whatever else the Spaniards do for the people they rule, they make them polite.

"What's doing in Chinatown these days?" I asked as he went on with his dressing.

He gave me a white-toothed smile.

"I take eleven bucks out of bean-game last night."

"And you're getting ready to take it back tonight?"

"Not all of 'em, sir! Five bucks I spend for this shirt."

"That's the stuff," I applauded his wisdom in investing part of his fan-tan profits. "What else is doing down there?"

"Nothing unusual, sir. You want to find something?"

"Yeah. Hear any talk about the killings down the country last week? The two Chinese women?"

"No, sir. Chinaboy don't talk much about things like that. Not like us Americans. I read about those things in newspapers, but I have not heard."

"Many strangers in Chinatown nowadays?"

"All the time there's strangers, sir. But I guess maybe some new Chinaboys are there. Maybe not, though."

"How would you like to do a little work for me?"

"Yes, sir! Yes, sir! Yes, sir!" He said it oftener than that, but that will give you the idea. While he was saying it he was down on his knees, dragging a valise from under the bed. Out of the valise he took a pair of brass knuckles and a shiny revolver.

"Here! I want some information. I don't want you to knock anybody off for me."

"I don't knock 'em," he assured me, stuffing his weapons in his hip pockets. "Just carry these—maybe I need 'em."

I let it go at that. If he wanted to make himself bow-legged carrying a ton of iron it was all right with me.

"Here's what I want. Two of the servants ducked out of the house down there." I described Yin Hung and Hoo Lun. "I want to find them. I want to find what anybody in Chinatown knows about the killings. I want to find who the dead women's friends and relatives are, where they came from, and the same thing for the two men. I want to know about those strange Chinese—where they hang out, where they sleep, what they're up to.

"Now, don't try to get all this in a night. You'll be doing fine if you get any of it in a week. Here's twenty dollars. Five of it is your night's pay. You can use the other to carry you around. Don't be foolish and poke your nose into a lot of grief. Take it easy and see what you can turn up for me. I'll drop in tomorrow."

From the Filipino's room I went to the office. Everybody except Fiske, the night man, was gone, but Fiske thought the Old Man would drop in for a few minutes later in the night.

I smoked, pretended to listen to Fiske's report on all the jokes that were at the Orpheum that week, and grouched over my job. I was too well known to get anything on the quiet in Chinatown. I wasn't sure Cipriano was going to be much help. I needed somebody who was in right down there.

This line of thinking brought me around to "Dummy" Uhl. Uhl was a dummerer who had lost his store. Five years before, he had been sitting on the world. Any day on which his sad face, his package of pins, and his I am deaf and dumb sign didn't take twenty dollars out of the office buildings along his route was a rotten day. His big card was his ability to play the statue when skeptical people yelled or made sudden noises behind him. When the Dummy was right, a gun off beside his ear wouldn't make him twitch an eye-lid. But too much heroin broke his nerves until a whisper was enough to make him jump. He put away his pins and his sign—another man whose social life had ruined him.

Since then Dummy had become an errand boy for whoever would stake him to the price of his necessary nose-candy. He slept somewhere in Chinatown, and he didn't care especially how he played the game. I had used him to get me some information on a window-smashing six months before. I decided to try him again.

I called "Loop" Pigatti's place—a dive down on Pacific Street, where Chinatown fringes into the Latin Quarter. Loop is a tough citizen, who runs a tough hole, and who minds his own business, which is making his dive show a profit. Everybody looks alike to Loop. Whether you're a yegg, stool-pigeon, detective, or settlement worker, you get an even break out of Loop and nothing else. But you can be sure that, unless it's something that might hurt his business, anything you tell Loop will get no further. And anything he tells you is more than likely to be right.

He answered the phone himself.

"Can you get hold of Dummy Uhl for me?" I asked after I had told him who I was.

"Maybe."

"Thanks. I'd like to see him tonight."

"You got nothin' on him?"

"No, Loop, and I don't expect to. I want him to get something for me."

"All right. Where d'you want him?"

"Send him up to my joint. I'll wait there for him."

"If he'll come," Loop promised and hung up.

I left word with Fiske to have the Old Man call me up when he came in, and then I went up to my rooms to wait for my informant.

He came in a little after ten—a short, stocky, pasty-faced man of forty or so, with mouse-colored hair streaked with yellow-white.

"Loop says y'got sumpin' f'r me."

"Yes," I said, waving him to a chair, and closing the door. "I'm buying news."

He fumbled with his hat, started to spit on the floor, changed his mind, licked his lips, and looked up at me.

"What kind o' news? I don't know nothin'."

I was puzzled. The Dummy's yellowish eyes should have showed the pinpoint pupils of the heroin addict. They didn't. The pupils were normal. That didn't mean he was off the stuff—he had put cocaine into them to distend them to normal. The puzzle was—why? He wasn't usually particular enough about his appearance to go to that trouble.

"Did you hear about the Chinese killings down the shore last week?" I asked him.

"No."

"Well," I said, paying no attention to the denial, "I'm hunting for the pair of yellow men who ducked out—Hoo Lun and Yin Hung. Know anything about them?"

"No."

"It's worth a couple of hundred dollars to you to find either of them for me. It's worth another couple hundred to find out about the killings for me. It's worth another to find the slim Chinese youngster with gold teeth who opened the door for the Shan girl and her maid."

"I don't know nothin' about them things," he said.

But he said it automatically while his mind was busy counting up the hundreds I had dangled before him. I suppose his dope-addled brains made the total somewhere in the thousands. He jumped up.

"I'll see what I c'n do. S'pose you slip me a hundred now, on account."

I didn't see that.

"You get it when you deliver."

We had to argue that point, but finally he went off grumbling and growling to get me my news.

I went back to the office. The Old Man hadn't come in yet. It was nearly midnight when he arrived.

"I'm using Dummy Uhl again," I told him, "and I've put a Filipino boy down there too. I've got another scheme, but I don't know anybody to handle it. I think if we offered the missing chauffeur and house-man jobs in some out-of-the-way place up the country, perhaps they'd fall for it. Do you know anybody who could pull it for us?"

"Exactly what have you in mind?"

"It must be somebody who has a house out in the country, the farther the better, the more secluded the better. They would phone one of the Chinese employment offices that they needed three servants—cook, house-man, and chauffeur. We throw in the cook for good measure, to cover the game. It's got to be air-tight on the other end, and, if we're going to catch our fish, we have to give 'em time to investigate. So whoever does it must have some servants, and must put up a bluff—I mean in his own neighborhood—that they are leaving, and the servants must be in on it. And we've got to wait a couple of days, so our friends here will have time to investigate. I think we'd better use Fong Yick's employment agency, on Washington Street.

"Whoever does it could phone Fong Yick tomorrow morning, and say he'd be in Thursday morning to look the applicants over. This is Monday—that'll be long enough. Our helper gets at the employment office at ten Thursday morning. Miss Shan and I arrive in a taxicab ten minutes later, when he'll be in the middle of questioning the applicants. I'll slide out of the taxi into Fong Yick's, grab anybody that looks like one of our missing servants. Miss Shan will come in a minute or two behind me and check me up—so there won't be any false-arrest mixups."

The Old Man nodded approval.

"Very well," he said. "I think I can arrange it. I will let you know tomorrow."

I went home to bed. Thus ended the first day.

3

AT NINE THE next morning, Tuesday, I was talking to Cipriano in the lobby of the apartment building that employs him. His eyes were black drops of ink in white saucers. He thought he had got something.

"Yes, sir! Strange Chinaboys are in town, some of them. They sleep in a house on Waverly Place—on the western side, four houses from the house of Jair Quon, where I sometimes play dice. And there is more—I talk to a white man who knows they are hatchet-men from Portland and Eureka and Sacramento. They are Hip Sing men—a tong war starts—pretty soon, maybe."

"Do these birds look like gunmen to you?"

Cipriano scratched his head.

"No, sir, maybe not. But a fellow can shoot sometimes if he don't look like it. This man tells me they are Hip Sing men."

"Who was this white man?"

"I don't know the name, but he lives there. A short man—snow-bird."

"Grey hair, yellowish eyes?"

"Yes, sir."

That, as likely as not, would be Dummy Uhl. One of my men was stringing the other. The tong stuff hadn't sounded right to me anyhow. Once in a while they mix things, but usually they are blamed for somebody else's crimes. Most wholesale killings in Chinatown are the result of family or clan feuds—such as the ones the "Four Brothers" used to stage.

"This house where you think the strangers are living—know anything about it?"

"No, sir. But maybe you could go through there to the house of Chang Li Ching on other street—Spofford Alley."

"So? And who is this Chang Li Ching?"

"I don't know, sir. But he is there. Nobody sees him, but all Chinaboys say he is great man."

"So? And his house is in Spofford Alley?"

"Yes, sir, a house with red door and red steps. You find it easy, but better not fool with Chang Li Ching."

I didn't know whether that was advice or just a general remark.

"A big gun, huh?" I probed.

But my Filipino didn't really know anything about this Chang Li Ching. He was basing his opinion of the Chinese's greatness on the attitude of his fellow countrymen when they mentioned him.

"Learn anything about the two Chinese men?" I asked after I had fixed this point.

"No, sir, but I will—you bet!"

I praised him for what he had done, told him to try it again that night, and went back to my rooms to wait for Dummy Uhl, who had promised to come there at ten-thirty. It was not quite ten when I got there, so I used some of my spare time to call up the office. The Old Man said Dick Foley—our shadow ace—was idle, so I borrowed him. Then I fixed my gun and sat down to wait for my stool-pigeon.

He rang the bell at eleven o'clock. He came in frowning tremendously.

"I don't know what t' hell to make of it, kid," he spoke

importantly over the cigarette he was rolling. "There's sumpin' makin' down there, an' that's a fact. Things ain't been anyways quiet since the Japs began buyin' stores in the Chink streets, an' maybe that's got sumpin' to do with it. But there ain't no strange Chinks in town—not a damn one! I got a hunch your men have gone down to L.A., but I expec' t' know f'r certain tonight. I got a Chink ribbed up t' get the dope; 'f I was you, I'd put a watch on the boats at San Pedro. Maybe those fellas'll swap papers wit' a coupla Chink sailors that'd like t' stay here."

"And there are no strangers in town?"

"Not any."

"Dummy," I said bitterly, "you're a liar, and you're a boob, and I've been playing you for a sucker. You were in on that killing, and so were your friends, and I'm going to throw you in the can, and your friends on top of you!"

I put my gun in sight, close to his scared-grey face.

"Keep yourself still while I do my phoning!"

Reaching for the telephone with my free hand, I kept one eye on the Dummy.

It wasn't enough. My gun was too close to him.

He yanked it out of my hand. I jumped for him.

The gun turned in his fingers. I grabbed it—too late. It went off, its muzzle less than a foot from where I'm thickest. Fire stung my body.

Clutching the gun with both hands I folded down to the floor. Dummy went away from there, leaving the door open behind him.

One hand on my burning belly, I crossed to the window and waved an arm at Dick Foley, stalling on a corner down the street. Then I went to the bathroom and looked to my wound. A blank cartridge does hurt if you catch it close up!

My vest and shirt and union suit were ruined, and I had a nasty scorch on my body. I greased it, taped a cushion over it, changed my clothes, loaded the gun again, and went down to the office to wait for word from Dick. The first trick in the game looked like mine. Heroin or no heroin, Dummy Uhl would not have jumped me if my guess—based on the trouble he was taking to make his eyes look right and the lie he had sprung on me about there being no strangers in Chinatown— hadn't hit close to the mark.

Dick wasn't long in joining me.

"Good pickings!" he said when he came in. The little Canadian talks like a thrifty man's telegram. "Beat it for phone. Called Hotel Irvington. Booth—couldn't get anything but number. Ought to be enough. Then Chinatown. Dived in cellar west side Waverly Place. Couldn't stick close enough to spot place. Afraid to take chance hanging around. How do you like it?"

"I like it all right. Let's look up 'The Whistler's' record."

A file clerk got it for us—a bulky envelope the size of a brief case, crammed with memoranda, clippings and letters. The gentleman's biography, as we had it, ran like this:

Neil Conyers, alias The Whistler, was born in Philadelphia— out on Whiskey Hill—in 1883. In '94, at the age of eleven, he was picked up by the Washington police. He had gone there to join Coxey's Army. They sent him home. In '98 he was arrested in his home town for stabbing another lad in a row over an election-night bonfire. This time he was released in his parents' custody. In 1901 the Philadelphia police grabbed

him again, charging him with being the head of the first orga-
nized automobile-stealing ring. He was released without trial,
for lack of evidence. But the district attorney lost his job in
the resultant scandal. In 1908 Conyers appeared on the Pacific
Coast—at Seattle, Portland, San Francisco, and Los Angeles—in company with a con-man known as "Duster" Hughes.
Hughes was shot and killed the following year by a man whom
he'd swindled in a fake airplane manufacturing deal. Conyers
was arrested on the same deal. Two juries disagreed and he was
turned loose. In 1910 the Post Office Department's famous
raid on get-rich-quick promoters caught him. Again there
wasn't enough evidence against him to put him away. In 1915
the law scored on him for the first time. He went to San Quentin for buncoing some visitors to the Panama-Pacific Inter-
national Exposition. He stayed there for three years. In 1919
he and a Jap named Hasegawa nicked the Japanese colony
of Seattle for $20,000, Conyers posing as an American who
had held a commission in the Japanese army during that late
war. He had a counterfeit medal of the Order of the Rising
Sun which the emperor was supposed to have pinned on him.
When the game fell through, Hasegawa's family made good
the $20,000—Conyers got out of it with a good profit and not
even any disagreeable publicity. The thing had been hushed.
He returned to San Francisco after that, bought the Hotel
Irvington, and had been living there now for five years without anybody being able to add another word to his criminal
record. He was up to something, but nobody could learn what.
There wasn't a chance in the world of getting a detective into
his hotel as a guest. Apparently the joint was always without
vacant rooms. It was as exclusive as the Pacific-Union Club.

This, then, was the proprietor of the hotel Dummy Uhl had got on the phone before diving into his hole in Chinatown.

I had never seen Conyers. Neither had Dick. There were a couple of photographs in his envelope. One was the profile and full-face photograph of the local police, taken when he had been picked up on the charge that led him to San Quentin. The other was a group picture: all rung up in evening clothes, with the phoney Japanese medal on his chest, he stood among half a dozen of the Seattle Japs he had trimmed—a flashlight picture taken while he was leading them to the slaughter.

These pictures showed him to be a big bird, fleshy, pompous-looking, with a heavy, square chin and shrewd eyes.

"Think you could pick him up?" I asked Dick.

"Sure."

"Suppose you go up there and see if you can get a room or apartment somewhere in the neighborhood—one you can watch the hotel from. Maybe you'll get a chance to tail him around now and then."

I put the pictures in my pocket, in case they'd come in handy, dumped the rest of the stuff back in its envelope, and went into the Old Man's office.

"I arranged that employment office stratagem," he said. "A Frank Paul, who has a ranch out beyond Martinez, will be in Fong Yick's establishment at ten Thursday morning, carrying out his part."

"That's fine! I'm going calling in Chinatown now. If you don't hear from me for a couple of days, will you ask the street-cleaners to watch what they're sweeping up?"

He said he would.

4

SAN FRANCISCO'S CHINATOWN jumps out of the shopping district at California Street and runs north to the Latin Quarter—a strip two blocks wide by six long. Before the fire nearly twenty-five thousand Chinese lived in those dozen blocks. I don't suppose the population is a third of that now.

Grant Avenue, the main street and spine of this strip, is for most of its length a street of gaudy shops catering to the tourist trade and flashy chop-suey houses, where the racket of American jazz orchestras drowns the occasional squeak of a Chinese flute. Farther out, there isn't so much paint and gilt, and you can catch the proper Chinese smell of spices and vinegar and dried things. If you leave the main thoroughfares and show places and start poking around in alleys and dark corners, and nothing happens to you, the chances are you'll find some interesting things—though you won't like some of them.

However, I wasn't poking around as I turned off Grant Avenue at Clay Street, and went up to Spofford Alley, hunting for the house with red steps and red door, which Cipriano had said was Chang Li Ching's. I did pause for a few seconds to look up Waverly Place when I passed it. The Filipino had told me the strange Chinese were living there, and that he thought their house might lead through to Chang Li Ching's; and Dick Foley had shadowed Dummy Uhl there.

But I couldn't guess which was the important house. Four doors from Jair Quon's gambling house, Cipriano had said, but I didn't know where Jair Quon's was. Waverly Place was a picture of peace and quiet just now. A fat Chinese was stacking crates of green vegetables in front of a grocery. Half a dozen small yellow boys were playing at marbles in the middle of the street. On the other side, a blond young man in tweeds was climbing the six steps from a cellar to the street, a painted Chinese woman's face showing for an instant before she closed the door behind him. Up the street a truck was unloading rolls of paper in front of one of the Chinese newspaper plants. A shabby guide was bringing four sightseers out of the Temple of the Queen of Heaven—a joss house over the Sue Hing headquarters.

I went on up to Spofford Alley and found my house with no difficulty at all. It was a shabby building with steps and door the color of dried blood, its windows solidly shuttered with thick, tight-nailed planking. What made it stand out from its neighbors was that its ground floor wasn't a shop or place of business. Purely residential buildings are rare in Chinatown: almost always the street floor is given to business, with the living quarters in cellar or upper stories.

I went up the three steps and tapped the red door with my knuckles.

Nothing happened.

I hit it again, harder. Still nothing. I tried it again, and this time was rewarded by the sounds of scraping and clicking inside.

At least two minutes of this scraping and clicking, and the door swung open—a bare four inches.

One slanting eye and a slice of wrinkled brown face looked out of the crack at me, above the heavy chain that held the door.

"Whata wan'?"

"I want to see Chang Li Ching."

"No savvy. Maybe closs stleet."

"Bunk! You fix your little door and run back and tell Chang Li Ching I want to see him."

"No can do! No savvy Chang."

"You tell him I'm here," I said, turning my back on the door. I sat down on the top step, and added, without looking around, "I'll wait."

While I got my cigarettes out there was silence behind me. Then the door closed softly and the scraping and clicking broke out behind it. I smoked a cigarette and another and let time go by, trying to look like I had all the patience there was. I hoped this yellow man wasn't going to make a chump of me by letting me sit there until I got tired of it.

Chinese passed up and down the alley, scuffling along in American shoes that can never be made to fit them. Some of them looked curiously at me, some gave me no attention at all. An hour went to waste, and a few minutes, and then the familiar scraping and clicking disturbed the door.

The chain rattled as the door swung open. I wouldn't turn my head.

"Go 'way! No catch 'em Chang!"

I said nothing. If he wasn't going to let me in he would have let me sit there without further attention.

A pause.

"Whata wan'?"

"I want to see Chang Li Ching," I said without looking around.

Another pause, ended by the banging of the chain against the door-frame.

"All light."

I chucked my cigarette into the street, got up and stepped into the house. In the dimness I could make out a few pieces of cheap and battered furniture. I had to wait while the Chinese put four arm-thick bars across the door and padlocked them there. Then he nodded at me and scuffled across the floor, a small, bent man with hairless yellow head and a neck like a piece of rope.

Out of this room, he led me into another, darker still, into a hallway, and down a flight of rickety steps. The odors of musty clothing and damp earth were strong. We walked through the dark across a dirt floor for a while, turned to the left, and cement was under my feet. We turned twice more in the dark, and then climbed a flight of unplaned wooden steps into a hall that was fairly light with the glow from shaded electric lights.

In this hall my guide unlocked a door, and we crossed a room where cones of incense burned, and where, in the light of an oil lamp, little red tables with cups of tea stood in front of wooden panels, marked with Chinese characters in gold paint, which hung on the walls. A door on the opposite side of this room let us into pitch blackness, where I had to hold the tail of my guide's loose made-to-order blue coat.

So far he hadn't once looked back at me since our tour began, and neither of us had said anything. This running upstairs and downstairs, turning to the right and turning to the left, seemed harmless enough. If he got any fun out of confusing me, he was welcome. I was confused enough now, so far as the directions were concerned. I hadn't the least idea where I might be. But that didn't disturb me so much. If I was going to be cut down, a knowledge of my geographical position wouldn't make it any more pleasant. If I was going to come out all right, one place was still as good as another.

We did a lot more of the winding around, we did some stair-climbing and some stair-descending, and the rest of the foolishness. I figured I'd been indoors nearly half an hour by now, and I had seen nobody but my guide.

Then I saw something else.

We were going down a long, narrow hall that had brown-painted doors close together on either side. All these doors were closed—secretive-looking in the dim light. Abreast of one of them, a glint of dull metal caught my eye—a dark ring in the door's center.

I went to the floor.

Going down as if I'd been knocked, I missed the flash. But I heard the roar, smelled the powder.

My guide spun around, twisting out of one slipper. In each of his hands was an automatic as big as a coal scuttle. Even while trying to get my own gun out I wondered how so puny a man could have concealed so much machinery on him.

The big guns in the little man's hands flamed at me. Chinese-fashion, he was emptying them—crash! crash! crash!

I thought he was missing me until I had my finger tight on my trigger. Then I woke up in time to hold my fire.

He wasn't shooting at me. He was pouring metal into the door behind me—the door from which I had been shot at.

I rolled away from it, across the hall.

The scrawny little man stepped closer and finished his bombardment. His slugs shredded the wood as if it had been paper. His guns clicked empty.

The door swung open, pushed by the wreck of a man who

was trying to hold himself up by clinging to the sliding panel in the door's center.

Dummy Uhl—all the middle of him gone—slid down to the floor and made more of a puddle than a pile there.

The hall filled with yellow men, black guns sticking out like briars in a blackberry patch.

I got up. My guide dropped his guns to his side and sang out a guttural solo. Chinese began to disappear through various doors, except four who began gathering up what twenty bullets had left of Dummy Uhl.

The stringy old boy tucked his empty guns away and came down the hall to me, one hand held out toward my gun.

"You give 'em," he said politely.

I gave 'em. He could have had my pants.

My gun stowed away in his shirt-bosom, he looked casually at what the four Chinese were carrying away, and then at me.

"No like 'em fella, huh?" he asked.

"Not so much," I admitted.

"All light. I take you."

Our two-man parade got under way again. The ring-around-the-rosy game went on for another flight of stairs and some right and left turns, and then my guide stopped before a door and scratched it with his finger-nails.

5

THE DOOR WAS opened by another Chinese. But this one was none of your Cantonese runts. He was a big meat-eating wrestler—bull-throated, mountain-shouldered, gorilla-armed, leather-skinned. The god that made him had plenty of material, and gave it time to harden.

Holding back the curtain that covered the door, he stepped to one side. I went in, and found his twin standing on the other side of the door.

The room was large and cubical, its doors and windows—if any—hidden behind velvet hangings of green and blue and silver. In a big black chair, elaborately carved, behind an inlaid black table, sat an old Chinese man. His face was round and plump and shrewd, with a straggle of thin white whiskers on his chin. A dark, close-fitting cap was on his head; a purple robe, tight around his neck, showed its sable lining at the bottom, where it had fallen back in a fold over his blue satin trousers.

He did not get up from his chair, but smiled mildly over his whiskers and bent his head almost to the tea things on the table.

"It was only the inability to believe that one of your excellency's heaven-born splendor would waste his costly time on so mean a clod that kept the least of your slaves from running down to prostrate himself at your noble feet as soon as he heard the Father of Detectives was at his unworthy door."

That came out smoothly in English that was a lot clearer than my own. I kept my face straight, waiting.

"If the Terror of Evildoers will honor one of my deplorable chairs by resting his divine body on it, I can assure him the chair shall be burned afterward, so no lesser being may use it. Or will the Prince of Thief-catchers permit me to send a servant to his palace for a chair worthy of him?"

I went slowly to a chair, trying to arrange words in my mind. This old joker was spoofing me with an exaggeration—a burlesque—of the well-known Chinese politeness. I'm not hard to get along with: I'll play anybody's game up to a certain point.

"It's only because I'm weak-kneed with awe of the mighty Chang Li Ching that I dare to sit down," I explained, letting myself down on the chair, and turning my head to notice that the giants who had stood beside the door were gone.

I had a hunch they had gone no farther than the other side of the velvet hangings that hid the door.

"If it were not that the King of Finders-out"—he was at it again—"knows everything, I should marvel that he had heard my lowly name."

"Heard it? Who hasn't?" I kidded back. "Isn't the word change, in English, derived from Chang? Change, meaning alter, is what happens to the wisest man's opinions after he has heard the wisdom of Chang Li Ching!" I tried to get away from this vaudeville stuff, which was a strain on my head. "Thanks for having your man save my life back there in the passage."

He spreads his hands out over the table.

"It was only because I feared the Emperor of Hawkshaws would find the odor of such low blood distasteful to his elegant nostrils that the foul one who disturbed your excellency was struck down quickly. If I have erred, and you would have chosen that he be cut to pieces inch by inch, I can only offer to torture one of my sons in his place."

"Let the boy live," I said carelessly, and turned to business. "I wouldn't have bothered you except that I am so ignorant that only the help of your great wisdom could ever bring me up to normal."

"Does one ask the way of a blind man?" the old duffer asked, cocking his head to one side. "Can a star, however willing, help the moon? If it pleases the Grandfather of Bloodhounds to flatter Chang Li Ching into thinking he can add to the great one's knowledge, who is Chang to thwart his master by refusing to make himself ridiculous?"

I took that to mean he was willing to listen to my questions.

"What I'd like to know is, who killed Lillian Shan's servants, Wang Ma and Wan Lan?"

He played with a thin strand of his white beard, twisting it in a pale, small finger.

"Does the stag-hunter look at the hare?" he wanted to know. "And when so mighty a hunter pretends to concern himself with the death of servants, can Chang think anything except that it pleases the great one to conceal his real object? Yet it may be, because the dead were servants and not girdle-wearers, that the Lord of Snares thought the lowly Chang Li Ching, insignificant one of the Hundred Names, might have knowledge of them. Do not rats know the way of rats?"

He kept this stuff up for some minutes, while I sat and listened and studied his round, shrewd yellow mask of a face, and hoped that something clear would come of it all. Nothing did.

"My ignorance is even greater than I had arrogantly supposed," he brought his speech to an end. "This simple question you put is beyond the power of my muddled mind. I do not know who killed Wang Ma and Wan Lan."

I grinned at him, and put another question:

"Where can I find Hoo Lun and Yin Hung?"

"Again I must grovel in my ignorance," he murmured, "only consoling myself with the thought that the Master of Mysteries knows the answers to his questions, and is pleased to conceal his infallibly accomplished purpose from Chang."

And that was as far as I got.

There were more crazy compliments, more bowing and scraping, more assurances of eternal reverence and love, and then I was following my rope-necked guide through winding, dark halls, across dim rooms, and up and down rickety stairs again.

At the street door—after he had taken down the bars—he slid my gun out of his shirt and handed it to me. I squelched the impulse to look at it then and there to see if anything had been done to it. Instead I stuck it in my pocket and stepped through the door.

"Thanks for the killing upstairs," I said.

The Chinese grunted, bowed, and closed the door.

I went up to Stockton Street, and turned toward the office, walking along slowly, punishing my brains.

First, there was Dummy Uhl's death to think over. Had it been arranged before-hand: to punish him for bungling that morning and, at the same time, to impress me? And how? And why? Or was it supposed to put me under obligations to the Chinese? And, if so, why? Or was it just one of those complicated tricks the Chinese like? I put the subject away and pointed my thoughts at the little plump yellow man in the purple robe.

I liked him. He had humor, brains, nerve, everything. To jam him in a cell would be a trick you'd want to write home about. He was my idea of a man worth working against.

But I didn't kid myself into thinking I had anything on him. Dummy Uhl had given me a connection between The Whistler's Hotel Irvington and Chang Li Ching. Dummy Uhl had gone into action when I accused him of being mixed up in the Shan killings. That much I had—and that was all, except that Chang had said nothing to show he wasn't interested in the Shan troubles.

In this light, the chances were that Dummy's death had not been a planned performance. It was more likely that he had seen me coming, had tried to wipe me out, and had been knocked off by my guide because he was interfering with the audience Chang had granted me. Dummy couldn't have had a very valuable life in the Chinese's eye—or in anybody else's.

I wasn't at all dissatisfied with the day's work so far. I hadn't done anything brilliant, but I had got a look at my destination, or thought I had. If I was butting my head against a stone wall, I at least knew where the wall was and had seen the man who owned it.

In the office, a message from Dick Foley was waiting for me. He had rented a front apartment up the street from the Irvington and had put in a couple of hours trailing The Whistler.

The Whistler had spent half an hour in "Big Fat" Thomson's place on Market Street, talking to the proprietor and some of the sure-thing gamblers who congregate there. Then he had taxi-cabbed out to an apartment house on O'Farrell Street—

the Glenway—where he had rung one of the bells. Getting no answer, he had let himself into the building with a key. An hour later he had come out and returned to his hotel. Dick hadn't been able to determine which bell he had rung, or which apartment he had visited.

I got Lillian Shan on the telephone.

"Will you be in this evening?" I asked. "I've something I want to go into with you, and I can't give it to you over the wire."

"I will be at home until seven-thirty."

"All right, I'll be down."

It was seven-fifteen when the car I had hired put me down at her front door. She opened the door for me. The Danish woman who was filling in until new servants were employed stayed there only in the daytime, returning to her own home—a mile back from the shore—at night.

The evening gown Lillian Shan wore was severe enough, but it suggested that if she would throw away her glasses and do something for herself, she might not be so unfeminine looking after all. She took me upstairs, to the library, where a clean-cut lad of twenty-something in evening clothes got up from a chair as we came in—a well-set-up boy with fair hair and skin.

His name, I learned when we were introduced, was Garthorne. The girl seemed willing enough to hold our conference in his presence. I wasn't. After I had done everything but insist point-blank on seeing her alone, she excused herself—calling him Jack—and took me out into another room.

By then I was a bit impatient.

"Who's that?" I demanded.

She put her eyebrows up for me.

"Mr. John Garthorne," she said.

"How well do you know him?"

"May I ask why you are so interested?"

"You may. Mr. John Garthorne is all wrong, I think."

"Wrong?"

I had another idea.

"Where does he live?"

She gave me an O'Farrell Street number.

"The Glenway Apartments?"

"I think so." She was looking at me without any affectation at all. "Will you please explain?"

"One more question and I will. Do you know a Chinese named Chang Li Ching?"

"No."

"All right. I'll tell you about Garthorne. So far I've run into two angles on this trouble of yours. One of them has to do with this Chang Li Ching in Chinatown, and one with an ex-convict named Conyers. This John Garthorne was in Chinatown today. I saw him coming out of a cellar that probably connects with Chang Li Ching's house. The ex-convict Conyers visited the building where Garthorne lives, early this afternoon."

Her mouth popped open and then shut.

"That is absurd!" she snapped. "I have known Mr. Garthorne for some time, and—"

"Exactly how long?"

"A long—several months."

"Where'd you meet him?"

"Through a girl I knew at college."

"What does he do for a living?"

She stood stiff and silent.

"Listen, Miss Shan," I said. "Garthorne may be all right, but

I've got to look him up. If he's in the clear there'll be no harm done. I want to know what you know about him."

I got it, little by little. He was, or she thought he was, the youngest son of a prominent Richmond, Virginia, family, in disgrace just now because of some sort of boyish prank. He had come to San Francisco four months ago, to wait until his father's anger cooled. Meanwhile his mother kept him in money, leaving him without the necessity of toiling during his exile. He had brought a letter of introduction from one of Lillian Shan's schoolmates. Lillian Shan had, I gathered, a lot of liking for him.

"You're going out with him tonight?" I asked when I had got this.

"Yes."

"In his car or yours?"

She frowned, but she answered my question.

"In his. We are going to drive down to Half Moon for dinner."

"I'll need a key, then, because I am coming back here after you have gone."

"You're what?"

"I'm coming back here. I'll ask you not to say anything about my more or less unworthy suspicions to him, but my honest opinion is that he's drawing you away for the evening. So if the engine breaks down on the way back, just pretend you see nothing unusual in it."

That worried her, but she wouldn't admit I might be right. I got the key, though, and then I told her of my employment agency scheme that needed her assistance, and she promised to be at the office at half past nine Thursday morning.

I didn't see Garthorne again before I left the house.

6

IN MY HIRED car again, I had the driver take me to the nearest village, where I bought a plug of chewing tobacco, a flashlight, and a box of cartridges at the general store. My gun is a .38 Special, but I had to take the shorter, weaker cartridges, because the storekeeper didn't keep the specials in stock.

My purchases in my pocket, we started back toward the Shan house again. Two bends in the road this side of it, I stopped the car, paid the chauffeur, and sent him on his way, finishing the trip afoot.

The house was dark all around.

Letting myself in as quietly as possible, and going easy with the flashlight, I gave the interior a combing from cellar to roof. I was the only occupant. In the kitchen, I looted the icebox for a bite or two, which I washed down with milk. I could have used some coffee, but coffee is too fragrant.

The luncheon done, I made myself comfortable on a chair in the passageway between the kitchen and the rest of the house. On one side of the passageway, steps led down to the basement. On the other, steps led upstairs. With every door in the house except the outer ones open, the passageway was the center of things so far as hearing noises was concerned.

An hour went by—quietly except for the passing of cars on the road a hundred yards away and the washing of the Pacific down in the little cove. I chewed on my plug of tobacco—a substitute for cigarettes—and tried to count up the hours of my life I'd spent like this, sitting or standing around waiting for something to happen.

The telephone rang.

I let it ring. It might be Lillian Shan needing help, but I couldn't take a chance. It was too likely to be some egg trying to find out if anybody was in the house.

Another half hour went by with a breeze springing up from the ocean, rustling trees outside.

A noise came that was neither wind nor surf nor passing car. Something clicked somewhere.

It was at a window, but I didn't know which. I got rid of my chew, got gun and flashlight out.

It sounded again, harshly.

Somebody was giving a window a strong play—too strong. The catch rattled, and something clicked against the pane. It was a stall. Whoever he was, he could have smashed the glass with less noise than he was making.

I stood up, but I didn't leave the passageway. The window noise was a fake to draw the attention of anyone who might be in the house. I turned my back on it, trying to see into the kitchen.

The kitchen was too black to see anything.

I saw nothing there. I heard nothing there.

Damp air blew on me from the kitchen.

That was something to worry about. I had company, and he was slicker than I. He could open doors or windows under my nose. That wasn't so good.

Weight on rubber heels, I backed away from my chair until the frame of the cellar door touched my shoulder. I wasn't sure I was going to like this party. I like an even break or better, and this didn't look like one.

So when a thin line of light danced out of the kitchen to hit the chair in the passsageway, I was three steps cellar-ward, my back flat against the stair-wall.

The light fixed itself on the chair for a couple of seconds, and then began to dart around the passageway, through it into the room beyond. I could see nothing but the light.

Fresh sounds came to me—the purr of automobile engines close to the house on the road side, the soft padding of feet on the back porch, on the kitchen linoleum, quite a few feet. An odor came to me—an unmistakable odor—the smell of unwashed Chinese.

Then I lost track of these things. I had plenty to occupy me close up.

The proprietor of the flashlight was at the head of the cellar steps. I had ruined my eyes watching the light: I couldn't see him.

The first thin ray he sent downstairs missed me by an inch— which gave me time to make a map there in the dark. If he was of medium size, holding the light in his left hand, a gun in his right, and exposing as little of himself as possible—his noodle should have been a foot and a half above the beginning of the light-beam, the same distance behind it, six inches to the left—my left.

The light swung sideways and hit one of my legs.

I swung the barrel of my gun at the point I had marked X in the night.

His gun-fire cooked my cheek. One of his arms tried to take me with him. I twisted away and let him dive alone into the cellar, showing me a flash of gold teeth as he went past.

The house was full of "Ah yahs" and pattering feet.

I had to move—or I'd be pushed.

Downstairs might be a trap. I went up to the passageway again.

The passageway was solid and alive with stinking bodies. Hands and teeth began to take my clothes away from me. I knew damned well I had declared myself in on something!

I was one of a struggling, tearing, grunting and groaning mob of invisibles. An eddy of them swept me toward the kitchen. Hitting, kicking, butting, I went along.

A high-pitched voice was screaming Chinese orders.

My shoulder scraped the door-frame as I was carried into the kitchen, fighting as best I could against enemies I couldn't see, afraid to use the gun I still gripped.

I was only one part of the mad scramble. The flash of my gun might have made me the center of it. These lunatics were fighting panic now: I didn't want to show them something tangible to tear apart.

I went along with them, cracking everything that got in my way, and being cracked back. A bucket got between my feet.

I crashed down, upsetting my neighbors, rolled over a body, felt a foot on my face, squirmed from under it, and came to rest in a corner, still tangled up with the galvanized bucket.

Thank God for that bucket!

I wanted these people to go away. I didn't care who or what they were. If they'd depart in peace I'd forgive their sins.

I put my gun inside the bucket and squeezed the trigger. I got the worst of the racket, but there was enough to go around. It sounded like a crump going off.

I cut loose in the bucket again, and had another idea. Two fingers of my left hand in my mouth, I whistled as shrill as I could while I emptied the gun.

It was a sweet racket!

When my gun had run out of bullets and my lungs out of air, I was alone. I was glad to be alone. I knew why men go off and live in caves by themselves. And I didn't blame them!

Sitting there alone in the dark, I reloaded my gun.

On hands and knees I found my way to the open kitchen door, and peeped out into the blackness that told me nothing. The surf made guzzling sounds in the cove. From the other side of the house came the noise of cars. I hoped it was my friends going away.

I shut the door, locked it, and turned on the kitchen light.

The place wasn't as badly upset as I had expected. Some pans and dishes were down and a chair had been broken, and the place smelled of unwashed bodies. But that was all—except a blue cotton sleeve in the middle of the floor, a straw sandal near the passageway door, and a handful of short black hairs, a bit blood-smeared, beside the sandal.

In the cellar I did not find the man I had sent down there. An open door showed how he had left me. His flashlight was there, and my own, and some of his blood.

Upstairs again, I went through the front of the house. The front door was open. Rugs had been rumpled. A blue vase was broken on the floor. A table was pushed out of place, and a couple of chairs had been upset. I found an old and greasy brown felt hat that had neither sweat-band nor hat-band. I found a grimy photograph of President Coolidge—apparently cut from a Chinese newspaper—and six wheat-straw cigarette papers.

I found nothing upstairs to show that any of my guests had gone up there.

It was half past two in the morning when I heard a car drive up to the front door. I peeped out of Lillian Shan's bedroom window, on the second floor. She was saying good-night to Jack Garthorne.

I went back to the library to wait for her.

"Nothing happened?" were her first words, and they sounded more like a prayer than anything else.

"It did," I told her, "and I suppose you had your breakdown."

For a moment I thought she was going to lie to me, but she nodded, and dropped into a chair, not as erect as usual.

"I had a lot of company," I said, "but I can't say I found out much about them. The fact is, I bit off more than I could chew, and had to be satisfied with chasing them out."

"You didn't call the sheriff's office?" There was something strange about the tone in which she put the question.

"No—I don't want Garthorne arrested yet."

That shook the dejection out of her. She was up, tall and straight in front of me, and cold.

"I'd rather not go into that again," she said.

That was all right with me, but:

"You didn't say anything to him, I hope."

"Say anything to him?" She seemed amazed. "Do you think I would insult him by repeating your guesses—your absurd guesses?"

"That's fine," I applauded her silence if not her opinion of my theories. "Now, I'm going to stay here tonight. There isn't a chance in a hundred of anything happening, but I'll play it safe."

She didn't seem very enthusiastic about that, but she finally went off to bed.

Nothing happened between then and sun-up, of course. I left the house as soon as daylight came and gave the grounds the once over. Footprints were all over the place, from water's edge to driveway. Along the driveway some of the sod was cut where machines had been turned carelessly.

Borrowing one of the cars from the garage, I was back in San Francisco before the morning was far gone.

In the office, I asked the Old Man to put an operative behind Jack Garthorne; to have the old hat, flashlight, sandal and the rest of my souvenirs put under the microscope and searched for finger prints, foot prints, tooth-prints or what have you; and to have our Richmond branch look up the Garthornes. Then I went up to see my Filipino assistant.

He was gloomy.

"What's the matter?" I asked. "Somebody knock you over?"

"Oh, no, sir!" he protested. "But maybe I am not so good a detective. I try to follow one fella, and he turns a corner and he is gone."

"Who was he, and what was he up to?"

"I do not know, sir. There is four automobiles with men getting out of them into that cellar of which I tell you the strange Chinese live. After they are gone in, one man comes out. He wears his hat down over bandage on his upper face, and he walks away rapidly. I try to follow him, but he turns that corner, and where is he?"

"What time did all this happen?"

"Twelve o'clock, maybe."

"Could it have been later than that, or earlier?"

"Yes, sir."

My visitors, no doubt, and the man Cipriano had tried to

shadow could have been the one I swatted. The Filipino hadn't thought to get the license numbers of the automobiles. He didn't know whether they had been driven by white men or Chinese, or even what make cars they were.

"You've done fine," I assured him. "Try it again tonight. Take it easy, and you'll get there."

From him I went to a telephone and called the Hall of Justice. Dummy Uhl's death had not been reported, I learned.

Twenty minutes later I was skinning my knuckles on Chang Li Ching's front door.

7

THE LITTLE OLD Chinese with the rope neck didn't open for me this time. Instead, a young Chinese with a small-pox-pitted face and a wide grin.

"You wanna see Chang Li Ching," he said before I could speak, and stepped back for me to enter.

I went in and waited while he replaced all the bars and locks. We went to Chang by a shorter route than before, but it was still far from direct. For a while I amused myself trying to map the route in my head as he went along, but it was too complicated, so I gave it up.

The velvet-hung room was empty when my guide showed me in, bowed, grinned, and left me. I sat down in a chair near the table and waited.

Chang Li Ching didn't put on the theatricals for me by materializing silently, or anything of the sort. I heard his soft slippers on the floor before he parted the hangings and came in. He was alone, his white whiskers ruffled in a smile that was grandfatherly.

"The Scatterer of Hordes honors my poor residence again," he greeted me, and went on at great length with the same sort of nonsense that I'd had to listen to on my first visit.

The Scatterer of Hordes part was cool enough—if it was a reference to last night's doings.

"Not knowing who he was until too late, I beaned one of your servants last night," I said when he had run out of flowers for the time. "I know there's nothing I can do to square myself for such a terrible act, but I hope you'll let me cut my throat and bleed to death in one of your garbage cans as a sort of apology."

A little sighing noise that could have been a smothered chuckle disturbed the old man's lips, and the purple cap twitched on his round head.

"The Disperser of Marauders knows all things," he murmured blandly, "even to the value of noise in driving away demons. If he says the man he struck was Chang Li Ching's servant, who is Chang to deny it?"

I tried him with my other barrel.

"I don't know much—not even why the police haven't yet heard of the death of the man who was killed here yesterday."

One of his hands made little curls in his white beard.

"I had not heard of the death," he said.

I could guess what was coming, but I wanted to take a look at it.

"You might ask the man who brought me here yesterday," I suggested.

Chang Li Ching picked up a little padded stick from the table and struck a tasseled gong that hung at his shoulder. Across the room the hangings parted to admit the pock-marked Chinese who had brought me in.

"Did death honor our hovel yesterday?" Chang asked in English.

"No, Ta Jen," the pock-marked one said.

"It was the nobleman who guided me here yesterday," I explained, "not this son of an emperor."

Chang imitated surprise.

"Who welcomed the King of Spies yesterday?" he asked the man at the door.

"I bring 'em, Ta Jen."

I grinned at the pock-marked man, he grinned back, and Chang smiled benevolently.

"An excellent jest," he said.

It was.

The pock-marked man bowed and started to duck back through the hangings. Loose shoes rattled on the boards behind him. He spun around. One of the big wrestlers I had seen the previous day loomed above him. The wrestler's eyes were bright with excitement, and grunted Chinese syllables poured out of his mouth. The pock-marked one talked back. Chang Li Ching silenced them with a sharp command. All this was in Chinese—out of my reach.

"Will the Grand Duke of Manhunters permit his servant to depart for a moment to attend to his distressing domestic affairs?"

"Sure."

Chang bowed with his hands together, and spoke to the wrestler.

"You will remain here to see that the great one is not disturbed and that any wishes he expresses are gratified."

The wrestler bowed and stood aside for Chang to pass through the door with the pock-marked man. The hangings swung over the door behind them.

I didn't waste any language on the man at the door, but got a cigarette going and waited for Chang to come back. The cigarette was half gone when a shot sounded in the building, not far away.

The giant at the door scowled.

Another shot sounded, and running feet thumped in the hall.

The pock-marked man's face came through the hangings. He poured grunts at the wrestler. The wrestler scowled at me and protested. The other insisted.

The wrestler scowled at me again, rumbled, "You wait," and was gone with the other.

I finished my cigarette to the tune of muffled struggle-sounds that seemed to come from the floor below. There were two more shots, far apart. Feet ran past the door of the room I was in. Perhaps ten minutes had gone since I had been left alone.

I found I wasn't alone.

Across the room from the door, the hangings that covered the wall were disturbed. The blue, green and silver velvet bulged out an inch and settled back in place.

The disturbance happened the second time perhaps ten feet farther along the wall. No movement for a while, and then a tremor in the far corner.

Somebody was creeping along between hangings and wall.

I let them creep, still slumping in my chair with idle hands. If the bulge meant trouble, action on my part would only bring it that much quicker.

I traced the disturbance down the length of that wall and halfway across the other, to where I knew the door was. Then I lost it for some time. I had just decided that the creeper had gone through the door when the curtains opened and the creeper stepped out.

She wasn't four and a half feet high—a living ornament from somebody's shelf. Her face was a tiny oval of painted beauty, its perfection emphasized by the lacquer-black hair that was flat and glossy around her temples. Gold earrings swung beside her smooth cheeks, a jade butterfly was in her hair. A lavender jacket, glittering with white stones, covered her from under her chin to her knees. Lavender stockings showed under her short lavender trousers, and her bound-small feet were in slippers of the same color, shaped like kittens, with yellow stones for eyes and aigrettes for whiskers.

The point of all this our-young-ladies'-fashion stuff is that she was impossibly dainty. But there she was—neither a carving nor a painting, but a living small woman with fear in her black eyes and nervous, tiny fingers worrying the silk at her bosom.

Twice as she came toward me—hurrying with the awkward, quick step of the foot-bound Chinese woman—her head twisted around for a look at the hangings over the door.

I was on my feet by now, going to meet her.

Her English wasn't much. Most of what she babbled at me I missed, though I thought "yung hel-lup" might have been meant for "You help?"

I nodded, catching her under the elbows as she stumbled against me.

She gave me some more language that didn't make the situation any clearer—unless "sul-lay-vee gull" meant slave-girl and "tak-ka wah" meant take away.

"You want me to get you out of here?" I asked.

Her head, close under my chin, went up and down, and her red flower of a mouth shaped a smile that made all the other smiles I could remember look like leers.

She did some more talking. I got nothing out of it. Taking one of her elbows out of my hand, she pushed up her sleeve, baring a forearm that an artist had spent a life-time carving out of ivory. On it were five finger-shaped bruises ending in cuts where the nails had punctured the flesh.

She let the sleeve fall over it again, and gave me more words. They didn't mean anything to me, but they tinkled prettily.

"All right," I said, sliding my gun out. "If you want to go, we'll go."

Both her hands went to the gun, pushing it down, and she talked excitedly into my face, winding up with a flicking of one hand across her collar—a pantomime of a throat being cut.

I shook my head from side to side and urged her toward the door.

She balked, fright large in her eyes.

One of her hands went to my watch-pocket. I let her take the watch out.

She put the tiny tip of one pointed finger over the twelve and then circled the dial three times. I thought I got that. Thirty-six hours from noon would be midnight of the following night—Thursday.

"Yes," I said.

She shot a look at the door and led me to the table where the tea things were. With a finger dipped in cold tea she began to draw on the table's inlaid top. Two parallel lines I took for a street. Another pair crossed them. The third pair crossed the second and paralleled the first.

"Waverly Place?" I guessed.

Her face bobbed up and down, delightedly.

On what I took for the east side of Waverly Place she drew a square—perhaps a house. In the square she set what could have been a rose. I frowned at that. She erased the rose and in its place put a crooked circle, adding dots. I thought I had it. The rose had been a cabbage. This thing was a potato. The square represented the grocery store I had noticed on Waverly Place. I nodded.

Her finger crossed the street and put a square on the other side, and her face turned up to mine, begging me to understand her.

"The house across the street from the grocer's," I said slowly, and then, as she tapped my watch-pocket, I added, "at midnight tomorrow."

I don't know how much of it she caught, but she nodded her little head until her earrings were swinging like crazy pendulums.

With a quick diving motion, she caught my right hand, kissed it, and with a tottering, hoppy run vanished behind the velvet curtains.

I used my handkerchief to wipe the map off the table and was smoking in my chair when Chang Li Ching returned some twenty minutes later.

I left shortly after that, as soon as we had traded a few dizzy compliments. The pock-marked man ushered me out.

At the office there was nothing new for me. Foley hadn't been able to shadow The Whistler the night before.

I went home for the sleep I had not got last night.

8

AT TEN MINUTES after ten the next morning Lillian Shan and I arrived at the front door of Fong Yick's employment agency on Washington Street.

"Give me just two minutes," I told her as I climbed out. "Then come in."

"Better keep your steam up," I suggested to the driver. "We might have to slide away in a hurry."

In Fong Yick's, a lanky, grey-haired man whom I thought was the Old Man's Frank Paul was talking around a chewed cigar to half a dozen Chinese. Across the battered counter a fat Chinese was watching them boredly through immense steel-rimmed spectacles.

I looked at the half-dozen. The third from me had a crooked nose—a short, squat man.

I pushed aside the others and reached for him.

I don't know what the stuff he tried on me was—jiu jitsu, maybe, or its Chinese equivalent. Anyhow, he crouched and moved his stiffly open hands trickily.

I took hold of him here and there, and presently had him by the nape of his neck, with one of his arms bent up behind him.

Another Chinese piled on my back. The lean, grey-haired man did something to his face, and the Chinese went over in a corner and stayed there.

That was the situation when Lillian Shan came in.

I shook the flat-nosed boy at her.

"Yin Hung!" she exclaimed.

"Hoo Lun isn't one of the others?" I asked, pointing to the spectators.

She shook her head emphatically, and began jabbering Chinese at my prisoner. He jabbered back, meeting her gaze.

"What are you going to do with him?" she asked me in a voice that wasn't quite right.

"Turn him over to the police to hold for the San Mateo sheriff. Can you get anything out of him?"

"No."

I began to push him toward the door. The steel-spectacled Chinese blocked the way, one hand behind him.

"No can do," he said.

I slammed Yin Hung into him. He went back against the wall.

"Get out!" I yelled at the girl.

The grey-haired man stopped two Chinese who dashed for the door, sent them the other way—back hard against the wall.

We left the place.

There was no excitement in the street. We climbed into the taxicab and drove the block and a half to the Hall of Justice, where I yanked my prisoner out. The rancher Paul said he wouldn't go in, that he had enjoyed the party, but now had some of his own business to look after. He went on up Kearney Street afoot.

Half-out of the taxicab, Lillian Shan changed her mind.

"Unless it's necessary," she said, "I'd rather not go in either. I'll wait here for you."

"Righto," and I pushed my captive across the sidewalk and up the steps.

Inside, an interesting situation developed.

The San Francisco police weren't especially interested in Yin Hung, though willing enough, of course, to hold him for the sheriff of San Mateo County.

Yin Hung pretended he didn't know any English, and I was curious to know what sort of story he had to tell, so I hunted around in the detectives' assembly room until I found Bill Thode of the Chinatown detail, who talks the language some.

He and Yin Hung jabbered at each other for some time.

Then Bill looked at me, laughed, bit off the end of a cigar, and leaned back in his chair.

"According to the way he tells it," Bill said, "that Wan Lan woman and Lillian Shan had a row. The next day Wan Lan's not anywheres around. The Shan girl and Wang Ma, her maid, say Wan Lan has left, but Hoo Lun tells this fellow he saw Wang Ma burning some of Wan Lan's clothes.

"So Hoo Lun and this fellow think something's wrong, and the next day they're damned sure of it, because this fellow misses a spade from his garden tools. He finds it again that night, and it's still wet with damp dirt, and he says no dirt was dug up anywheres around the place—not outside of the house anyways. So him and Hoo Lun put their heads together, didn't like the result, and decided they'd better dust out before they went wherever Wan Lan had gone. That's the message."

"Where is Hoo Lun now?"

"He says he don't know."

"So Lillian Shan and Wang Ma were still in the house when this pair left?" I asked. "They hadn't started for the East yet?"

"So he says."

"Has he got any idea why Wan Lan was killed?"

"Not that I've been able to get out of him."

"Thanks, Bill! You'll notify the sheriff that you're holding him?"

"Sure."

Of course Lillian Shan and the taxicab were gone when I came out of the Hall of Justice door.

I went back into the lobby and used one of the booths to phone the office. Still no report from Dick Foley—nothing of any value—and none from the operative who was trying to shadow Jack Garthorne. A wire had come from the Richmond branch. It was to the effect that the Garthornes were a wealthy and well-known local family, that young Jack was usually in trouble, that he had slugged a Prohibition agent during a café raid a few months ago, that his father had taken him out of his will and chased him from the house, but that his mother was believed to be sending him money.

That fit in with what the girl had told me.

A street car carried me to the garage where I had stuck the roadster I had borrowed from the girl's garage the previous morning. I drove around to Cipriano's apartment building. He had no news of any importance for me. He had spent the night hanging around Chinatown, but had picked up nothing.

I was a little inclined toward grouchiness as I turned the roadster west, driving out through Golden Gate Park to the Ocean Boulevard. The job wasn't getting along as snappily as I wanted it to.

I let the roadster slide down the boulevard at a good clip, and the salt air blew some of my kinks away.

A bony-faced man with pinkish mustache opened the door when I rang Lillian Shan's bell. I knew him—Tucker, a deputy sheriff.

"Hullo," he said. "What d'you want?"

"I'm hunting for her too."

"Keep on hunting," he grinned. "Don't let me stop you."

"Not here, huh?"

"Nope. The Swede woman that works for her says she was in and out half an hour before I got here, and I've been here about ten minutes now."

"Got a warrant for her?" I asked.

"You bet you! Her chauffeur squawked."

"Yes, I heard him," I said. "I'm the bright boy who gathered him in."

I spent five or ten minutes more talking to Tucker and then climbed in the roadster again.

"Will you give the agency a ring when you nab her?" I asked as I closed the door.

"You bet you."

I pointed the roadster at San Francisco again.

Just outside of Daly City a taxicab passed me, going south. Jack Garthorne's face looked through the window.

I snapped on the brakes and waved my arm. The taxicab turned and came back to me. Garthorne opened the door, but did not get out.

I got down into the road and went over to him.

"There's a deputy sheriff waiting in Miss Shan's house, if that's where you're headed."

His blue eyes jumped wide, and then narrowed as he looked suspiciously at me.

"Let's go over to the side of the road and have a little talk," I invited.

He got out of the taxicab and we crossed to a couple of

comfortable-looking boulders on the other side.

"Where is Lil—Miss Shan?" he asked.

"Ask The Whistler," I suggested.

This blond kid wasn't so good. It took him a long time to get his gun out. I let him go through with it.

"What do you mean?" he demanded.

I hadn't meant anything. I had just wanted to see how the remark would hit him. I kept quiet.

"Has The Whistler got her?"

"I don't think so," I admitted, though I hated to do it. "But the point is that she has had to go in hiding to keep from being hanged for the murders The Whistler framed."

"Hanged?"

"Uh-huh. The deputy waiting in her house has a warrant for her—for murder."

He put away his gun and made gurgling noises in his throat.

"I'll go there! I'll tell everything I know!"

He started for his taxicab.

"Wait!" I called. "Maybe you'd better tell me what you know first. I'm working for her, you know."

He spun around and came back.

"Yes, that's right. You'll know what to do."

"Now what do you really know, if anything?" I asked when he was standing in front of me.

"I know the whole thing!" he cried. "About the deaths and the booze and—"

"Easy! Easy! There's no use wasting all that knowledge on the chauffeur."

He quieted down, and I began to pump him. I spent nearly an hour getting all of it.

9

THE HISTORY OF his young life, as he told it to me, began with his departure from home after falling into disgrace through slugging the Prohi. He had come to San Francisco to wait until his father cooled off. Meanwhile his mother kept him in funds, but she didn't send him all the money a young fellow in a wild city could use.

That was the situation when he ran into The Whistler, who suggested that a chap with Garthorne's front could pick up some easy money in the rum-running game if he did what he was told to do. Garthorne was willing enough. He didn't like Prohibition—it had caused most of his troubles. Rum-running sounded romantic to him—shots in the dark, signal lights off the starboard bow, and so on.

The Whistler, it seemed, had boats and booze and waiting customers, but his landing arrangements were out of whack. He had his eye on a little cove down the shore line that was an ideal spot to land hooch. It was neither too close nor too far from San Francisco. It was sheltered on either side by rocky points, and screened from the road by a large house and high hedges. Given the use of that house, his troubles would be over. He could land his hooch in the cove, run it into the house, repack it innocently there, put it through the front door into his automobiles, and shoot it to the thirsty city.

The house, he told Garthorne, belonged to a Chinese girl named Lillian Shan, who would neither sell nor rent it. Garthorne was to make her acquaintance—The Whistler was already supplied with a letter of introduction written by a former classmate of the girl's, a classmate who had fallen a lot since university days—and try to work himself in with her to a degree of intimacy that would permit him to make her an offer for the use of the house. That is, he was to find out if she was the sort of person who could be approached with a more or less frank offer of a share in the profits of The Whistler's game.

Garthorne had gone through with his part, or the first of it, and had become fairly intimate with the girl, when she suddenly left for the East, sending him a note saying she would be gone several months. That was fine for the rum-runners. Garthorne, calling at the house, the next day, had learned that Wang Ma had gone with her mistress, and that the three other servants had been left in charge of the house.

That was all Garthorne knew first-hand. He had not taken part in the landing of the booze, though he would have liked to. But The Whistler had ordered him to stay away, so that he could continue his original part when the girl returned.

The Whistler told Garthorne he had bought the help of the three Chinese servants, but that the woman, Wan Lan, had been killed by the two men in a fight over their shares of the money. Booze had been run through the house once during Lillian Shan's absence. Her unexpected return gummed things. The house still held some of the booze. They had to grab her and Wang Ma and stick them in a closet until they got the stuff away. The strangling of Wang Ma had been accidental—a rope tied too tight.

The worst complication, however, was that another cargo was scheduled to land in the cove the following Tuesday night, and there was no way of getting word out to the boat that the place was closed. The Whistler sent for our hero and ordered him to get the girl out of the way and keep her out of the way until at least two o'clock Wednesday morning.

Garthorne had invited her to drive down to Half Moon with him for dinner that night. She had accepted. He had faked engine trouble, and had kept her away from the house until two-thirty, and The Whistler had told him later that everything had gone through without a hitch.

After this I had to guess at what Garthorne was driving at— he stuttered and stammered and let his ideas rattle looser than ever. I think it added up to this: he hadn't thought much about the ethics of his play with the girl. She had no attraction for him—too severe and serious to seem really feminine. And he had not pretended—hadn't carried on what could possibly be called a flirtation with her. Then he suddenly woke up to the fact that she wasn't as indifferent as he. That had been a shock to him—one he couldn't stand. He had seen things straight for the first time. He had thought of it before as simply a wit-matching game. Affection made it different—even though the affection was all on one side.

"I told The Whistler I was through this afternoon," he finished.

"How did he like it?"

"Not a lot. In fact, I had to hit him."

"So? And what were you planning to do next?"

"I was going to see Miss Shan, tell her the truth, and then— then I thought I'd better lay low."

"I think you'd better. The Whistler might not like being hit."

"I won't hide now! I'll go give myself up and tell the truth."

"Forget it!" I advised him. "That's no good. You don't know enough to help her."

That wasn't exactly the truth, because he did know that the chauffeur and Hoo Lun had still been in the house the day after her departure for the East. But I didn't want him to get out of the game yet.

"If I were you," I went on, "I'd pick out a quiet hiding place and stay there until I can get word to you. Know a good place?"

"Yes," slowly. "I have a—a friend who will hide me—down near—near the Latin Quarter."

"Near the Latin Quarter?" That could be Chinatown. I did some sharp-shooting. "Waverly Place?"

He jumped.

"How did you know?"

"I'm a detective. I know everything. Ever hear of Chang Li Ching?"

"No."

I tried to keep from laughing into his puzzled face.

The first time I had seen this cut-up he was leaving a house in Waverly Place, with a Chinese woman's face showing dimly in the doorway behind him. The house had been across the street from a grocery. The Chinese girl with whom I had talked at Chang's had given me a slave-girl yarn and an invitation to that same house. Big-hearted Jack here had fallen for the same game, but he didn't know that the girl had anything to do with Chang Li Ching, didn't know that Chang existed, didn't know Chang and The Whistler were playmates. Now Jack is in trouble, and he's going to the girl to hide!

I didn't dislike this angle of the game. He was walking into a trap, but that was nothing to me—or, rather, I hoped it was going to help me.

"What's your friend's name?" I asked.

He hesitated.

"What is the name of the tiny woman whose door is across the street from the grocery?" I made myself plain.

"Hsiu Hsiu."

"All right," I encouraged him in his foolishness. "You go there. That's an excellent hiding place. Now if I want to get a Chinese boy to you with a message, how will he find you?"

"There's a flight of steps to the left as you go in. He'll have to skip the second and third steps, because they are fitted with some sort of alarm. So is the handrail. On the second floor you turn to the left again. The hall is dark. The second door to the right—on the right-hand side of the hall—lets you into a room. On the other side of the room is a closet, with a door hidden behind old clothes. There are usually people in the room the door opens into, so he'll have to wait for a chance to get through it. This room has a little balcony outside, that you can get to from either of the windows. The balcony's sides are solid, so if you crouch low you can't be seen from the street or from other houses. At the other end of the balcony there are two loose floor boards. You slide down under them into a little room between walls. The trap-door there will let you down into another just like it where I'll probably be. There's another way out of the bottom room, down a flight of steps, but I've never been that way."

A fine mess! It sounded like a child's game. But even with all this frosting on the cake our young chump hadn't tumbled. He took it seriously.

"So that's how it's done!" I said. "You'd better get there as soon as you can, and stay there until my messenger gets to you. You'll know him by the cast in one of his eyes, and maybe I'd better give him a password. Haphazard—that'll be the word. The street door—is it locked?"

"No. I've never found it locked. There are forty or fifty Chinamen—or perhaps a hundred—living in that building, so I don't suppose the door is ever locked."

"Good. Beat it now."

10

AT 10:15 THAT night I was pushing open the door opposite the grocery in Waverly Place—an hour and three-quarters early for my date with Hsiu Hsiu. At 9:55 Dick Foley had
phoned that The Whistler had gone into the red-painted door
on Spofford Alley.

I found the interior dark, and closed the door softly, concen-
trating on the childish directions Garthorne had given me.
That I knew they were silly didn't help me, since I didn't know
any other route.

The stairs gave me some trouble, but I got over the second
and third without touching the handrail, and went on up.
I found the second door in the hall, the closet in the room
behind it, and the door in the closet. Light came through the
cracks around it. Listening, I heard nothing.

I pushed the door open—the room was empty. A smoking
oil lamp stunk there. The nearest window made no sound as I
raised it. That was inartistic—a squeak would have impressed
Garthorne with his danger.

I crouched low on the balcony, in accordance with instructions, and found the loose floorboards that opened up a black
hole. Feet first, I went down in, slanting at an angle that made
descent easy. It seemed to be a sort of slot cut diagonally
through the wall. It was stuffy, and I don't like narrow holes. I
went down swiftly, coming into a small room, long and narrow,
as if placed inside a thick wall.

No light was there. My flashlight showed a room perhaps

eighteen feet long by four wide, furnished with table, couch and two chairs. I looked under the one rug on the floor. The trapdoor was there—a crude affair that didn't pretend it was part of the floor.

Flat on my belly, I put an ear to the trapdoor. No sound. I raised it a couple of inches. Darkness and a faint murmuring of voices. I pushed the trapdoor wide, let it down easily on the floor and stuck head and shoulders into the opening, discovering then that it was a double arrangement. Another door was below, fitting no doubt in the ceiling of the room below.

Cautiously I let myself down on it. It gave under my foot. I could have pulled myself up again, but since I had disturbed it I chose to keep going.

I put both feet on it. It swung down. I dropped into light. The door snapped up over my head. I grabbed Hsiu Hsiu and clapped a hand over her tiny mouth in time to keep her quiet.

"Hello," I said to the startled Garthorne; "this is my boy's evening off, so I came myself."

"Hello," he gasped.

This room, I saw, was a duplicate of the one from which I had dropped, another cupboard between walls, though this one had an unpainted wooden door at one end.

I handed Hsiu Hsiu to Garthorne.

"Keep her quiet," I ordered, "while—"

The clicking of the door's latch silenced me. I jumped to the wall on the hinged side of the door just as it swung open—the opener hidden from me by the door.

The door opened wide, but not much wider than Jack Garthorne's blue eyes, nor than this mouth. I let the door go back against the wall and stepped out behind my balanced gun.

The queen of something stood there!

She was a tall woman, straight-bodied and proud. A butter-fly-shaped headdress decked with the loot of a dozen jewelry stores exaggerated her height. Her gown was amethyst fili-greed with gold above, a living rainbow below. The clothes were nothing!

She was—maybe I can make it clear this way. Hsiu Hsiu was as perfect a bit of feminine beauty as could be imagined. She was perfect! Then comes this queen of something—and Hsiu Hsiu's beauty went away. She was a candle in the sun. She was still pretty—prettier than the woman in the doorway, if it came to that—but you didn't pay any attention to her. Hsiu Hsiu was a pretty girl: this royal woman in the doorway was—I don't know the words.

"My God!" Garthorne was whispering harshly. "I never knew it!"

"What are you doing here?" I challenged the woman.

She didn't hear me. She was looking at Hsiu Hsiu as a tigress might look at an alley cat. Hsiu Hsiu was looking at her as an alley cat might look at a tigress. Sweat was on Garthorne's face and his mouth was the mouth of a sick man.

"What are you doing here?" I repeated, stepping closer to Lillian Shan.

"I am here where I belong," she said slowly, not taking her eyes from the slave-girl. "I have come back to my people."

That was a lot of bunk. I turned to the goggling Garthorne.

"Take Hsiu Hsiu to the upper room, and keep her quiet, if you have to strangle her. I want to talk to Miss Shan."

Still dazed, he pushed the table under the trapdoor, climbed up on it, hoisted himself through the ceiling, and reached down. Hsiu Hsiu kicked and scratched, but I heaved her up to him. Then I closed the door through which Lillian Shan had come, and faced her.

"How did you get here?" I demanded.

"I went home after I left you, knowing what Yin Hung would say, because he had told me in the employment office, and when I got home— When I got home I decided to come here where I belong."

"Nonsense!" I corrected her. "When you got home you found a message there from Chang Li Ching, asking you—ordering you to come here."

She looked at me, saying nothing.

"What did Chang want?"

"He thought perhaps he could help me," she said, "and so I stayed here."

More nonsense.

"Chang told you Garthorne was in danger—had split with The Whistler."

"The Whistler?"

"You made a bargain with Chang," I accused her, paying no attention to her question. The chances were she didn't know The Whistler by that name.

She shook her head, jiggling the ornaments on her headdress.

"There was no bargain," she said, holding my gaze too steadily.

I didn't believe her. I said so.

"You gave Chang your house—or the use of it—in exchange for his promise that"—the boob were the first words I thought of, but I changed them—"Garthorne would be saved from The Whistler, and that you would be saved from the law."

She drew herself up.

"I did," she said calmly.

I caught myself weakening. This woman who looked like the queen of something wasn't easy to handle the way I wanted to handle her. I made myself remember that I knew her when she was homely as hell in mannish clothes.

"You ought to be spanked!" I growled at her. "Haven't you had enough trouble without mixing yourself now with a flock of highbinders? Did you see The Whistler?"

"There was a man up there," she said, "I don't know his name."

I hunted through my pocket and found the picture of him taken when he was sent to San Quentin.

"That is he," she told me when I showed it to her.

"A fine partner you picked," I raged. "What do you think his word on anything is worth?"

"I did not take his word for anything. I took Chang Li Ching's word."

"That's just as bad. They're mates. What was your bargain?"

She balked again, straight, stiff-necked and level-eyed. Because she was getting away from me with this Manchu princess stuff I got peevish.

"Don't be a chump all your life!" I pleaded. "You think you made a deal. They took you in! What do you think they're using your house for?"

She tried to look me down. I tried another angle of attack.

"Here, you don't mind who you make bargains with. Make one with me. I'm still one prison sentence ahead of The Whistler, so if his word is any good at all, mine ought to be highly valuable. You tell me what the deal was. If it's half-way decent. I'll promise you to crawl out of here and forget it. If you don't tell me, I'm going to empty a gun out of the first window I can find. And you'd be surprised how many cops a shot will draw in this part of town, and how fast it'll draw them."

The threat took some of the color out of her face.

"If I tell, you will promise to do nothing?"

"You missed part of it," I reminded her. "If I think the deal is half-way on the level I'll keep quiet."

She bit her lips and let her fingers twist together, and then it came.

"Chang Li Ching is one of the leaders of the anti-Japanese movement in China. Since the death of Sun Wen—or Sun Yat-Sen, as he is called in the south of China and here—the Japanese have increased their hold on the Chinese government until it is greater than it ever was. It is Sun Wen's work that Chang Li Ching and his friends are carrying on.

"With their own government against them, their immediate necessity is to arm enough patriots to resist Japanese aggression when the time comes. That is what my house is used for. Rifles and ammunition are loaded into boats there and sent out to ships lying far offshore. This man you call The Whistler is the owner of the ships that carry the arms to China."

"And the death of the servants?" I asked.

"Wan Lan was a spy for the Chinese government—for the Japanese. Wang Ma's death was an accident, I think, though she, too, was suspected of being a spy. To a patriot, the death of traitors is a necessary thing, you can understand that? Your people are like that too when your country is in danger."

"Garthorne told me a rum-running story," I said. "How about it?"

"He believed it," she said, smiling softly at the trapdoor

through which he had gone. "They told him that, because they did not know him well enough to trust him. That is why they would not let him help in the loading."

One of her hands came out to rest on my arm.

"You will go away and keep silent?" she pleaded. "These things are against the law of your country, but would you not break another country's laws to save your own country's life? Have not four hundred million people the right to fight an alien race that would exploit them? Since the day of Taou-kwang my country has been the plaything of more aggressive nations. Is any price too great for patriotic Chinese to pay to end that period of dishonor? You will not put yourself in the way of my people's liberty?"

"I hope they win," I said, "but you've been tricked. The only guns that have gone through your house have gone through in pockets! It would take a year to get a shipload through there. Maybe Chang is running guns to China. It's likely. But they don't go through your place.

"The night I was there coolies went through—coming in, not going out. They came from the beach, and they left in machines. Maybe The Whistler is running the guns over for Chang and bringing coolies back. He can get anything from a thousand dollars up for each one he lands. That's about the how of it. He runs the guns over for Chang, and brings his own stuff—coolies and no doubt some opium—back, getting his big profit on the return trip. There wouldn't be enough money in the guns to interest him.

"The guns would be loaded at a pier, all regular, masquerading as something else. Your house is used for the return. Chang may or may not be tied up with the coolie and opium game, but it's a cinch he'll let The Whistler do whatever he likes if only The Whistler will run his guns across. So, you see, you have been gypped!"

"But—"

"But nothing! You're helping Chang by taking part in the coolie traffic. And, my guess is, your servants were killed, not because they were spies, but because they wouldn't sell you out."

She was white-faced and unsteady on her feet. I didn't let her recover.

"Do you think Chang trusts The Whistler? Did they seem friendly?"

I knew he couldn't trust him, but I wanted something specific.

"No-o-o," she said slowly. "There was some talk about a missing boat."

That was good.

"They still together?"

"Yes."

"How do I get there?"

"Down these steps, across the cellar—straight across—and up two flights of steps on the other side. They were in a room to the right of the second-floor landing."

Thank God I had a direct set of instructions for once!

I jumped up on the table and rapped on the ceiling.

"Come on down, Garthorne, and bring your chaperon."

"Don't either of you budge out of here until I'm back," I told the boob and Lillian Shan when we were all together again. "I'm going to take Hsiu Hsiu with me. Come on, sister, I want you to talk to any bad men I meet. We go to see Chang Li Ching, you understand?" I made faces. "One yell out of you, and—" I put my fingers around her collar and pressed them lightly.

She giggled, which spoiled the effect a little.

"To Chang," I ordered, and, holding her by one shoulder, urged her toward the door.

We went down into the dark cellar, across it, found the other stairs, and started to climb them. Our progress was slow. The girl's bound feet weren't made for fast walking.

A dim light burned on the first floor, where we had to turn to go up to the second floor. We had just made the turn when footsteps sounded behind us.

I lifted the girl up two steps, out of the light, and crouched beside her, holding her still. Four Chinese in wrinkled street clothes came down the first-floor hall, passed our stairs without a glance, and started on.

Hsiu Hsiu opened her red flower of a mouth and let out a squeal that could have been heard over in Oakland.

I cursed, turned her loose, and started up the steps. The four Chinese came after me. On the landing ahead one of Chang's big wrestlers appeared—a foot of thin steel in his paw. I looked back.

Hsiu Hsiu sat on the bottom step, her head over her shoulder, experimenting with different sorts of yells and screams, enjoyment all over her laughing doll's face. One of the climbing yellow men was loosening an automatic.

My legs pushed me on up toward the man-eater at the head of the steps.

When he crouched close above me I let him have it.

My bullet cut the gullet out of him.

I patted his face with my gun as he tumbled down past me.

A hand caught one of my ankles.

Clinging to the railing, I drove my other foot back. Something stopped my foot. Nothing stopped me.

A bullet flaked some of the ceiling down as I made the head of the stairs and jumped for the door to the right.

Pulling it open, I plunged in.

The other of the big man-eaters caught me—caught my plunging hundred and eighty-some pounds as a boy would catch a rubber ball.

Across the room, Chang Li Ching ran plump fingers through his thin whiskers and smiled at me. Beside him, a man I knew for The Whistler started up from his chair, his beefy face twitching.

"The Prince of Hunters is welcome," Chang said, and added something in Chinese to the man-eater who held me.

The man-eater set me down on my feet, and turned to shut the door on my pursuers.

The Whistler sat down again, his red-veined eyes shifty on me, his bloated face empty of enjoyment.

I tucked my gun inside my clothes before I started across the room toward Chang. And crossing the room, I noticed something.

Behind The Whistler's chair the velvet hangings bulged just the least bit, not enough to have been noticed by anyone who hadn't seen them bulge before. So Chang didn't trust his confederate at all!

"I have something I want you to see," I told the old Chinese when I was standing in front of him, or, rather, in front of the table that was in front of him.

"That eye is privileged indeed which may gaze on anything brought by the Father of Avengers."

"I have heard," I said, as I put my hand in my pocket, "that all that starts for China doesn't get there."

The Whistler jumped up from his chair again, his mouth a snarl, his face a dirty pink. Chang Li Ching looked at him, and he sat down again.

I brought out the photograph of The Whistler standing in a group of Japs, the medal of the Order of the Rising Sun on his chest. Hoping Chang had not heard of the swindle and would not know the medal for a counterfeit, I dropped the photograph on the table.

The Whistler craned his neck, but could not see the picture.

Chang Li Ching looked at it for a long moment over his clasped hands, his old eyes shrewd and kindly, his face gentle. No muscle in his face moved. Nothing changed in his eyes.

The nails of his right hand slowly cut a red gash across the back of the clasped left hand.

"It is true," he said softly, "that one acquires wisdom in the company of the wise."

He unclasped his hands, picked up the photograph, and held it out to the beefy man. The Whistler seized it. His face drained grey, his eyes bulged out.

"Why, that's—" he began, and stopped, let the photograph drop to his lap, and slumped down in an attitude of defeat.

That puzzled me. I had expected to argue with him, to convince Chang that the medal was not the fake it was.

"You may have what you wish in payment for this," Chang Li Ching was saying to me.

"I want Lillian Shan and Garthorne cleared, and I want your fat friend here, and I want anybody else who was in on the killings."

Chang's eyes closed for a moment—the first sign of weariness I had seen on his round face.

"You may have them," he said.

"The bargain you made with Miss Shan is all off, of course," I pointed out. "I may need a little evidence to make sure I can hang this baby," nodding at The Whistler.

Chang smiled dreamily.

"That, I am regretful, is not possible."

"Why—?" I began, and stopped.

There was no bulge in the velvet curtain behind The Whistler now, I saw. One of the chair legs glistened in the light. A red pool spread on the floor under him. I didn't have to see his back to know he was beyond hanging.

"That's different," I said, kicking a chair over to the table. "Now we'll talk business."

I sat down and we went into conference.

11

TWO DAYS LATER everything was cleared up to the satisfaction of police, press and public. The Whistler had been found in a dark street, hours dead from a cut in his back, killed in a bootlegging war, I heard. Hoo Lun was found. The gold-toothed Chinese who had opened the door for Lillian Shan was found. Five others were found. These seven, with Yin Hung, the chauffeur, eventually drew a life sentence apiece. They were The Whistler's men, and Chang sacrificed them without batting an eye. They had as little proof of Chang's complicity as I had, so they couldn't hit back, even if they knew that Chang had given me most of my evidence against them.

Nobody but the girl, Chang and I knew anything about Garthorne's part, so he was out, with liberty to spend most of his time at the girl's house.

I had no proof that I could tie on Chang, couldn't get any. Regardless of his patriotism, I'd have given my right eye to put the old boy away. That would have been something to write home about. But there hadn't been a chance of nailing him, so I had had to be content with making a bargain whereby he turned everything over to me except himself and his friends.

I don't know what happened to Hsiu Hsiu, the squealing slave-girl. She deserved to come through all right. I might have gone back to Chang's to ask about her, but I stayed away. Chang had learned that the medal in the photo was a trick one. I had a note from him:

Greetings and Great Love to the Unveiler of Secrets:

One whose patriotic fervor and inherent stupidity combined to blind him, so that he broke a valuable tool, trusts that the fortunes of worldly traffic will not again ever place his feeble wits in opposition to the irresistible will and dazzling intellect of the Emperor of Untanglers.

You can take that any way you like. But I know the man who wrote it, and I don't mind admitting that I've stopped eating in Chinese restaurants, and that if I never have to visit Chinatown again it'll be soon enough.

The Gutting of Couffignal

.

1

WEDGE-SHAPED COUFFIGNAL IS not a large island, and not far from the mainland, to which it is linked by a wooden bridge. Its western shore is a high, straight cliff that jumps abruptly up out of San Pablo Bay. From the top of this cliff the island slopes eastward, down to a smooth pebble beach that runs into the water again, where there are piers and a clubhouse and moored pleasure boats.

Couffignal's main street, paralleling the beach, has the usual bank, hotel, moving-picture theater, and stores. But it differs from most main streets of its size in that it is more carefully arranged and preserved. There are trees and hedges and strips of lawn on it, and no glaring signs. The buildings seem to belong beside one another, as if they had been designed by the same architect, and in the stores you will find goods of a quality to match the best city stores.

The intersecting streets—running between rows of neat cottages near the foot of the slope—become winding hedged roads as they climb toward the cliff. The higher these roads get, the farther apart and larger are the houses they lead to. The occupants of these higher houses are the owners and rulers of the island. Most of them are well-fed old gentlemen who, the profits they took from the world with both hands in their younger days now stowed away at safe percentages, have bought into the island colony so they may spend what is left of their lives nursing their livers and improving their golf among their kind. They admit to the island only as many storekeepers, working-people, and similar riffraff as are needed to keep them comfortably served.

That is Couffignal.

It was some time after midnight. I was sitting in a second-story room in Couffignal's largest house, surrounded by wedding presents whose value would add up to something between fifty and a hundred thousand dollars.

Of all the work that comes to a private detective (except divorce work, which the Continental Detective Agency doesn't handle) I like weddings as little as any. Usually I manage to avoid them, but this time I hadn't been able to. Dick Foley, who had been slated for the job, had been handed a black eye by an unfriendly pickpocket the day before. That let Dick out and me in. I had come up to Couffignal—a two-hour ride from San Francisco by ferry and auto stage—that morning, and would return the next.

This had been neither better nor worse than the usual wedding detail. The ceremony had been performed in a little stone church down the hill. Then the house had begun to fill with reception guests. They had kept it filled to overflowing until some time after the bride and groom had sneaked off to their eastern train.

The world had been well represented. There had been an admiral and an earl or two from England; an ex-president of a South American country; a Danish baron; a tall young Russian princess surrounded by lesser titles, including a fat, bald, jovial and black-bearded Russian general who had talked to me for a solid hour about prize fights, in which he had a lot of interest, but not so much knowledge as was possible; an ambassador from one of the Central European countries; a justice of the

The GUTTING OF COUFFIGNAL

By Dashiell Hammett

Supreme Court; and a mob of people whose prominence and near-prominence didn't carry labels.

In theory, a detective guarding wedding presents is supposed to make himself indistinguishable from the other guests. In practice, it never works out that way. He has to spend most of his time within sight of the booty, so he's easily spotted. Besides that, eight or ten people I recognized among the guests were clients or former clients of the Agency, and so knew me. However, being known doesn't make so much difference as you might think, and everything had gone off smoothly.

A couple of the groom's friends, warmed by wine and the necessity of maintaining their reputations as cut-ups, had tried to smuggle some of the gifts out of the room where they were displayed and hide them in the piano. But I had been expecting that familiar trick, and blocked it before it had gone far enough to embarrass anybody.

Shortly after dark a wind smelling of rain began to pile storm clouds up over the bay. Those guests who lived at a distance, especially those who had water to cross, hurried off for their homes. Those who lived on the island stayed until the first raindrops began to patter down. Then they left.

The Hendrixson house quieted down. Musicians and extra servants left. The weary house servants began to disappear in the direction of their bedrooms. I found some sandwiches, a couple of books and a comfortable armchair, and took them up to the room where the presents were now hidden under grey-white sheeting.

Keith Hendrixson, the bride's grandfather—she was an orphan—put his head in at the door.

"Have you everything you need for your comfort?" he asked.

"Yes, thanks."

He said good night and went off to bed—a tall old man, slim as a boy.

The wind and the rain were hard at it when I went downstairs to give the lower windows and doors the up-and-down. Everything on the first floor was tight and secure, everything in the cellar. I went upstairs again.

Pulling my chair over by a floor lamp, I put sandwiches, books, ash-tray, gun and flashlight on a small table beside it. Then I switched off the other lights, set fire to a Fatima, sat down, wriggled my spine comfortably into the chair's padding, picked up one of the books, and prepared to make a night of it.

The book was called The Lord of the Sea, and had to do with a strong, tough and violent fellow named Hogarth, whose modest plan was to hold the world in one hand. There were plots and counterplots, kidnappings, murders, prison-breakings, forgeries and burglaries, diamonds large as hats and floating forts larger than Couffignal. It sounds dizzy here, but in the book it was as real as a dime.

Hogarth was still going strong when the lights went out.

2

IN THE DARK, I got rid of the glowing end of my cigarette by grinding it in one of the sandwiches. Putting the book
down, I picked up gun and flashlight, and moved away from
the chair.

Listening for noises was no good. The storm was making
hundreds of them. What I needed to know was why the lights
had gone off. All the other lights in the house had been turned
off some time ago. So the darkness of the hall told me nothing.

I waited. My job was to watch the presents. Nobody had
touched them yet. There was nothing to get excited about.

Minutes went by, perhaps ten of them.

The floor swayed under my feet. The windows rattled with a
violence beyond the strength of the storm. The dull boom of
a heavy explosion blotted out the sounds of wind and falling
water. The blast was not close at hand, but not far enough away
to be off the island.

Crossing to the window, peering through the wet glass, I
could see nothing. I should have seen a few misty lights far
down the hill. Not being able to see them settled one point.
The lights had gone out all over Couffignal, not only in the
Hendrixson house.

That was better. The storm could have put the lighting system
out of whack, could have been responsible for the explosion—
maybe.

Staring through the black window, I had an impression of
great excitement down the hill, of movement in the night. But

all was too far away for me to have seen or heard even had there been lights, and all too vague to say what was moving. The impression was strong but worthless. It didn't lead anywhere. I told myself I was getting feeble-minded, and turned away from the window.

Another blast spun me back to it. This explosion sounded nearer than the first, maybe because it was stronger. Peering through the glass again, I still saw nothing. And still had the impression of things that were big moving down there.

Bare feet pattered in the hall. A voice was anxiously calling my name. Turning from the window again, I pocketed my gun and snapped on the flashlight. Keith Hendrixson, in pajamas and bathrobe, looking thinner and older than anybody could be, came into the room.

"Is it—"

"I don't think it's an earthquake," I said, since that is the first calamity your Californian thinks of. "The lights went off a little while ago. There have been a couple of explosions down the hill since the—"

I stopped. Three shots, close together, had sounded. Rifle-shots, but of the sort that only the heaviest of rifles could make. Then, sharp and small in the storm, came the report of a far-away pistol.

"What is it?" Hendrixson demanded.

"Shooting."

More feet were pattering in the halls, some bare, some shod. Excited voices whispered questions and exclamations. The butler, a solemn, solid block of a man, partly dressed, and carrying a lighted five-pronged candlestick, came in.

"Very good, Brophy," Hendrixson said as the butler put the

candlestick on the table beside my sandwiches. "Will you try to learn what is the matter?"

"I have tried, sir. The telephone seems to be out of order, sir. Shall I send Oliver down to the village?"

"No-o. I don't suppose it's that serious. Do you think it is anything serious?" he asked me.

I said I didn't think so, but I was paying more attention to the outside than to him. I had heard a thin screaming that could have come from a distant woman, and a volley of small-arms shots. The racket of the storm muffled these shots, but when the heavier firing we had heard before broke out again, it was clear enough.

To have opened the window would have been to let in gallons of water without helping us to hear much clearer. I stood with an ear tilted to the pane, trying to arrive at some idea of what was happening outside.

Another sound took my attention from the window—the ringing of the doorbell. It rang loudly and persistently.

Hendrixson looked at me. I nodded.

"See who it is, Brophy," he said.

The butler went solemnly away, and came back even more solemnly.

"Princess Zhukovski," he announced.

She came running into the room—the tall Russian girl I had seen at the reception. Her eyes were wide and dark with excitement. Her face was very white and wet. Water ran in streams down her blue waterproof cape, the hood of which covered her dark hair.

"Oh, Mr. Hendrixson!" She had caught one of his hands in both of hers. Her voice, with nothing foreign in its accents, was the voice of one who is excited over a delightful surprise. "The bank is being robbed, and the—what do you call him?—marshal of police has been killed!"

"What's that?" the old man exclaimed, jumping awkwardly, because water from her cape had dripped down on one of his bare feet. "Weegan killed? And the bank robbed?"

"Yes! Isn't it terrible?" She said it as if she were saying wonderful. "When the first explosion woke us, the general sent Ignati down to find out what was the matter, and he got down there just in time to see the bank blown up. Listen!"

We listened, and heard a wild outbreak of mixed gun-fire.

"That will be the general arriving!" she said. "He'll enjoy himself most wonderfully. As soon as Ignati returned with the news, the general armed every male in the household from Aleksandr Sergyeevich to Ivan the cook, and led them out happier than he's been since he took his division to East Prussia in 1914."

"And the duchess?" Hendrixson asked.

"He left her at home with me, of course, and I furtively crept out and away from her while she was trying for the first time in her life to put water in a samovar. This is not the night for one to stay at home!"

"H-m-m," Hendrixson said, his mind obviously not on her words. "And the bank!"

He looked at me. I said nothing. The racket of another volley came to us.

"Could you do anything down there?" he asked.

"Maybe, but—" I nodded at the presents under their covers.

"Oh, those!" the old man said. "I'm as much interested in the bank as in them; and, besides, we will be here."

"All right!" I was willing enough to carry my curiosity down the hill. "I'll go down. You'd better have the butler stay in here, and plant the chauffeur inside the front door. Better give them guns if you have any. Is there a raincoat I can borrow? I brought only a light overcoat with me."

Brophy found a yellow slicker that fit me. I put it on, stowed gun and flashlight conveniently under it, and found my hat while Brophy was getting and loading an automatic pistol for himself and a rifle for Oliver, the mulatto chauffeur.

Hendrixson and the princess followed me downstairs. At the door I found she wasn't exactly following me—she was going with me.

"But, Sonya!" the old man protested.

"I'm not going to be foolish, though I'd like to," she promised him. "But I'm going back to my Irinia Androvana, who will perhaps have the samovar watered by now."

"That's a sensible girl!" Hendrixson said, and let us out into the rain and the wind.

It wasn't weather to talk in. In silence we turned downhill between two rows of hedging, with the storm driving at our backs. At the first break in the hedge I stopped, nodding toward the black blot a house made.

"That is your—"

Her laugh cut me short. She caught my arm and began to urge me down the road again.

"I only told Mr. Hendrixson that so he would not worry," she explained. "You do not think I am not going down to see the sights."

3

SHE WAS TALL. I am short and thick. I had to look up to
see her face—to see as much of it as the rain-grey night would
let me see.

"You'll be soaked to the hide, running around in this rain," I
objected.

"What of that? I am dressed for it."

She raised a foot to show me a heavy waterproof boot and a
woolen-stockinged leg.

"There's no telling what we'll run into down there, and I've
got work to do," I insisted. "I can't be looking out for you."

"I can look out for myself."

She pushed her cape aside to show me a square automatic
pistol in one hand.

"You'll be in my way."

"I will not," she retorted. "You'll probably find I can help you.
I'm as strong as you, and quicker, and I can shoot."

The reports of scattered shooting had punctuated our argument,
but now the sound of heavier firing silenced the dozen objections
to her company that I could still think of. After all, I could slip
away from her in the dark if she became too much of a nuisance.

"Have it your own way," I growled, "but don't expect
anything from me."

"You're so kind," she murmured as we got under way again,
hurrying now, with the wind at our backs speeding us along.

Occasionally dark figures moved on the road ahead of us,
but too far away to be recognizable. Presently a man passed us,

running uphill—a tall man whose nightshirt hung out of his trousers, down below his coat, identifying him as a resident.

"They've finished the bank and are at Medcraft's!" he yelled as he went by.

"Medcraft is the jeweler," the girl informed me.

The sloping under our feet grew less sharp. The houses—dark but with faces vaguely visible here and there at windows—came closer together. Below, the flash of a gun could be seen now and then—orange streaks in the rain.

Our road put us into the lower end of the main street just as a staccato rat-ta-tat broke out.

I pushed the girl into the nearest doorway, and jumped in after her.

Bullets ripped through walls with the sound of hail tapping on leaves.

That was the thing I had taken for an exceptionally heavy rifle—a machine gun.

The girl had fallen back in a corner, all tangled up with something. I helped her up. The something was a boy of seventeen or so, with one leg and a crutch.

"It's the boy who delivers papers," Princess Zhukovski said, "and you've hurt him with your clumsiness."

The boy shook his head, grinning as he got up.

"No'm, I ain't hurt none, but you kind of scared me, jumping on me like that."

She had to stop and explain that she hadn't jumped on him, that she had been pushed into him by me, and that she was sorry and so was I.

"What's happening?" I asked the newsboy when I could get a word in.

"Everything," he boasted, as if some of the credit were his. "There must be a hundred of them, and they've blowed the bank wide open, and now some of 'em is in Medcraft's, and I guess they'll blow that up, too. And they killed Tom Weegan. They got a machine gun on a car in the middle of the street. That's it shooting now."

"Where's everybody—all the merry villagers?"

"Most of 'em are up behind the Hall. They can't do nothing, though, because the machine gun won't let 'em get near enough to see what they're shooting at, and that smart Bill Vincent told me to clear out, 'cause I've only got one leg, as if I couldn't shoot as good as the next one, if I only had something to shoot with!"

"That wasn't right of them," I sympathized. "But you can do something for me. You can stick here and keep your eye on this end of the street, so I'll know if they leave in this direction."

"You're not just saying that so I'll stay here out of the way, are you?"

"No," I lied. "I need somebody to watch. I was going to leave the princess here, but you'll do better."

"Yes," she backed me up, catching the idea. "This gentleman is a detective, and if you do what he asks you'll be helping more than if you were up with the others."

The machine gun was still firing, but not in our direction now.

"I'm going across the street," I told the girl. "If you—"

"Aren't you going to join the others?"

"No. If I can get around behind the bandits while they're busy with the others, maybe I can turn a trick."

"Watch sharp now!" I ordered the boy, and the princess and I made a dash for the opposite sidewalk.

We reached it without drawing lead, sidled along a building for a few yards, and turned into an alley. From the alley's other end came the smell and wash and the dull blackness of the bay.

While we moved down this alley I composed a scheme by which I hoped to get rid of my companion, sending her off on a safe wild-goose chase. But I didn't get a chance to try it out.

The big figure of a man loomed ahead of us.

Stepping in front of the girl, I went on toward him. Under my slicker I held my gun on the middle of him.

He stood still. He was larger than he had looked at first. A big, slope-shouldered, barrel-bodied husky. His hands were empty. I spotted the flashlight on his face for a split second. A flat-cheeked, thick-featured face, with high cheek-bones and a lot of ruggedness in it.

"Ignati!" the girl exclaimed over my shoulder.

He began to talk what I suppose was Russian to the girl. She laughed and replied. He shook his big head stubbornly, insisting on something. She stamped her foot and spoke sharply. He shook his head again and addressed me.

"General Pleshskev, he tell me bring Princess Sonya to home."

His English was almost as hard to understand as his Russian. His tone puzzled me. It was as if he was explaining some absolutely necessary thing that he didn't want to be blamed for, but that nevertheless he was going to do.

While the girl was speaking to him again, I guessed the answer. This big Ignati had been sent out by the general to bring the girl home, and he was going to obey his orders if he had to carry her. He was trying to avoid trouble with me by explaining the situation.

"Take her," I said, stepping aside.

The girl scowled at me, laughed.

"Very well, Ignati," she said in English, "I shall go home," and she turned on her heel and went back up the alley, the big man close behind her.

Glad to be alone, I wasted no time in moving in the opposite direction until the pebbles of the beach were under my feet. The pebbles ground harshly under my heels. I moved back to more silent ground and began to work my way as swiftly as I could up the shore toward the center of action.

The machine gun barked on. Smaller guns snapped. Three concussions, close together—bombs, hand grenades, my ears and my memory told me.

The stormy sky glared pink over a roof ahead of me and to the left. The boom of the blast beat my ear-drums. Fragments I couldn't see fell around me. That, I thought, would be the jeweler's safe blowing apart.

I crept on up the shore line. The machine gun went silent. Lighter guns snapped, snapped, snapped. Another grenade went off. A man's voice shrieked pure terror.

Risking the crunch of pebbles, I turned down to the water's edge again. I had seen no dark shape on the water that could have been a boat. There had been boats moored along this beach in the afternoon. With my feet in the water of the bay I still saw no boat. The storm could have scattered them, but I didn't think it had. The island's western height shielded this shore. The wind was strong here, but not violent.

My feet sometimes on the edge of the pebbles, sometimes in the water, I went on up the shore line. Now I saw a boat. A gently bobbing black shape ahead. No light was on it. Nothing I could see moved on it. It was the only boat on that shore. That made it important.

Foot by foot, I approached.

A shadow moved between me and the dark rear of a building. I froze. The shadow, man-size, moved again, in the direction from which I was coming.

Waiting, I didn't know how nearly invisible, or how plain, I might be against my background. I couldn't risk giving myself away by trying to improve my position.

Twenty feet from me the shadow suddenly stopped.

I was seen. My gun was on the shadow.

"Come on," I called softly. "Keep coming. Let's see who you are."

The shadow hesitated, left the shelter of the building, drew nearer. I couldn't risk the flashlight. I made out dimly a handsome face, boyishly reckless, one cheek dark-stained.

"Oh, how d'you do?" the face's owner said in a musical baritone voice. "You were at the reception this afternoon."

"Yes."

"Have you seen Princess Zhukovski? You know her?"

"She went home with Ignati ten minutes or so ago."

"Excellent!" He wiped his stained cheek with a stained handkerchief, and turned to look at the boat. "That's Hendrixson's boat," he whispered. "They've got it and they've cast the others off."

"That would mean they are going to leave by water."

"Yes," he agreed, "unless— Shall we have a try at it?"

"You mean jump it?"

"Why not?" he asked. "There can't be very many aboard. God knows there are enough of them ashore. You're armed. I've a pistol."

"We'll size it up first," I decided, "so we'll know what we're jumping."

"That is wisdom," he said, and led the way back to the shelter of the buildings.

Hugging the rear walls of the buildings, we stole toward the boat.

The boat grew clearer in the night. A craft perhaps forty-five feet long, its stern to the shore, rising and falling beside a small pier. Across the stern something protruded. Something I couldn't quite make out. Leather soles scuffled now and then on the wooden deck. Presently a dark head and shoulders showed over the puzzling thing in the stern.

The Russian lad's eyes were better than mine.

"Masked," he breathed in my ear. "Something like a stocking over his head and face."

The masked man was motionless where he stood. We were motionless where we stood.

"Could you hit him from here?" the lad asked.

"Maybe, but night and rain aren't a good combination for sharpshooting. Our best bet is to sneak as close as we can, and start shooting when he spots us."

"That is wisdom," he agreed.

Discovery came with our first step forward. The man in the boat grunted. The lad at my side jumped forward. I recognized the thing in the boat's stern just in time to throw out a leg and trip the young Russian. He tumbled down, all sprawled out on the pebbles. I dropped behind him.

The machine gun in the boat's stern poured metal over our heads.

4

"NO GOOD RUSHING that!" I said. "Roll out of it!"

I set the example by revolving toward the back of the building we had just left.

The man at the gun sprinkled the beach, but sprinkled it at random, his eyes no doubt spoiled for night-seeing by the flash of his gun.

Around the corner of the building, we sat up.

"You saved my life by tripping me," the lad said coolly.

"Yes. I wonder if they've moved the machine gun from the street, or if—"

The answer to that came immediately. The machine gun in the street mingled its vicious voice with the drumming of the one in the boat.

"A pair of them!" I complained. "Know anything about the layout?"

"I don't think there are more than ten or twelve of them," he said, "although it is not easy to count in the dark. The few I have seen are completely masked—like the man in the boat. They seem to have disconnected the telephone and light lines first and then to have destroyed the bridge. We attacked them while they were looting the bank, but in front they had a machine gun mounted in an automobile, and we were not equipped to combat on equal terms."

"Where are the islanders now?"

"Scattered, and most of them in hiding, I fancy, unless General Pleshskev has succeeded in rallying them again."

I frowned and beat my brains together. You can't fight machine guns and hand grenades with peaceful villagers and retired capitalists. No matter how well led and armed they are, you can't do anything with them. For that matter, how could anybody do much against a game of that toughness?

"Suppose you stick here and keep your eye on the boat," I suggested. "I'll scout around and see what's doing further up, and if I can get a few good men together, I'll try to jump the boat again, probably from the other side. But we can't count on that. The get-away will be by boat. We can count on that, and try to block it. If you lie down you can watch the boat around the corner of the building without making much of a target of yourself. I wouldn't do anything to attract attention until the break for the boat comes. Then you can do all the shooting you want."

"Excellent!" he said. "You'll probably find most of the islanders up behind the church. You can get to it by going straight up the hill until you come to an iron fence, and then follow that to the right."

"Right."

I moved off in the direction he had indicated.

At the main street I stopped to look around before venturing across. Everything was quiet there. The only man I could see was spread out face-down on the sidewalk near me.

On hands and knees I crawled to his side. He was dead. I didn't stop to examine him further, but sprang up and streaked for the other side of the street.

Nothing tried to stop me. In a doorway, flat against a wall, I peeped out. The wind had stopped. The rain was no longer a driving deluge, but a steady down-pouring of small drops.

Couffignal's main street, to my senses, was a deserted street.

I wondered if the retreat to the boat had already started. On the sidewalk, walking swiftly toward the bank, I heard the answer to that guess.

High up on the slope, almost up to the edge of the cliff, by the sound, a machine gun began to hurl out its stream of bullets.

Mixed with the racket of the machine gun were the sounds of smaller arms, and a grenade or two.

At the first crossing, I left the main street and began to run up the hill. Men were running toward me. Two of them passed, paying no attention to my shouted, "What's up now?"

The third man stopped because I grabbed him—a fat man whose breath bubbled, and whose face was fish-belly white.

"They've moved the car with the machine gun on it up behind us," he gasped when I had shouted my question into his ear again.

"What are you doing without a gun?" I asked.

"I—I dropped it."

"Where's General Pleshskev?"

"Back there somewhere. He's trying to capture the car, but he'll never do it. It's suicide! Why don't help come?"

Other men had passed us, running downhill, as we talked. I let the white-faced man go, and stopped four men who weren't running so fast as the others.

"What's happening now?" I questioned them.

"They's going through the houses up the hill," a sharp-featured man with a small mustache and a rifle said.

"Has anybody got word off the island yet?" I asked.

"Can't," another informed me. "They blew up the bridge first thing."

"Can't anybody swim?"

"Not in that wind. Young Catlan tried it and was lucky to get out again with a couple of broken ribs."

"The wind's gone down," I pointed out.

The sharp-featured man gave his rifle to one of the others and took off his coat.

"I'll try it," he promised.

"Good! Wake up the whole country, and get word through to the San Francisco police boat and to the Mare Island Navy Yard. They'll lend a hand if you tell 'em the bandits have machine guns. Tell 'em the bandits have an armed boat waiting to leave in. It's Hendrixson's."

The volunteer swimmer left.

"A boat?" two of the men asked together.

"Yes. With a machine gun on it. If we're going to do anything, it'll have to be now, while we're between them and their get-away. Get every man and every gun you can find down there. Tackle the boat from the roofs if you can. When the bandits' car comes down there, pour it into it. You'll do better from the buildings than from the street."

The three men went on downhill. I went uphill, toward the crackling of firearms ahead. The machine gun was working irregularly. It would pour out its rat-tat-tat for a second or so, and then stop for a couple of seconds. The answering fire was thin, ragged.

I met more men, learned from them that the general, with less than a dozen men, was still fighting the car. I repeated the advice I had given the other men. My informants went down to join them. I went on up.

A hundred yards farther along, what was left of the general's dozen broke out of the night, around and past me, flying downhill, with bullets hailing after them.

The road was no place for mortal man. I stumbled over two bodies, scratched myself in a dozen places getting over a hedge. On soft, wet sod I continued my uphill journey.

The machine gun on the hill stopped its clattering. The one in the boat was still at work.

The one ahead opened again, firing too high for anything near at hand to be its target. It was helping its fellow below, spraying the main street.

Before I could get closer it had stopped. I heard the car's motor racing. The car moved toward me.

Rolling into the hedge, I lay there, straining my eyes through the spaces between the stems. I had six bullets in a gun that hadn't yet been fired on this night that had seen tons of powder burned.

When I saw wheels on the lighter face of the road, I emptied my gun, holding it low.

The car went on.

I sprang out of my hiding-place.

The car was suddenly gone from the empty road.

There was a grinding sound. A crash. The noise of metal folding on itself. The tinkle of glass.

I raced toward those sounds.

5

OUT OF A black pile where an engine sputtered, a black figure leaped—to dash off across the soggy lawn. I cut after it, hoping that the others in the wreck were down for keeps.

I was less than fifteen feet behind the fleeing man when he cleared a hedge. I'm no sprinter, but neither was he. The wet grass made slippery going.

He stumbled while I was vaulting the hedge. When we straightened out again I was not more than ten feet behind him.

Once I clicked my gun at him, forgetting I had emptied it. Six cartridges were wrapped in a piece of paper in my vest pocket, but this was no time for loading.

I was tempted to chuck the empty gun at his head. But that was too chancy.

A building loomed ahead. My fugitive bore off to the right, to clear the corner.

To the left a heavy shotgun went off.

The running man disappeared around the house-corner.

"Sweet God!" General Pleshskev's mellow voice complained. "That with a shotgun I should miss all of a man at the distance!"

"Go round the other way!" I yelled, plunging around the corner after my quarry.

His feet thudded ahead. I could not see him. The general puffed around from the other side of the house.

"You have him?"

"No."

In front of us was a stone-faced bank, on top of which ran a path. On either side of us was a high and solid hedge.

"But, my friend," the general protested. "How could he have—?"

A pale triangle showed on the path above a triangle that could have been a bit of shirt showing above the opening of a vest.

"Stay here and talk!" I whispered to the general, and crept forward.

"It must be that he has gone the other way," the general carried out my instructions, rambling on as if I were standing beside him, "because if he had come my way I should have seen him, and if he had raised himself over either of the hedges or the embankment, one of us would surely have seen him against …"

He talked on and on while I gained the shelter of the bank on which the path sat, while I found places for my toes in the rough stone facing.

The man on the road, trying to make himself small with his back in a bush, was looking at the talking general. He saw me when I had my feet on the path.

He jumped, and one hand went up.

I jumped, with both hands out.

A stone, turning under my foot, threw me sidewise, twisting my ankle, but saving my head from the bullet he sent at it.

My outflung left arm caught his legs as I spilled down. He came over on top of me. I kicked him once, caught his gun-arm, and had just decided to bite it when the general puffed up over the edge of the path and prodded the man off me with the muzzle of the shotgun.

When it came my turn to stand up, I found it not so good. My twisted ankle didn't like to support its share of my hundred-and-eighty-some pounds. Putting most of my weight on the other leg, I turned my flashlight on the prisoner.

"Hello, Flippo!" I exclaimed.

"Hello!" he said without joy in the recognition.

He was a roly-poly Italian youth of twenty-three or -four. I had helped send him to San Quentin four years ago for his part in a payroll stick-up. He had been out on parole for several months now.

"The prison board isn't going to like this," I told him.

"You got me wrong," he pleaded. "I ain't been doing a thing. I was up here to see some friends. And when this thing busted loose I had to hide, because I got a record, and if I'm picked up I'll be railroaded for it. And now you got me, and you think I'm in on it!"

"You're a mind reader," I assured him, and asked the general: "Where can we pack this bird away for a while, under lock and key?"

"In my house there is a lumber-room with a strong door and not a window."

"That'll do it. March, Flippo!"

General Pleshskev collared the youth, while I limped along behind them, examining Flippo's gun, which was loaded except for the one shot he had fired at me, and reloading my own.

We had caught our prisoner on the Russian's grounds, so we didn't have far to go.

The general knocked on the door and called out something in his language. Bolts clicked and grated, and the door was swung open by a heavily mustached Russian servant. Behind him the princess and a stalwart older woman stood.

We went in while the general was telling his household about the capture, and took the captive up to the lumber-room. I frisked him for his pocket-knife and matches—he had nothing else that could help him get out—locked him in and braced the door solidly with a length of board. Then we went downstairs again.

"You are injured!" the princess, seeing me limp across the floor, cried.

"Only a twisted ankle," I said. "But it does bother me some. Is there any adhesive tape around?"

"Yes," and she spoke to the mustached servant, who went out of the room and presently returned, carrying rolls of gauze and tape and a basin of steaming water.

"If you'll sit down," the princess said, taking these things from the servant.

But I shook my head and reached for the adhesive tape.

"I want cold water, because I've got to go out in the wet again. If you'll show me the bathroom, I can fix myself up in no time."

We had to argue about that, but I finally got to the bathroom, where I ran cold water on my foot and ankle, and strapped it with adhesive tape, as tight as I could without stopping the circulation altogether. Getting my wet shoe on again was a job, but when I was through I had two firm legs under me, even if one of them did hurt some.

When I rejoined the others I noticed that the sound of firing no longer came up the hill, and that the patter of rain was lighter, and a grey streak of coming daylight showed under a drawn blind.

I was buttoning my slicker when the knocker rang on the front door. Russian words came through, and the young Russian I had met on the beach came in.

"Aleksandr, you're—" the stalwart older woman screamed when she saw the blood on his cheek, and fainted.

He paid no attention to her at all, as if he was used to having her faint.

"They've gone in the boat," he told me while the girl and two men servants gathered up the woman and laid her on an ottoman.

"How many?" I asked.

"I counted ten, and I don't think I missed more than one or two, if any."

"The men I sent down there couldn't stop them?"

He shrugged.

"What would you? It takes a strong stomach to face a machine gun. Your men had been cleared out of the buildings almost before they arrived."

The woman who had fainted had revived by now and was pouring anxious questions in Russian at the lad. The princess was getting into her blue cape. The woman stopped questioning the lad and asked her something.

"It's all over," the princess said. "I am going to view the ruins."

That suggestion appealed to everybody. Five minutes later all of us, including the servants, were on our way downhill. Behind us, around us, in front of us, were other people going downhill, hurrying along in the drizzle that was very gentle now, their faces tired and excited in the bleak morning light.

Halfway down, a woman ran out of a cross-path and began to tell me something. I recognized her as one of Hendrixson's maids.

I caught some of her words.

"Presents gone. ... Mr. Brophy murdered. ... Oliver. ..."

6

"I'LL BE DOWN later," I told the others, and set out after the maid.

She was running back to the Hendrixson house. I couldn't run, couldn't even walk fast. She and Hendrixson and more of his servants were standing on the front porch when I arrived.

"They killed Oliver and Brophy," the old man said.

"How?"

"We were in the back of the house, the rear second story, watching the flashes of the shooting down in the village. Oliver was down here, just inside the front door, and Brophy in the room with the presents. We heard a shot in there, and immediately a man appeared in the doorway of our room, threatening us with two pistols, making us stay there for perhaps ten minutes. Then he shut and locked the door and went away. We broke the door down—and found Brophy and Oliver dead."

"Let's look at them."

The chauffeur was just inside the front door. He lay on his back, with his brown throat cut straight across the front, almost back to the vertebræ. His rifle was under him. I pulled it out and examined it. It had not been fired.

Upstairs, the butler Brophy was huddled against a leg of one of the tables on which the presents had been spread. His gun was gone. I turned him over, straightened him out, and found a bullet-hole in his chest. Around the hole his coat was charred in a large area.

Most of the presents were still here. But the most valuable

pieces were gone. The others were in disorder, lying around any which way, their covers pulled off.

"What did the one you saw look like?" I asked.

"I didn't see him very well," Hendrixson said. "There was no light in our room. He was simply a dark figure against the candle burning in the hall. A large man in a black rubber raincoat, with some sort of black mask that covered his whole head and face, with small eyeholes."

"No hat?"

"No, just the mask over his entire face and head."

As we went downstairs again I gave Hendrixson a brief account of what I had seen and heard and done since I had left him. There wasn't enough of it to make a long tale.

"Do you think you can get information about the others from the one you caught?" he asked, as I prepared to go out.

"No. But I expect to bag them just the same."

Couffignal's main street was jammed with people when I limped into it again. A detachment of Marines from Mare Island was there, and men from a San Francisco police boat. Excited citizens in all degrees of partial nakedness boiled around them. A hundred voices were talking at once, recounting their personal adventures and braveries and losses and what they had seen. Such words as machine gun, bomb, bandit, car, shot, dynamite, and killed sounded again and again, in every variety of voice and tone.

The bank had been completely wrecked by the charge that had blown the vault. The jewelry store was another ruin. A grocer's across the street was serving as a field hospital. Two doctors were toiling there, patching up damaged villagers.

I recognized a familiar face under a uniform cap—Sergeant

Roche of the harbor police—and pushed through the crowd to him.

"Just get here?" he asked as we shook hands. "Or were you in on it?"

"In on it."

"What do you know?"

"Everything."

"Who ever heard of a private detective that didn't," he joshed as I led him out of the mob.

"Did you people run into an empty boat out in the bay?" I asked when we were away from audiences.

"Empty boats have been floating around the bay all night," he said.

I hadn't thought of that.

"Where's your boat now?" I asked him.

"Out trying to pick up the bandits. I stayed with a couple of men to lend a hand here."

"You're in luck," I told him. "Now sneak a look across the street. See the stout old boy with the black whiskers? Standing in front of the druggist's."

General Pleshskev stood there, with the woman who had fainted, the young Russian whose bloody cheek had made her faint, and a pale, plump man of forty-something who had been with them at the reception. A little to one side stood big Ignati, the two menservants I had seen at the house, and another who was obviously one of them. They were chatting together and watching the excited antics of a red-faced property-owner who was telling a curt lieutenant of Marines that it was his own personal private automobile that the bandits had stolen to mount their machine gun on, and what he thought should be done about it.

"Yes," said Roche, "I see your fellow with the whiskers."

"Well, he's your meat. The woman and two men with him are also your meat. And those four Russians standing to the left are some more of it. There's another missing, but I'll take care of that one. Pass the word to the lieutenant, and you can round up those babies without giving them a chance to fight back. They think they're safe as angels."

"Sure, are you?" the sergeant asked.

"Don't be silly!" I growled, as if I had never made a mistake in my life.

I had been standing on my one good prop. When I put my weight on the other to turn away from the sergeant, it stung me all the way to the hip. I pushed my back teeth together and began to work painfully through the crowd to the other side of the street.

The princess didn't seem to be among those present. My idea was that, next to the general, she was the most important member of the push. If she was at their house, and not yet suspicious, I figured I could get close enough to yank her in without a riot.

Walking was hell. My temperature rose. Sweat rolled out on me.

"Mister, they didn't none of 'em come down that way."

The one-legged newsboy was standing at my elbow. I greeted him as if he were my pay-check.

"Come on with me," I said, taking his arm. "You did fine down there, and now I want you to do something else for me."

Half a block from the main street I led him up on the porch of a small yellow cottage. The front door stood open, left that way when the occupants ran down to welcome police and

Marines, no doubt. Just inside the door, beside a hall rack, was a wicker porch chair. I committed unlawful entry to the extent of dragging that chair out on the porch.

"Sit down, son," I urged the boy.

He sat, looking up at me with puzzled freckled face. I took a firm grip on his crutch and pulled it out of his hand.

"Here's five bucks for rental," I said, "and if I lose it I'll buy you one of ivory and gold."

And I put the crutch under my arm and began to propel myself up the hill.

It was my first experience with a crutch. I didn't break any records. But it was a lot better than tottering along on an unassisted bum ankle.

The hill was longer and steeper than some mountains I've seen, but the gravel walk to the Russians' house was finally under my feet.

I was still some dozen feet from the porch when Princess Zhukovski opened the door.

7

"OH!" SHE EXCLAIMED, and then, recovering from her surprise, "your ankle is worse!"

She ran down the steps to help me climb them. As she came I noticed that something heavy was sagging and swinging in the right-hand pocket of her grey flannel jacket.

With one hand under my elbow, the other arm across my back, she helped me up the steps and across the porch. That assured me she didn't think I had tumbled to the game. If she had, she wouldn't have trusted herself within reach of my hands. Why, I wondered, had she come back to the house after starting downhill with the others?

While I was wondering we went into the house, where she planted me in a large and soft leather chair.

"You must certainly be starving after your strenuous night," she said. "I will see if—"

"No, sit down." I nodded at a chair facing mine. "I want to talk to you."

She sat down, clasping her slender white hands in her lap. In neither face nor pose was there any sign of nervousness, not even of curiosity. And that was overdoing it.

"Where have you cached the plunder?" I asked.

The whiteness of her face was nothing to go by. It had been white as marble since I had first seen her. The darkness of her eyes was as natural. Nothing happened to her other features. Her voice was smoothly cool.

"I am sorry," she said. "The question doesn't convey anything to me."

"Here's the point," I explained. "I'm charging you with complicity in the gutting of Couffignal, and in the murders that went with it. And I'm asking you where the loot has been hidden."

Slowly she stood up, raised her chin, and looked at least a mile down at me.

"How dare you? How dare you speak so to me, a Zhukovski!"

"I don't care if you're one of the Smith Brothers!" Leaning forward, I had pushed my twisted ankle against a leg of the chair, and the resulting agony didn't improve my disposition. "For the purpose of this talk you are a thief and a murderer."

Her strong slender body became the body of a lean crouching animal. Her white face became the face of an enraged animal. One hand—claw now—swept to the heavy pocket of her jacket.

Then, before I could have batted an eye—though my life seemed to depend on my not batting it—the wild animal had vanished. Out of it—and now I know where the writers of the old fairy stories got their ideas—rose the princess again, cool and straight and tall.

She sat down, crossed her ankles, put an elbow on an arm of her chair, propped her chin on the back of that hand, and looked curiously into my face.

"However," she murmured, "did you chance to arrive at so strange and fanciful a theory?"

"It wasn't chance, and it's neither strange nor fanciful," I said. "Maybe it'll save time and trouble if I show you part of the score against you. Then you'll know how you stand and won't waste your brains pleading innocence."

"I should be grateful," she smiled, "very!"

I tucked my crutch in between one knee and the arm of my chair, so my hands would be free to check off my points on my fingers.

"First—whoever planned the job knew the island—not fairly well, but every inch of it. There's no need to argue about that. Second—the car on which the machine gun was mounted was local property, stolen from the owner here. So was the boat in which the bandits were supposed to have escaped. Bandits from the outside would have needed a car or a boat to bring their machine guns, explosives, and grenades here and there doesn't seem to be any reason why they shouldn't have used that car or boat instead of stealing a fresh one. Third—there wasn't the least hint of the professional bandit touch on this job. If you ask me, it was a military job from beginning to end. And the worst safe-burglar in the world could have got into both the bank vault and the jeweler's safe without wrecking the buildings. Fourth—bandits from the outside wouldn't have destroyed the bridge. They might have blocked it, but they wouldn't have destroyed it. They'd have saved it in case they had to make their get-away in that direction. Fifth—bandits figuring on a get-away by boat would have cut the job short, wouldn't have spread it over the whole night. Enough racket was made here to wake up California all the way from Sacramento to Los Angeles. What you people did was to send one man out in the boat, shooting, and he didn't go far. As soon as he was at a safe distance, he went overboard, and swam back to the island. Big Ignati could have done it without turning a hair."

That exhausted my right hand. I switched over, counting on my left.

"Sixth—I met one of your party, the lad, down on the beach, and he was coming from the boat. He suggested that we jump it. We were shot at, but the man behind the gun was playing with us. He could have wiped us out in a second if he had been in earnest, but he shot over our heads. Seventh—that same lad is the only man on the island, so far as I know, who saw the departing bandits. Eighth—all of your people that I ran into were especially nice to me, the general even spending an hour talking to me at the reception this afternoon. That's a distinctive amateur crook trait. Ninth—after the machine gun car had been wrecked I chased its occupant. I lost him around this house. The Italian boy I picked up wasn't him. He couldn't have climbed up on the path without my seeing him. But he could have run around to the general's side of the house and vanished indoors there. The general liked him, and would have helped him. I know that, because the general performed a downright miracle by missing him at some six feet with a shotgun. Tenth—you called at Hendrixson's house for no other purpose than to get me away from there."

That finished the left hand. I went back to the right.

"Eleventh—Hendrixson's two servants were killed by someone they knew and trusted. Both were killed at close quarters and without firing a shot. I'd say you got Oliver to let you into the house, and were talking to him when one of your men cut his throat from behind. Then you went upstairs and probably shot the unsuspecting Brophy yourself. He wouldn't have been on his guard against you. Twelfth—but that ought to be enough, and I'm getting a sore throat from listing them."

She took her chin off her hand, took a fat white cigarette out of a thin black case, and held it in her mouth while I put a match to the end of it. She took a long pull at it—a draw that accounted for a third of its length—and blew the smoke down at her knees.

"That would be enough," she said when all these things had been done, "if it were not that you yourself know it was impossible for us to have been so engaged. Did you not see us—did not everyone see us—time and time again?"

"That's easy!" I argued. "With a couple of machine guns, a trunkful of grenades, knowing the island from top to bottom, in the darkness and in a storm, against bewildered civilians—it was duck soup. There are nine of you that I know of, including two women. Any five of you could have carried on the work, once it was started, while the others took turns appearing here and there, establishing alibis. And that is what you did. You took turns slipping out to alibi yourselves. Everywhere I went I ran into one of you. And the general! That whiskered old joker running around leading the simple citizens to battle! I'll bet he led 'em plenty! They're lucky there are any of 'em alive this morning!"

She finished her cigarette with another inhalation, dropped the stub on the rug, ground out the light with one foot, sighed wearily, put her hands on her hips, and asked:

"And now what?"

"Now I want to know where you have stowed the plunder."

The readiness of her answer surprised me.

"Under the garage, in a cellar we dug secretly there some months ago."

I didn't believe that, of course, but it turned out to be the truth.

I didn't have anything else to say. When I fumbled with my

borrowed crutch, preparing to get up, she raised a hand and spoke gently:

"Wait a moment, please. I have something to suggest."

Half standing, I leaned toward her, stretching out one hand until it was close to her side.

"I want the gun," I said.

She nodded, and sat still while I plucked it from her pocket, put it in one of my own, and sat down again.

8

"YOU SAID A little while ago that you didn't care who I was," she began immediately. "But I want you to know. There are so many of us Russians who once were somebodies and who now are nobodies that I won't bore you with the repetition of a tale the world has grown tired of hearing. But you must remember that this weary tale is real to us who are its subjects. However, we fled from Russia with what we could carry of our property, which fortunately was enough to keep us in bearable comfort for a few years.

"In London we opened a Russian restaurant, but London was suddenly full of Russian restaurants, and ours became, instead of a means of livelihood, a source of loss. We tried teaching music and languages, and so on. In short, we hit on all the means of earning our living that other Russian exiles hit upon, and so always found ourselves in overcrowded, and thus unprofitable, fields. But what else did we know—could we do?

"I promised not to bore you. Well, always our capital shrank, and always the day approached on which we should be shabby and hungry, the day when we should become familiar to readers of your Sunday papers—charwomen who had been princesses, dukes who now were butlers. There was no place for us in the world. Outcasts easily become outlaws. Why not? Could it be said that we owed the world any fealty? Had not the world sat idly by and seen us despoiled of place and property and country?

"We planned it before we had heard of Couffignal. We could

find a small settlement of the wealthy, sufficiently isolated, and, after establishing ourselves there, we would plunder it. Couffignal, when we found it, seemed to be the ideal place. We leased this house for six months, having just enough capital remaining to do that and to live properly here while our plans matured. Here we spent four months establishing ourselves, collecting our arms and our explosives, mapping our offensive, waiting for a favorable night. Last night seemed to be that night, and we had provided, we thought, against every eventuality. But we had not, of course, provided against your presence and your genius. They were simply others of the unforeseen misfortunes to which we seem eternally condemned."

She stopped, and fell to studying me with mournful large eyes that made me feel like fidgeting.

"It's no good calling me a genius," I objected. "The truth is you people botched your job from beginning to end. Your general would get a big laugh out of a man without military training who tried to lead an army. But here are you people with absolutely no criminal experience trying to swing a trick that needed the highest sort of criminal skill. Look at how you all played around with me! Amateur stuff! A professional crook with any intelligence would have either let me alone or knocked me off. No wonder you flopped! As for the rest of it—your troubles—I can't do anything about them."

"Why?" very softly. "Why can't you?"

"Why should I?" I made it blunt.

"No one else knows what you know." She bent forward to put a white hand on my knee. "There is wealth in that cellar beneath the garage. You may have whatever you ask."

I shook my head.

"You aren't a fool!" she protested. "You know—"

"Let me straighten this out for you," I interrupted. "We'll disregard whatever honesty I happen to have, sense of loyalty to employers, and so on. You might doubt them, so we'll throw them out. Now I'm a detective because I happen to like the work. It pays me a fair salary, but I could find other jobs that would pay more. Even a hundred dollars more a month would be twelve hundred a year. Say twenty-five or thirty thousand dollars in the years between now and my sixtieth birthday.

"Now I pass up that twenty-five or thirty thousand of honest gain because I like being a detective, like the work. And liking work makes you want to do it as well as you can. Otherwise there'd be no sense to it. That's the fix I am in. I don't know anything else, don't enjoy anything else, don't want to know or enjoy anything else. You can't weigh that against any sum of money. Money is good stuff. I haven't anything against it. But in the past eighteen years I've been getting my fun out of chasing crooks and tackling puzzles, my satisfaction out of catching crooks and solving riddles. It's the only kind of sport I know anything about, and I can't imagine a pleasanter future than twenty-some years more of it. I'm not going to blow that up!"

She shook her head slowly, lowering it, so that now her dark eyes looked up at me under the thin arcs of her brows.

"You speak only of money," she said. "I said you may have whatever you ask."

That was out. I don't know where these women get their ideas.

"You're still all twisted up," I said brusquely, standing now and adjusting my borrowed crutch. "You think I'm a man and you're a woman. That's wrong. I'm a manhunter and you're something that has been running in front of me. There's nothing human about it. You might just as well expect a hound to play tiddly-winks with the fox he's caught. We're wasting time anyway. I've been thinking the police or Marines might come up here and save me a walk. You've been waiting for your mob to come back and grab me. I could have told you they were being arrested when I left them."

That shook her. She had stood up. Now she fell back a step, putting a hand behind her for steadiness, on her chair. An exclamation I didn't understand popped out of her mouth. Russian, I thought, but the next moment I knew it had been Italian.

"Put your hands up."

It was Flippo's husky voice. Flippo stood in the doorway, holding an automatic.

9

I RAISED MY hands as high as I could without dropping my supporting crutch, meanwhile cursing myself for having been too careless, or too vain, to keep a gun in my hand while I talked to the girl.

So this was why she had come back to the house. If she freed the Italian, she had thought, we would have no reason for suspecting that he hadn't been in on the robbery, and so we would look for the bandits among his friends. A prisoner, of course, he might have persuaded us of his innocence. She had given him the gun so he could either shoot his way clear, or, what would help her as much, get himself killed trying.

While I was arranging these thoughts in my head, Flippo had come up behind me. His empty hand passed over my body, taking away my own gun, his, and the one I had taken from the girl.

"A bargain, Flippo," I said when he had moved away from me, a little to one side, where he made one corner of a triangle whose other corners were the girl and I. "You're out on parole, with some years still to be served. I picked you up with a gun on you. That's plenty to send you back to the big house. I know you weren't in on this job. My idea is that you were up here on a smaller one of your own, but I can't prove that and don't want to. Walk out of here, alone and neutral, and I'll forget I saw you."

Little thoughtful lines grooved the boy's round, dark face.

The princess took a step toward him.

"You heard the offer I just now made him?" she asked. "Well, I make that offer to you, if you will kill him."

The thoughtful lines in the boy's face deepened.

"There's your choice, Flippo," I summed up for him. "All I can give you is freedom from San Quentin. The princess can give you a fat cut of the profits in a busted caper, with a good chance to get yourself hanged."

The girl, remembering her advantage over me, went at him hot and heavy in Italian, a language in which I know only four words. Two of them are profane and the other two obscene. I said all four.

The boy was weakening. If he had been ten years older, he'd have taken my offer and thanked me for it. But he was young and she—now that I thought of it—was beautiful. The answer wasn't hard to guess.

"But not to bump him off," he said to her, in English, for my benefit. "We'll lock him up in there where I was at."

I suspected Flippo hadn't any great prejudice against murder. It was just that he thought this one unnecessary, unless he was kidding me to make the killing easier.

The girl wasn't satisfied with his suggestion. She poured more hot Italian at him. Her game looked sure-fire, but it had a flaw. She couldn't persuade him that his chances of getting any of the loot away were good. She had to depend on her charms to swing him. And that meant she had to hold his eye.

He wasn't far from me.

She came close to him. She was singing, chanting, crooning Italian syllables into his round face.

She had him.

He shrugged. His whole face said yes. He turned—

I knocked him on the noodle with my borrowed crutch.

The crutch splintered apart. Flippo's knees bent. He stretched up to his full height. He fell on his face on the floor. He lay there, dead-still, except for a thin worm of blood that crawled out of his hair to the rug.

A step, a tumble, a foot or so of hand-and-knee scrambling put me within reach of Flippo's gun.

The girl, jumping out of my path, was half-way to the door when I sat up with the gun in my hand.

"Stop!" I ordered.

"I shan't," she said, but she did, for the time at least. "I am going out."

"You are going out when I take you."

She laughed, a pleasant laugh, low and confident.

"I'm going out before that," she insisted good-naturedly.

I shook my head.

"How do you purpose stopping me?" she asked.

"I don't think I'll have to," I told her. "You've got too much sense to try to run while I'm holding a gun on you."

She laughed again, an amused ripple.

"I've got too much sense to stay," she corrected me. "Your crutch is broken, and you're lame. You can't catch me by running after me, then. You pretend you'll shoot me, but I don't believe you. You'd shoot me if I attacked you, of course, but I shan't do that. I shall simply walk out, and you know you won't shoot me for that. You'll wish you could, but you won't. You'll see."

Her face turned over her shoulder, her dark eyes twinkling at me, she took a step toward the door.

"Better not count on that!" I threatened.

For answer to that she gave me a cooing laugh. And took another step.

"Stop, you idiot!" I bawled at her.

Her face laughed over her shoulder at me. She walked without haste to the door, her short skirt of grey flannel shaping itself to the calf of each grey wool-stockinged leg as its mate stepped forward.

Sweat greased the gun in my hand.

When her right foot was on the doorsill, a little chuckling sound came from her throat.

"Adieu!" she said softly.

And I put a bullet in the calf of her left leg.

She sat down—plump! Utter surprise stretched her white face. It was too soon for pain.

I had never shot a woman before. I felt queer about it.

"You ought to have known I'd do it!" My voice sounded harsh and savage and like a stranger's in my ears. "Didn't I steal a crutch from a cripple?"

Creeping Siamese

1

STANDING BESIDE THE cashier's desk in the front office of the Continental Detective Agency's San Francisco branch, I was watching Porter check up my expense account when the man came in. He was a tall man, raw-boned, hard-faced. Grey clothes bagged loosely from his wide shoulders. In the late afternoon sunlight that came through partially drawn blinds, his skin showed the color of new tan shoes.

He opened the door briskly, and then hesitated, standing in the doorway, holding the door open, turning the knob back and forth with one bony hand. There was no indecision in his face. It was ugly and grim, and its expression was the expression of a man who is remembering something disagreeable.

Tommy Howd, our freckled and snub-nosed office boy, got up from his desk and went to the rail that divided the office.

"Do you—?" Tommy began, and jumped back.

The man had let go the doorknob. He crossed his long arms over his chest, each hand gripping a shoulder. His mouth stretched wide in a yawn that had nothing to do with relaxation. His mouth clicked shut. His lips snarled back from clenched yellow teeth.

"Hell!" he grunted, full of disgust, and pitched down on the floor.

I heaved myself over the rail, stepped across his body, and went out into the corridor.

Four doors away, Agnes Braden, a plump woman of thirty-something who runs a public stenographic establishment, was going into her office.

"Miss Braden!" I called, and she turned, waiting for me to come up. "Did you see the man who just came in our office?"

"Yes." Curiosity put lights in her green eyes. "A tall man who came up in the elevator with me. Why?"

"Was he alone?"

"Yes. That is, he and I were the only ones who got off at this floor. Why?"

"Did you see anybody close to him?"

"No, though I didn't notice him in the elevator. Why?"

"Did he act funny?"

"Not that I noticed. Why?"

"Thanks. I'll drop in and tell you about it later."

I made a circuit of the corridors on our floor, finding nothing.

The raw-boned man was still on the floor when I returned to the office, but he had been turned over on his back. He was as dead as I had thought. The Old Man, who had been examining him, straightened up as I came in. Porter was at the telephone, trying to get the police. Tommy Howd's eyes were blue half-dollars in a white face.

"Nothing in the corridors," I told the Old Man. "He came up in the elevator with Agnes Braden. She says he was alone, and she saw nobody close to him."

"Quite so." The Old Man's voice and smile were as pleasantly polite as if the corpse at his feet had been a part of the pattern in the carpet. Fifty years of sleuthing have left him with no more emotion than a pawnbroker. "He seems to have been stabbed in the left breast, a rather large wound that was staunched with this piece of silk"—one of his feet poked at a rumpled ball of red cloth on the floor—"which seems to be a sarong."

Today is never Tuesday to the Old Man: it seems to be Tuesday.

"On his person," he went on, "I have found some nine hundred dollars in bills of various denominations, and some silver; a gold watch and a pocket knife of English manufacture; a Japanese silver coin, 50 sen; tobacco, pipe and matches; a Southern Pacific timetable; two handkerchiefs without laundry marks; a pencil and several sheets of blank paper; four two-cent stamps; and a key labeled Hotel Montgomery, Room 540.

"His clothes seem to be new. No doubt we shall learn something from them when we make a more thorough examination, which I do not care to make until the police come. Meanwhile, you had better go to the Montgomery and see what you can learn there."

In the Hotel Montgomery's lobby the first man I ran into was the one I wanted: Pederson, the house copper, a blond-mustached ex-bartender who doesn't know any more about gum-shoeing than I do about saxophones, but who does know people and how to handle them, which is what his job calls for.

"Hullo!" he greeted me. "What's the score?"

"Six to one, Seattle, end of the fourth. Who's in 540, Pete?"

"They're not playing in Seattle, you chump! Portland! A man that hasn't got enough civic spirit to know where his team—"

"Stop it, Pete! I've got no time to be fooling with your childish pastimes. A man just dropped dead in our joint with one of your room-keys in his pocket—540."

Civic spirit went blooey in Pederson's face.

"540?" He stared at the ceiling. "That would be that fellow Rounds. Dropped dead, you say?"

"Dead. Tumbled down in the middle of the floor with a knife-cut in him. Who is this Rounds?"

"I couldn't tell you much off-hand. A big bony man with leathery skin. I wouldn't have noticed him excepting he was such a sour looking body."

"That's the bird. Let's look him up."

At the desk we learned that the man had arrived the day before, registering as H.R. Rounds, New York, and telling the clerk he expects to leave within three days. There was no record of mail or telephone calls for him. Nobody knew when he had gone out, since he had not left his key at the desk. Neither elevator boys nor bell-hops could tell us anything.

His room didn't add much to our knowledge. His baggage consisted of one pigskin bag, battered and scarred, and covered with the marks of labels that had been scraped off. It was locked, but traveling bags locks don't amount to much. This one held us up about five minutes.

Rounds' clothes—some in the bag, some in the closet—were neither many nor expensive, but they were all new. The washable stuff was without laundry marks. Everything was of popular makes, widely advertised brands that could be bought in any city in the country. There wasn't a piece of paper with anything written on it. There wasn't an identifying tag. There wasn't anything in the room to tell where Rounds had come from or why.

Pederson was peevish about it.

"I guess if he hadn't got killed he'd of beat us out of a week's bill! These guys that don't carry anything to identify 'em, and that don't leave their keys at the desk when they go out, ain't to be trusted too much!"

We had just finished our search when a bell-hop brought Detective Sergeant O'Gar, of the police department Homicide Detail, into the room.

"Been down to the Agency?" I asked him.

"Yeah, just came from there."

"What's new?"

O'Gar pushed back his wide-brimmed black village-constable's hat and scratched his bullet head.

"Not a heap. The doc says he was opened with a blade at least six inches long by a couple wide, and that he couldn't of lived two hours after he got the blade—most likely not more'n one. We didn't find any news on him. What've you got here?"

"His name is Rounds. He registered here yesterday from New York. His stuff is new, and there's nothing on any of it to tell us anything except that he didn't want to leave a trail. No letters, no memoranda, nothing. No blood, no signs of a row, in the room."

O'Gar turned to Pederson.

"Any brown men been around the hotel? Hindus or the like?"

"Not that I saw," the house copper said. "I'll find out for you."

"Then the red silk was a sarong?" I asked.

"And an expensive one," the detective sergeant said. "I saw a lot of 'em the four years I was soldiering on the islands, but I never saw as good a one as that."

"Who wears them?"

"Men and women in the Philippines, Borneo, Java, Sumatra, Malay Peninsula, parts of India."

"Is it your idea that whoever did the carving advertised himself by running around in the streets in a red petticoat?"

"Don't try to be funny!" he growled at me. "They're often

enough twisted or folded up into sashes or girdles. And how do I know he was knifed in the street? For that matter, how do I know he wasn't cut down in your joint?"

"We always bury our victims without saying anything about 'em. Let's go down and give Pete a hand in the search for your brown men."

That angle was empty. Any brown men who had snooped around the hotel had been too good at it to be caught.

I telephoned the Old Man, telling him what I had learned—which didn't cost me much breath—and O'Gar and I spent the rest of the evening sharp-shooting around without ever getting on the target once. We questioned taxicab drivers, questioned the three Roundses listed in the telephone book, and our ignorance was as complete when we were through as when we started.

The morning papers, on the streets at a little after eight o'clock that evening, had the story as we knew it.

At eleven o'clock O'Gar and I called it a night, separating in the direction of our respective beds.

We didn't stay apart long.

2

I OPENED MY eyes sitting on the side of my bed in the dim light of a moon that was just coming up, with the ringing telephone in my hand.

O'Gar's voice: "1856 Broadway! On the hump!"

"1856 Broadway," I repeated, and he hung up.

I finished waking up while I phoned for a taxicab, and then wrestled my clothes on. My watch told me it was 12:55 A.M. as I went downstairs. I hadn't been fifteen minutes in bed.

1856 Broadway was a three-story house set behind a pocket-size lawn in a row of like houses behind like lawns. The others were dark. 1856 shed light from every window, and from the open front door. A policeman stood in the vestibule.

"Hello, Mac! O'Gar here?"

"Just went in."

I walked into a brown and buff reception hall, and saw the detective sergeant going up the wide stairs.

"What's up?" I asked as I joined him.

"Don't know."

On the second floor we turned to the left, going into a library or sitting room that stretched across the front of the house.

A man in pajamas and bathrobe sat on a davenport there, with one bared leg stretched out on a chair in front of him. I recognized him when he nodded to me: Austin Richter, owner of a Market Street moving picture theater. He was a round-faced man of forty-five or so, partly bald, for whom the Agency had done some work a year or so before in connection with a ticket-seller who had departed without turning in the day's receipts.

In front of Richter a thin white-haired man with doctor written all over him stood looking at Richter's leg, which was wrapped in a bandage just below the knee. Beside the doctor, a tall woman in a fur-trimmed dressing-gown stood, a roll of gauze and a pair of scissors in her hands. A husky police corporal was writing in a notebook at a long narrow table, a thick hickory walking stick laying on the bright blue table cover at his elbow.

All of them looked around at us as we came into the room. The corporal got up and came over to us.

"I knew you were handling the Rounds job, sergeant, so I thought I'd best get word to you as soon as I heard they was brown men mixed up in this."

"Good work, Flynn," O'Gar said. "What happened here?"

"Burglary, or maybe only attempted burglary. They was four of them—crashed the kitchen door."

Richter was sitting up very straight, and his blue eyes were suddenly excited, as were the brown eyes of the woman.

"I beg your pardon," he said, "but is there—you mentioned brown men in connection with another affair—is there another?"

O'Gar looked at me.

"You haven't seen the morning papers?" I asked the theatre owner.

"No."

"Well, a man came into the Continental office late this afternoon, with a stab in his chest, and died there. Pressed against the wound, as if to stop the bleeding, was a sarong, which is where we got the brown men idea."

"His name?"

"Rounds, H.R. Rounds."

The name brought no recognition into Richter's eyes.

"A tall man, thin, with dark skin?" he asked. "In a grey suit?"

"All of that."

Richter twisted around to look at the woman.

"Molloy!" he exclaimed.

"Molloy!" she exclaimed.

"So you know him?"

Their faces came back toward me.

"Yes. He was here this afternoon. He left—"

Richter stopped, to turn to the woman again, questioningly.

"Yes, Austin," she said, putting gauze and scissors on the table, and sitting down beside him on the davenport. "Tell them."

He patted her hand and looked up at me again with the expression of a man who has seen a nice spot on which to lay down a heavy load.

"Sit down. It isn't a long story, but sit down."

We found ourselves chairs.

"Molloy—Sam Molloy—that is his name, or the name I have always known him by. He came here this afternoon. He'd either called up the theater or gone there, and they had told him I was home. I hadn't seen him for three years. We could see—both my wife and I—that there was something the matter with him when he came in.

"When I asked him, he said he'd been stabbed, by a Siamese, on his way here. He didn't seem to think the wound amounted to much, or pretended he didn't. He wouldn't let us fix it for him, or look at it. He said he'd go to a doctor after he left, after he'd got rid of the thing. That was what he had come to me for. He wanted me to hide it, to take care of it until he came for it again.

"He didn't talk much. He was in a hurry, and suffering. I didn't ask him any questions. I couldn't refuse him anything. I couldn't question him even though he as good as told us that it was illegal as well as dangerous. He saved our lives once—more than my wife's life—down in Mexico, where we first knew him. That was in 1916. We were caught down there during the Villa troubles. Molloy was running guns over the border, and he had enough influence with the bandits to have us released when it looked as if we were done for.

"So this time, when he wanted me to do something for him, I couldn't ask him about it. I said, 'Yes,' and he gave me the package. It wasn't a large package: about the size of—well—a loaf of bread, perhaps, but quite heavy for its size. It was wrapped in brown paper. We unwrapped it after he had gone, that is, we took the paper off. But the inner wrapping was of canvas, tied with silk cord, and sealed, so we didn't open that. We put it upstairs in the pack room, under a pile of old magazines.

"Then, at about a quarter to twelve tonight—I had only been in bed a few minutes, and hadn't gone to sleep yet—I heard a noise in here. I don't own a gun, and there's nothing you could properly call a weapon in the house, but that walking stick"— indicating the hickory stick on the table—"was in a closet in our bedroom. So I got that and came in here to see what the noise was.

"Right outside the bedroom door I ran into a man. I could see him better than he could see me, because this door was open and he showed against the window. He was between me and it, and the moonlight showed him fairly clear. I hit him with the stick, but didn't knock him down. He turned and ran in here. Foolishly, not thinking that he might not be alone, I ran after him. Another man shot me in the leg just as I came through the door.

"I fell, of course. While I was getting up, two of them came in with my wife between them. There were four of them. They were medium-sized men, brown-skinned, but not so dark. I took it for granted that they were Siamese, because Molloy had spoken of Siamese. They turned on the lights here, and one of them, who seemed to be the leader, asked me:

" 'Where is it?'

"His accent was pretty bad, but you could understand his words good enough. Of course I knew they were after what Molloy had left, but I pretended I didn't. They told me, or rather the leader did, that he knew it had been left here, but they called Molloy by another name—Dawson. I said I didn't know any Dawson, and nothing had been left here, and I tried to get them to tell me what they expected to find. They wouldn't, though—they just called it 'it.'

"They talked among themselves, but of course I couldn't make out a word of what they were saying, and then three of them went out, leaving one here to guard us. He had a Luger pistol. We could hear the others moving around the house. The search must have lasted an hour. Then the one I took for the leader came in, and said something to our guard. Both of them looked quite elated.

" 'It is not wise if you will leave this room for many minutes,' the leader said to me, and they left us—both of them—closing the door behind them.

"I knew they were going, but I couldn't walk on this leg. From what the doctor says, I'll be lucky if I walk on it inside of a couple of months. I didn't want my wife to go out, and perhaps run into one of them before they'd got away, but she insisted on going. She found they'd gone, and she phoned the police, and then ran up to the pack room and found Molloy's package was gone."

"And this Molloy didn't give you any hint at all as to what was in the package?" O'Gar asked when Richter had finished.

"Not a word, except that it was something the Siamese were after."

"Did he know the Siamese who stabbed him?" I asked.

"I think so," Richter said slowly, "though I am not sure he said he did."

"Do you remember his words?"

"Not exactly, I'm afraid."

"I think I remember them," Mrs. Richter said. "My husband, Mr. Richter, asked him, 'What's the matter, Molloy? Are you hurt, or sick?'

"Molloy gave a little laugh, putting a hand on his chest, and said, 'Nothing much. I run into a Siamese who was looking for me on my way here, and got careless and let him scratch me. But I kept my little bundle!' And he laughed again, and patted the package."

"Did he say anything else about the Siamese?"

"Not directly," she replied, "though he did tell us to watch out for any Asiatics we saw around the neighborhood. He said he wouldn't leave the package if he thought it would make trouble for us, but that there was always a chance that something would go wrong, and we'd better be careful. And he told my husband"—nodding at Richter—"that the Siamese had been dogging him for months, but now that he had a safe place for the package he was going to 'take them for a walk and forget to bring them back.' That was the way he put it."

"How much do you know about Molloy?"

"Not a great deal, I'm afraid," Richter took up the answering again. "He liked to talk about the places he had been and the things he had seen, but you couldn't get a word out of him about his own affairs. We met him first in Mexico, as I have told you, in 1916. After he saved us down there and got us away, we didn't see him again for nearly four years. He rang the bell one night, and came in for an hour or two. He was on his way to China, he said, and had a lot of business to attend to before he left the next day.

"Some months later I had a letter from him, from the Queen's Hotel in Kandy, asking me to send him a list of the importers and exporters in San Francisco. He wrote me a letter thanking me for the list, and I didn't hear from him again until he came to San Francisco for a week, about a year later. That was in 1921, I think.

"He was here for another week about a year after that, telling us that he had been in Brazil, but, as usual, not saying what he had been doing there. Some months later I had a letter from him, from Chicago, saying he would be here the following week. However, he didn't come. Instead, some time later, he wrote from Vladivostok, saying he hadn't been able to make it. Today was the first we'd heard of him since then."

"Where's his home? His people?"

"He always says he has neither. I've an idea he was born in England, though I don't know that he ever said so, or what made me think so."

"Got any more questions?" I asked O'Gar.

"No. Let's give the place the eye, and see if the Siamese left any leads behind 'em."

The eye we gave the house was thorough. We didn't split the territory between us, but went over everything together—everything from roof to cellar—every nook, drawer, corner.

The cellar did most for us: it was there, in the cold furnace, that we found the handful of black buttons and the fire-darkened garter clasps. But the upper floors hadn't been altogether worthless: in one room we had found the crumpled sales slip of an Oakland store, marked 1 table cover; and in another room we had found no garters.

"Of course it's none of my business," I told Richter when O'Gar and I joined the others again, "but I think maybe if you plead self-defense you might get away with it."

He tried to jump up from the davenport, but his shot leg failed him.

The woman got up slowly.

"And maybe that would leave an out for you," O'Gar told her. "Why don't you try to persuade him?"

"Or maybe it would be better if you plead the self-defense," I suggested to her. "You could say that Richter ran to your help when your husband grabbed you, that your husband shot him and was turning his gun on you when you stabbed him. That would sound smooth enough."

"My husband?"

"Uh-huh, Mrs. Rounds-Molloy-Dawson. Your late husband, anyway."

Richter got his mouth far enough closed to get words out of it.

"What is the meaning of this damned nonsense?" he demanded.

"Them's harsh words to come from a fellow like you," O'Gar growled at him. "If this is nonsense, what do you make of that yarn you told us about creeping Siamese and mysterious bundles, and God knows what all?"

"Don't be too hard on him," I told O'Gar. "Being around movies all the time has poisoned his idea of what sounds plausible. If it hadn't, he'd have known better than to see a Siamese in the moonlight at 11:45, when the moon was just coming up at somewhere around 12:45, when you phoned me."

Richter stood up on his one good leg.

The husky police corporal stepped close to him.

"Hadn't I better frisk him, sergeant?"

O'Gar shook his bullet head.

"Waste of time. He's got nothing on him. They cleaned the place of weapons. The chances are the lady dropped them in the bay when she rode over to Oakland to get a table cover to take the place of the sarong her husband carried away with him."

That shook the pair of them. Richter pretended he hadn't gulped, and the woman had a fight of it before she could make her eyes stay still on mine.

O'Gar struck while the iron was hot by bringing the buttons and garters clasps we had salvaged out of his pocket, and letting them trickle from one hand to another. That used up the last bit of the facts we had.

I threw a lie at them.

"Never me to knock the press, but you don't want to put too much confidence in what the papers say. For instance, a fellow might say a few pregnant words before he died, and the papers might say he didn't. A thing like that would confuse things."

The woman reared up her head and looked at O'Gar.

"May I speak to Austin alone?" she asked. "I don't mean out of your sight."

The detective sergeant scratched his head and looked at me. This letting your victims go into conference is always a ticklish business: they may decide to come clean, and then again, they may frame up a new out. On the other hand, if you don't let them, the chances are they get stubborn on you, and you can't get anything out of them. One way was as risky as another. I grinned at O'Gar and refused to make a suggestion. He could decide for himself, and, if he was wrong, I'd have him to dump the blame on. He scowled at me, and then nodded to the woman.

"You can over into that corner and whisper together for a couple of minutes," he said, "but no foolishness."

She gave Richter the hickory stick, took his other arm, helped him hobble to a far corner, pulled a chair over there for him. He sat with his back to us. She stood behind him, leaning over his shoulder, so that both their faces were hidden from us.

O'Gar came closer to me.

"What do you think?" he muttered.

"I think they'll come through."

"That shot of yours about being Molloy's wife hit center. I missed that one. How'd you make it?"

"When she was telling us what Molloy had said about the Siamese she took pains both times she said 'my husband' to show that she meant Richter."

"So? Well—"

The whispering in the far corner had been getting louder,

so that the s's had become sharp hisses. Now a clear emphatic sentence came from Richter's mouth.

"I'll be damned if I will!"

Both of them looked furtively over their shoulders, and they lowered their voices again, but not for long. The woman was apparently trying to persuade him to do something. He kept shaking his head. He put a hand on her arm. She pushed it away, and kept on whispering.

He said aloud, deliberately:

"Go ahead, if you want to be a fool. It's your neck. I didn't put the knife in him."

She jumped away from him, her eyes black blazes in a white face. O'Gar and I moved softly toward them.

"You rat!" she spat at Richter, and spun to face us.

"I killed him!" she cried. "This thing in the chair tried to and—"

Richter swung the hickory stick.

I jumped for it—missed—crashed into the back of his chair. Hickory stick, Richter, chair, and I sprawled together on the floor. The corporal helped me up. He and I picked Richter up and put him on the davenport again.

The woman's story poured out of her angry mouth:

"His name wasn't Molloy. It was Lange, Sam Lange. I married him in Providence in 1913 and went to China with him—to Canton, where he had a position with a steamship line. We didn't stay there long, because he got into some trouble through being mixed up in the revolution that year. After that we drifted around, mostly around Asia.

"We met this thing"—she pointed at the now sullenly quiet Richter—"in Singapore, in 1919, I think—right after the World

War was over. His name is Holley, and Scotland Yard can tell you something about him. He had a proposition. He knew of a gem-bed in upper Burma, one of many that were hidden from the British when they took the country. He knew the natives who were working it, knew where they were hiding their gems.

"My husband went in with him, with two other men that were killed. They looted the natives' cache, and got away with a whole sackful of sapphires, topazes and even a few rubies. The two other men were killed by the natives and my husband was badly wounded.

"We didn't think he could live. We were hiding in a hut near the Yunnan border. Holley persuaded me to take the gems and run away with them. It looked as if Sam was done for, and if we stayed there long we'd be caught. I can't say that I was crazy about Sam anyway; he wasn't the kind you would be, after living with him for a while.

"So Holley and I took it and lit out. We had to use a lot of the stones to buy our way through Yunnan and Kwangsi and Kwangtung, but we made it. We got to San Francisco with enough to buy this house and the movie theater, and we've been here since. We've been honest since we came here, but I don't suppose that means anything. We had enough money to keep us comfortable.

"Today Sam showed up. We hadn't heard of him since we left him on his back in Burma. He said he'd been caught and jailed for three years. Then he'd got away, and had spent the other three hunting for us. He was that kind. He didn't want me back, but he did want money. He wanted everything we had. Holley lost his nerve. Instead of bargaining with Sam, he lost his head and tried to shoot him.

"Sam took his gun away from him and shot him in the leg. In the scuffle Sam had dropped a knife—a kris, I think. I picked it up, but he grabbed me just as I got it. I don't know how it happened. All I saw was Sam staggering back, holding his chest with both hands—and the kris shining red in my hand.

"Sam had dropped his gun. Holley got it and was all for shooting Sam, but I wouldn't let him. It happened in this room. I don't remember whether I gave Sam the sarong we used for a cover on the table or not. Anyway, he tried to stop the blood with it. He went away then, while I kept Holley from shooting him.

"I knew Sam wouldn't go to the police, but I didn't know what he'd do. And I knew he was hurt bad. If he dropped dead somewhere, the chances are he'd be traced here. I watched from a window as he went down the street, and nobody seemed to pay any attention to him, but he looked so conspicuously wounded to me that I thought everybody would be sure to remember him if it got into the papers that he had been found dead somewhere.

"Holley was even more scared than I. We couldn't run away, because he had a shot leg. So we made up that Siamese story, and I went over to Oakland, and bought the table cover to take the place of the sarong. We had some guns and even a few oriental knives and swords here. I wrapped them up in paper, breaking the swords, and dropped them off the ferry when I went to Oakland.

"When the morning papers came out we read what had happened, and then we went ahead with what we had planned. We burned the suit Holley had worn when he was shot, and his garters—because the pants had a bullet-hole in them, and the bullet had cut one garter. We fixed a hole in his pajama-leg, unbandaged his leg,—I had fixed it as well as I could,—and washed away the clotted blood until it began to bleed again. Then I gave the alarm."

She raised both hands in a gesture of finality and made a clucking sound with her tongue.

"And there you are," she said.

"You got anything to say?" I asked Holley, who was staring at his bandaged leg.

"To my lawyer," he said without looking up.

O'Gar spoke to the corporal.

"The wagon, Flynn."

Ten minutes later we were in the street, helping Holley and the woman into a police car.

Around the corner on the other side of the street came three brown-skinned men, apparently Malay sailors. The one in the middle seemed to be drunk, and the other two were supporting him. One of them had a package that could have held a bottle under his arm.

O'Gar looked from them to me and laughed.

"We wouldn't be doing a thing to those babies right now if we had fallen for that yarn, would we?" he whispered.

"Shut up, you, you big heap!" I growled back, nodding at Holley, who was in the car by now. "If that bird sees them he'll identify 'em as his Siamese, and God knows what a jury would make of it!"

We made the puzzled driver twist the car six blocks out of his way to be sure we'd miss the brown men. It was worth it, because nothing interfered with the twenty years apiece that Holley and Mrs. Lange drew.